A THREAD IN TIME

Barrie Day

KDP
Kindle Direct Publishing

Copyright © Barrie Day

First Printed 2020

ISBN 978-1-912181-33-9

For Sue,
our children
and
our children's children

From Amazon reviews of
'The Breath I Would Give You'
Any teacher can relate to the feelings of the main character as he battles to inspire his, not always enthusiastic, students. The writer has raised some very real issues and does so in such a way as to make the reader frighteningly aware of the potential for devastation.
This book gripped me from the start; I loved the cleverly interwoven story lines that slowly revealed each character's true character. A compelling first novel.
Beautifully written in a style that allows the deep nature of the subject matter to be honestly felt.

From Amazon reviews of 'Not Behind The Bike Sheds'
A life so colourful and full of incident and it all comes through with such charm and modesty that the reader feels able to be part of the experience rather than look at it from the outside.
A fascinating journey from Birmingham to Cumbria via Jamaica, Lancaster and Florida with a gifted teacher of English.
An interesting collection of tales of a teacher working in vastly different cultures. Always engaging, touching and thought-provoking.

From a review of 'A Thread in Time'
'a dramatic and enrapturing read...a story that is sure to captivate a wide audience....'
R.Slack for Austin Macauley Publishers

"Music gives a soul to the universe, wings to the mind, flight to the imagination and life to everything"
— Plato

"Each and every event in the past is connected to the present by invisible threads"
— Momofuku Ando

CONTENTS

PART ONE: The Unravelling

May 2016

David sat on the carpet surrounded by the debris of his father's life - papers, loose leaf files, books, old newspapers, photographs. It had been a long slow death. 'Death in life' they called it, the way a person gradually evaporates as the dementia progresses leaving only the husk slumped in a chair in a care home. No recognition, no communication. Just a blankness, an aching blankness until the final death which had come two weeks ago.

But there had been that moment, that startling moment back in September. He had gone to visit his father as usual. It was a Saturday morning of bright autumn sunshine - in the old days his father would have loved it - the trees turning shades of bronze, the cobalt sky, the dry, cold edge to the air. And when he entered the lounge of the care home there he was, as usual, sitting by the window, staring out. The other care home 'inmates' sat in their usual places, apart from Muriel, who was always wandering, mithering, muttering to herself and feverishly rinsing her hands.

There was classical music playing in the background. David sat down in front of his father. 'Hi, dad,' he said touching his father on his hand and holding it. The hand was cold. 'Cold hands, dad, that's not like you.' The head moved slowly and the eyes looked towards the hand which touched his. And then the head lifted and the eyes stared at David and looked through him. No recognition. Nothing.

'How about if I wheel you out into the garden; it's one of those great autumn mornings.'

He waited. Hoped. But nothing. Outside, the garden was still a blaze of colour. Once his father would have been there, hands in the soil, nurturing. But now. Nada.

1

The music changed and David suddenly felt his father's body tense and saw his eyes start to move from side to side. At the same time as the new melody started so he felt the squeeze of his own hand. It was quite a gentle melody but it seemed to stir something in his father whose body was shifting restlessly in the chair. Then his head started to shake with a kind of ague and both hands went and clasped over his ears. As the music swelled in a crescendo David's father grasped the arms of the chair and tried to stand: 'My..oh!' he shouted. 'Don't go!'

'Dad, it's alright, there, there, it's okay,' murmured David close to his father's ear, 'it's okay.' But in that moment he turned, looked at David and still shaking his head, sobbed the words, 'She's gone! She's gone!' He slumped back into the chair, head bent, hands over his face, chest heaving with great gulping sobs.

It had taken another fifteen minutes for the tension in his father's body to subside and then he sank into a deep, snoring sleep. When he had shouted, the duty nurse had hurried over and put her arm round him.

'What was the music that was playing?' asked David.

'Some playlist we use.'

'It seemed to affect my father; stirred something in him.'

'Let me find out,' said the nurse.

She returned with a piece of paper which showed the playlist. 'Seems it was this one,' she said.

David read the words: *Andante : Piano Concerto No. 2. Shostakovich.* 'Thank you,' he said nodding at the nurse.

Since that day he had listened to the piece a number of times on his phone. He still felt the squeeze of his father's hand, the eyes darting, the tensing of the body and the words 'She's gone'. And the sobbing. Something deep in his father had surfaced for that brief moment. And it nagged at David like a haunting.

'Dad, can I take this?'

Joe stood at the door holding an old hand drill. 'Pops used to use this in the workshop. He showed me how it worked. Could I take it? To remember him, kind of.'

David looked at his eleven-year old son. 'Of course,' he nodded. 'Anything else you want?'

'There's so much stuff.' Joe shrugged. 'It's like he's still here.' He turned and went down the hallway.

They'd had such a great relationship - Joe and his 'Pops', as he called him. The affection between them had been strong since Joe was a toddler and he had found it confusing when Pops didn't recognise him. 'Why doesn't he talk to us anymore?' Joe had asked after a visit to the care home.

How to explain dementia to a child. To David, the tragedy of it was like a perpetual ache, a longing that it could be other than it was. It had come gradually after his mother had died. First there was the random forgetfulness, his father becoming impatient with losing his keys, forgetting what he'd gone to order at a pub bar, repeating the same story only a few moments later. Forgetting that David and Anna had divorced, he once asked where Anna was and then with a flicker of memory he pointed a finger at David and shouted: 'You did it, you drove her away with your foolish, selfish drinking. You neglected that wonderful girl.'

It was true, he was to blame, but David didn't need to hear it repeated again and again and he felt it was driving a wedge of resentment between himself and his father. They had been so close for so many years but now there were these unprovoked outbursts from his father which David couldn't counter. He told himself it was the dementia which was speaking, but he knew that it was the unspoken which was now being voiced by his father and there was no reasoning with him.

And it got worse as the weeks passed. His father would bite at him for no apparent reason and if it was the end of a long working day David would bite back, weary and frustrated at these unprovoked outbursts and accusations. On one occasion he accused David of being cruel to his mother, of hastening his mother's illness. This was so wounding and unfair but his father was now beyond the reach of any reason or logic.

It was only when the dementia was diagnosed and the GP explained to David about the personality changes that the disease could cause that he realised that he had lost the father he had known and they could never find the love and reconciliation that he craved. Then he was weighed down with guilt - guilt that he should have realised what was happening; guilt that he should not have risen to the accusations but responded with more compassion. But it was too late. There was a gulf between them.

And then came the wandering. For the past few years his father had taken to doing a walk to the old promontory which used to carry the railway across the Solway to Annan. Now it was just a pier of sandstone blocks thrusting out into the estuary tides. He said it was a place that he was drawn to. He would sit for hours staring westwards, watching the changing light on the tidal channels and the distant hump of Criffel on the Scottish side fading into translucency as the sun dropped behind it. When the tide was coming in he would walk along the road to where it rose over the old railway cutting and then branch down along the gorse covered embankment along a path which snaked to the open pier where the wind was strong and the sea salt scoured the air.

When the tide was out, however, he would walk along the sand and wade across the muddy tidal creeks to get to the pier. David had often warned him against this but, as the dementia progressed, his father became increasingly belligerent and would snap back at him: 'Just leave me be. If I'm going to drown, so be it. And who cares anyway!' This was not the voice of the father he had grown up with and it pained him deeply. This was some impostor who was wrestling demons that David could not fathom.

Sometimes David would arrive at the house to find the back door open, no sign of his father until he picked up the binoculars and focused on the old promontory. Often he was there, a lone figure staring out to sea. The danger came when he went, not by the road, but along the foreshore. There were quicksands, hidden gullies and deep salt pannes - pools of brackish water left by the outgoing tide. It was easy to lose your footing and get stuck. And that's what happened one evening in March.

David arrived at the house to find the front and back doors open and no sign of his father. The tide was low and David guessed where his father might be. He found footprints in the wet sand just below the house, footprints which led away towards the distant pier. He scanned the estuary mud flats with the binoculars, focused on the end of the pier where his father usually sat, but spotted nothing. He set off at a steady jog along the wet sand following the line of footprints and checking the grassy gullies and salt pannes for any sign of his dad. The sun was dropping and there was only the sound of the odd curlew spilling its song down the funnels of wind.

'Dad! Dad!' David's voice spun away across the mud flats. 'Dad! Dad!'

Then he saw him. He was waist deep in a muddy gully and he was barely moving. 'Dad, for Christ's sake!' David knew how treacherous this mud could be. It sucked you in and there was nothing firm to help you to pull yourself out. He searched the grassy foreshore for branches or driftwood and spotted a plank half sunk into one of the salt pannes. 'Hold on, dad, I'm coming for you,' he yelled. He pulled the plank onto the grass, heaved it down to the edge of the gully and pushed it down the slope to where his father was now up to his chest in mud. He crawled out on the plank and grasped his father's outstretched hand. He looked into his face. There was a blankness in his eyes, tears on his cheeks as he shook his head slowly. 'Leave me,' he moaned. 'There's no hope left. Nothing to live for. She's gone.'

David pulled against the grip of the mud but it was hopeless. He clawed at his pocket for his phone. 'Hold on, dad, I'm getting help.' He made the call and then put his arms round his father's chest and held him from sinking further. He buried his head against his father's neck. 'You mustn't say that, dad. I need you. Joe needs you.'

His dad's voice was a low murmur against David's ear. 'You'll never understand. How could you?'

It was ten minutes later that David heard the sirens and saw the blue flashing lights. The rescue team had to use ropes under his armpits to pull his father out. They put his muddy body onto a stretcher and carried him across the marsh grass to the road where an ambulance and police car were standing.

They kept him in hospital overnight for observation but he was discharged the next day. David moved into the house with him for a week and used the time to find a care home which would take him in. It had to happen. Besides this narrow escape, his father had become a danger to himself in the house, leaving saucepans to boil dry, singeing clothes draped over chairs too close to the open fire. His father was a lost soul, deeply troubled, inhabiting a world of vacancy and listlessness. He didn't fight the move, for he was barely aware of what was happening to him. David was consumed with guilt at first but then relieved when he saw the way the care workers mothered his father. The empty house on the Solway echoed with ghosts and so many memories that reduced David to tears when he was there alone. He coped better when Joe was there but it was never easy visiting the place.

He continued sorting through the piles of papers on the carpet. There was an envelope of photographs. The colours had faded or were that strange tone of bluey-green that older photos often took on. These were holiday snaps - his father and mother on a beach somewhere and him making sand castles. The date written on the back in biro - 1981.

Then a photo of *Jamaya,* his father's sailing boat, the boat which had taken them on so many holidays to the Western Isles of Scotland. They would drive from their home on the edge of the Solway Firth, travel north of the border, then along the western shore of Loch Lomond, turn left at Crianlarich and then south from Lochgilphead into the wooded delights of Argyll, along the shore of Loch Sween to where the boat was anchored in the sheltered anchorage of Tayvallich. David knew the route by heart and he cherished the sailing adventures they'd had on *Jamaya.* Seared into his memory was when they dived for clams and collected mussels just off the Ardnamurchan headland. Then they had anchored and taken the dinghy to the wide sandy beach of Sanna Bay, collected driftwood, coaxed a fire against a stiff breeze, sizzled their catch on a skillet and warmed their bare feet on the stones around the fire.

Such memories. And when Joe was five they had sailed south to the island of Gigha, just off the Kintyre peninsula. It was the first time Joe was old enough to begin to understand what sailing was all about. Pops had held Joe's hands against the wheel and explained how they had to steer the boat to catch the wind and curve the sails smooth. Joe had listened and nodded and held the wheel tightly and Pops had hugged his little grandson in the same way he had hugged David when he was little.

It wasn't a long voyage but it was the final straw for David's marriage with Anna. She hated the sailing and was sick on the voyage back. They'd had a blazing row when they landed back at Tayvallich. A few weeks later the truth came out about Anna's affair with a colleague at work. The divorce was quick but the settlement fairly amicable with shared custody of Joe.

He was lucky - it could have been otherwise. Anna could have cited his poor record as a husband and a father to the new baby; the way his work had come between them, his obsession to succeed and prove himself. She said she had watched it happening, the gradual rift with him working unreasonable hours, coming home late and smelling of whisky. He claimed he was 'building the business' but she felt it was excessive. He realised he had been competing with his old school buddies who had gone into finance and already had the badges of status - the flash cars, the foreign holidays. And what did he have? A small semi in a village in north Cumbria, a modest lifestyle and what Anna had at first hoped for - a pleasure in the simple life. But for David it was not enough. That is, until his mother's death and the decline of his father. Then he seemed to wake up to what was really important. But for Anna it was too late. They'd lost each other. But she said she didn't want to punish him further. He was suffering enough and so she instructed her divorce solicitor not to push too hard. She could have pressed for total custody of Joe but she didn't. Joe must not be made to suffer for their failings, she had said. Yes he was lucky.

David felt in his pocket for his phone - found his playlist and chose one of his father's favourites - Rod Stewart's 'Sailing'. His eyes burned and welled at the memories and the loss of those great times. There was only Joe now. He had lost his mother, his father and his wife. Joe was his main concern. With both parents gone it was time to fully grow up. No-one to depend on or turn to. This was it.

But he was doing okay. His design business was pulling in more projects. He'd coped on his own for four years now, Joe living with him for part of the week and with regular visits to his father in the care home which had sadly become increasingly depressing and exhausting. Now he had to sort his father's house, clear it, sell it and then start a new chapter. Like emerging from a dark tunnel into the light.

*

Joe returned to the workshop. It stood across the yard from the house. He had always loved the smell as you opened the wooden door and went inside - wood shavings and oil. Pops had said it was the resin from the wood which gave it that scent. A comforting smell. But without Pops there it was not the same. He had told Joe the story of building the workshop - of having the wooden planks and beams delivered from the sawmill and building the frame on the ground then hoisting it into place with the help of his friends. Joe liked that idea, of friends coming together to build a workshop.

He ran his fingers along the edge of the workbench, looked at the tools all fitting neatly into their places - the shape of each tool inked in black and the tool fitting inside the outline so that you didn't put the tool in the wrong place. He remembered the tools he had used - the clamps for holding the wood firmly on the bench when you were sawing, the hacksaw for cutting metal, the tenon saw for cutting straight down into the wood and you always cut across the grain of the wood, he remembered that; and the row of pliers of different sizes, good for pulling nails out of a piece of wood. There were hammers and mallets of different sizes: a claw hammer for pulling out nails, a hammer with one end made of copper for beating metal into shape. 'And always use a mallet for hitting a wood chisel, never a hammer,' Pops had said sternly one day when Joe was having a go at chiselling a piece of wood. He'd never forgotten the sound of Pops' voice and the serious look in his eyes.

At the end of the bench was a row of hooks and hanging from one of the hooks was a small sack. Joe remembered - it was the sack of special stones which Pops collected when he went to different places. He pulled the draw string at the neck of the sack and carefully tipped the contents onto the bench. The stones were different colours and shapes - some flat, good for skimming, others as round and smooth as an egg. On each stone was a name - Arisaig, Sanna Bay, Gigha, Jura, Ben Nevis, Gairloch, Barra. He felt the egg-shaped stone from Barra - smooth and dark grey, almost black with tiny glinting crystals. He had found it on a beach near where there had been a terrible shipwreck years ago. Many people had drowned in the surf just off the sandy beach. He and his dad had flown to Barra on a small Flybe plane which landed on the sand and taxied to a small Arrival building close to the beach. The planes could only land when the tide was out.

They had met Pops at the harbour. He had sailed out to Barra a few days earlier and they spent three days sailing round Barra and the next island which was called Eriskay. Joe remembered seeing seals nosing their funny heads above the water as if they were curious to know what was going on. And that was the last time he had sailed with his grandad on *Jamaya*.

Underneath the workbench and along one wall there were cupboards. Each had a label telling you what was inside. At the end of the bench was an antique chair in front of an old office desk. The desk had drawers down one side and a cupboard on the other. It was where Pops would sit when he was drawing plans for his projects. There was an old mug crammed with rulers and pencils and in the drawers there were workshop books and tool catalogues. Joe had never sat in Pops' chair before. It had a shiny, green cushion on the seat and the arms were curved in such a way that they wrapped round to form the back of the chair. Joe sat down and ran has hands down the smooth curves of the arms. He leaned back and placed his hands on the top of the desk, ran his fingers along the edge of the desk following the curving grain of the wood.

In the front of the desk just above Joe's knees there was a desk drawer. He pulled it open. Inside were more pencils, a small set square and a tiny spirit level with polished brass ends. Joe opened the drawer a little further. To the rear of the drawer there was a wooden box with some intricate patterning across the edge. He brought it out into the light and set it down on the top of the desk.

It was a cigar box with an elaborate design on the front: a crown on the top of what looked like an arch of red curtains with gold fringing like on a theatre stage. Next to the curtains two gold coins on each side and in the middle, between the curtains, centre stage, a circular badge which read *Royal Jamaica* in gold lettering. Underneath the central badge were the words *Jamaica Tobacco Co. Ltd.*

When Joe opened the lid of the box there were no cigars but still the vague hint of tobacco. Filling most of the box, however, was a notebook with a dark blue hard cover. In the bottom right hand corner of the cover some handwriting, small and neat. It read:

Will Pearson's Jamaica Journal - 1974

*

David was looking at a photograph of his mother, Beth. She was much younger, maybe in her thirties. Her hair was long and straight and she wore a kaftan type dress, patterned with swirls of colour. Very hippyish. Very Seventies. He knew a little of when she had met William, his dad. The story was that his father had returned from living abroad and was working on a building project in the Lake District. His mother was working in a local hotel as a receptionist, the hotel where his dad was lodging for the duration of the project. 'Very romantic,' his dad had said. 'I took your mother sailing on Derwentwater and then for a slap-up meal at the Swiss Lodore Hotel at the end of the lake. And that was it. I'd hooked her.'

'But you didn't reel me in immediately,' Beth had insisted. 'I was the one who kept you dangling for a while.'

It had been a warm, close, affectionate relationship and when David's mother was diagnosed with cancer and died suddenly at the age of sixty, his father was devastated. That was ten years ago now. But it probably hastened the dementia, David reckoned.

He turned at the sound of running footsteps along the hall.

'Dad, I found something.' Joe stood at the door panting after running from the workshop. He went across to David and handed him the cigar box. 'There's a book inside,' he said. 'I think it's a diary.'

David opened the box and frowned as he looked at the cover of the notebook. Jamaica? His dad had never mentioned ever being in Jamaica. He opened the cover and started reading.

THE JAMAICA JOURNAL OF WILL PEARSON
My first venture into serious writing.
Here's to posterity!

August 20th 1974
Kingston airport- Getting off the plane the heat slaps you like a hot towel. Air thick with humidity. The Blue Mountains, hazy in the distance beyond the city. Tricky landing. You approach over the harbour towards this thin spit of land which branches like a curved arm out from the coast. They call it the Palisadoes Peninsula. Where the pirate Henry Morgan had his hideout at Port Royal

until it was destroyed by an earthquake. Lots of noise and clamour at the airport. Young Jamaican guys in cowboy hats arriving from Miami - meeting their families. Lots of swagger 'Hey brudder, you lookin' cool man.' I'm picking up on the accent.

Met by Jim Suarez, young American guy, also with the company. Clean cut, friendly. Took me by car to the Sheraton Hotel where I'm booked in. Then to an old plantation mansion called Devon House, just down the road - Hope Road, close to where the Prime Minister's place is. Drank my first Jamaican rum punch. Very exotic like a fruit cocktail. Kingston's a mish mash of some new high rise offices and apartment blocks but a lot of beat up shacks with donkey carts and goats in the street and market women sitting by the roadside selling fruit and other stuff. Quite a culture shock, but exciting!

August 23rd

Starting to get my bearings. I'll be at the Sheraton for a few weeks before I get an apartment. Went out to the project yesterday. Uptown, along Hope Road past Devon House and then first glimpse of King's House where I think the Governor General lives - a white mansion set back amid broad lawns - very grand. The footings for the project have been done. Jim described a weird ceremony which went on at the ground-breaking. Some old Jamaican high priest guy came and they slaughtered a cockerel and a goat and had to pour the blood plus white rum in the corners of the site for good luck. Then the goat was cooked and the managers had to sit through a kind of banquet at which the goat's testicles were offered to the MD as a gesture of great honour. Maxim, the MD, did the business and ate them, much to the approval of the local Jamaican guys. Jim said it was hilarious but they had to take it very seriously.

David closed the journal. This was bizarre. A period in his father's life he knew nothing about. His

13

mother had never mentioned a connection with Jamaica. He knew his father had worked abroad as a young man, somewhere in central America, he thought. And his dad certainly had a passion for reggae and had sat with David when he was younger and watched a documentary on Bob Marley. But he'd never talked about living in Jamaica.

'So what does it say, dad?' asked Joe.

'Seems that Pops lived and worked in Jamaica before he married Nan.'

'Didn't you know?'

David shrugged: 'It's news to me.' He placed the book back in the cigar box and closed the lid. 'I'll read some more when we get home and let you know what I find out.' He looked at his watch. 'C'mon, let's call it a day and go get a burger at McDonald's.'

'Great!' said Joe. 'Mine's a double cheese.'

'We'll see,' said David, and he patted Joe's hair lightly as they went down the hallway to the front door.

Before closing the door behind him David took in the familiar view. It was the view that he had gazed at all his life - across the Solway estuary to Scotland. This was the house he had grown up in and the sea had been ever present in his waking hours and lulling him to sleep. The tide was coming in, the sand of the foreshore was dry and across the water the humped dome of Criffel on the Scottish side was hedged with sea mist. The house was the last house in the village, the place where Hadrian's Wall ended in marsh and mud flats. Some of the sandstone blocks which were the cornerstones of the house were probably salvaged from the Wall itself back in the 1800s. This had been his father's outpost, facing the weather which bowled in from the Atlantic, facing westwards, where, maybe, his father's early memories were lodged.

That evening after Joe had gone to bed, David made himself a coffee, threw a log on the fire and settled down to read more of the journal.

August 26th. Didn't realise Jamaica was such a magnet for celebrities. Chatted to one of Mick Jagger's roadies this morning at breakfast. The Rolling Stones are here doing some recording at Chris Blackwell's studio in the Blue Mountains - it's a place called Strawberry Hill. Blackwell is the Island Records' chief. There's lots in the newspapers about him promoting local singer, Bob Marley. Been trying to get a feel for the country by reading the two main newspapers - the Daily Gleaner and the Daily News. Seems there's quite a battle going on between the government party - the PNP and the Opposition - the JLP. Regular shootings in Western Kingston - but uptown things seem ok.

August 30th. Finally got myself a car. Weird system. Had to go to the bank to beg for a loan and the manager checks what car I want to buy before he decides whether he's going to give me the money. I'd seen a nice Austin Allegro. Manager said it was a 'shit' car for Jamaican roads. Told me to find a VW and then come back to him. So now I'm the proud owner of a VW Beetle. Bit of a tank, but he's right about the roads - potholes everywhere. Had to get it tested and licensed. What a shock that was, driving through western Kingston to the test centre. Never seen poverty like it. Corpses of rusting cars along Spanish Town Road. Side roads lined with small shacks of patched corrugated iron. Children sitting in the roadside dust, barefoot, playing with hoops and sticks. Donkeys and goats scavenging in the rubbish which is vomited onto the road from the dustbins.
Jim had said to lock doors and windows and I'm glad I did. As the streets narrowed so I had to drive more slowly between crowds of raggedy people. Pavements and side

streets oozed black bodies like oil. On the pavements women sat cross-legged on pieces of old sacking in front of small selections of fruit and veg - paw-paws, yams, avocados, sugar cane, bananas (I can now identify some of the new fruits!). Saw a young boy walking - dirty, naked and I felt a sense of guilt - at being white, having a car, money in my pocket....

Sept.4th. Now I've seen the extremes. Seems that the area I drove in Western Kingston to get the car tested is close to Trenchtown - famous for shootouts between rival gangs and it's also where local hero, Bob Marley, grew up. But last night I saw the other end of the social spectrum. The MD, or CEO (Chief Executive Officer) as the American guys call the top man in the organisation, invited us to his house for a party. I had to drive further up Hope Road and then to this district called Beverly Hills. I thought it was a joke when I heard the name but that's what it's called. And it lives up to its name. It's where the Kingston elite live. Extravagant homes built on concrete stilts and projecting out from the hillside called Long Mountain - balconies which look out over the city below - a fantasy of twinkling lights. Up here, in the less humid, balmy air of wealth and privilege it's a different Jamaica - the party candles shimmer against the curve of the cocktail glasses, moisture freckles the buckets of ice, the flames from the barbecue illuminate the dark faces of the chefs and servants and the chatter from Americans, English and pale-skinned Jamaicans floats out over the city lights like so much confetti.

Listen to me getting all kind of poetic - but this place brings out a kind of wonder and awe at what feels like a dreamscape. I have to pinch myself that it's real and it's happening to little old suburban me! But more difficult is to hang some notion of reality on it all.

I chatted to various people working on the project - designers, architects, finance guys. The CEO, Maxim Moreno, is from the Middle East - or his ancestors were.

Seems there are many rich Syrians among the Jamaican elite. He asked me if I was settling in and talked about how he admired British designers and architects and hoped I'd enjoy contributing to the success of the project. I felt kind of honoured that he'd taken a few moments to speak to me. His wife, Camilla, who's American, was the classic hostess - bejewelled, and wearing a striking lemon dress, drifting around the guests with a touch here, a few words there, introducing people - in fact she made a point of coming across and welcoming me. 'So you must be William, from England. Maxim tells me you just arrived last week.' I felt a little tongue-tied faced by this glamorous woman who clearly swam so comfortably in this gathering of style and elegance. I mumbled some appropriate pleasantries and was surprised when she took my arm and drew me across the balcony. 'Thought you ought to meet my friend, Carl,' she said. 'He's looking for crew for a yacht race in two weeks time. Whad'ya reckon. Are you a sailor?' I mentioned that I'd sailed in college and that seemed to seal the deal. 'Perfect,' she said. And she introduced me to this suave olive-skinned Jamaican called Carl Da Costa. Seems he's in the import business, fitting out hotels on the north coast. Friendly guy, he's invited me to crew on his boat in a couple of weeks time. It's some sort of yacht race to some islands south east of Jamaica called the Morant Cays. Sounds exciting.

Sept. 10th. I'm enjoying the challenge of writing this journal. Trying to capture the people, the places, the moments, is not easy. But I'm working at it. I feel this adventure needs recording - it's pretty special and I want to be able to look back in years to come and relive it. It's all so, so different from my life in little ol' England. I'm reading more critically from magazines and books - trying to work out how writers make it so vivid for the reader. That's what I'm working on. Trying to bring it alive on the page. Not sure I'm succeeding but that's my mission.

Finally moved out of the Sheraton into my own apartment. It's near the university at Mona. First floor with a balcony view of the sea! Can't believe my luck. And it comes with Eveline, who's like a good fairy - local woman who is employed to maintain the apartment block - takes the washing, will prepare food if I want it, cleans etc.. I'm feeling like a guilty colonial - but that's the way it is here. I'm shouldering my 'white man's burden' with a rum and ginger in my hand - tough life this! Eveline has relations in 'Hengland' so she's really interested to quiz me about the home country. She says she mostly deals with Americans so to meet a real 'Henglish mon' gets her really excited. Can't understand her half the time - she speaks with a strong line in local patois so I get every 4th word. But it's fun and 'Me gettin' a likkle bitta deh Jamaican twang, nah mon!'

Sept. 12th. Jim invited me to a concert downtown at a place called The Little Theatre. It was the Jamaican Philharmonic Orchestra. Hadn't associated Jim with classical music - doesn't fit the American stereotype somehow. Rubbed shoulders with the Jamaican elite - all dressed in their finery. Some stunning women in the most flamboyant colours, some with coiled scarves on their heads, men in what they call Kariba suits - kind of safari jackets, with matching trousers - very smart and cool looking. The current prime minister, Michael Manley, has made the style very popular. Wasn't sure classical music would appeal but I was wrong. It was curious to see black musicians in an orchestra - threw me somehow. Never seen a black person playing a violin and creating this sort of wonderful sound. Black musicians are usually playing guitars or banging drums. To see the young men in tuxedos and the women in evening gowns was a revelation. The programme was a mix of pieces, Debussy,

Chopin but the piece which held me was a truly beautiful section of the Shostakovich Piano Concerto, the Andante ……

David suddenly stopped reading as he felt a knot tighten in his stomach. He searched for his phone in his jacket pocket and checked his downloads. There it was - the *Shostakovich Andante*, the piece his father had reacted to so strongly.

…… I was mesmerised first by the music itself but then by one of the violinists - a young woman wearing a bright orange dress. She sat near the front of the stage, was probably one of the lead violinists, but I was held by the profile of her face, the lustre of her dark skin, the slender neck, a slight frown above the eyes, the curve of her back as she moved with the motion of the violin bow. It was intoxicating - the music, the sensuality of this young woman, the smoulder of emotion I felt as I watched. Afterwards I wanted to hang around in the foyer, hoping to get a second glimpse of her, but Jim was eager to get a cold beer and we left soon after the concert finished. But the allure of that young woman haunted me for hours afterwards.

David closed the journal. He was intrigued. A few days earlier he'd discovered that the Jamaican Daily Gleaner newspaper was available online. He wondered how far back it went. Might this concert have been reported on? He opened his laptop and Googled *Daily Gleaner archives.*
The page appeared and he typed in *Little Theatre concert, September, 1974.* Like the magic that was Google, a rather blurry page appeared and down the side was a report entitled *'Concert audience thrilled'.* There was reference to the *'brilliance of the virtuoso pianist Calvin Richardson playing the Shostakovich 2nd Piano Concerto'* . He scanned the page for other items. There

was a report on shootings in Trenchtown, the place his father had written about earlier in the diary, a report on a planned visit by the prime minister, Michael Manley, to Cuba to meet Fidel Castro and details of a new hotel being built in a place called Ocho Rios.

David sat back in his chair and stared out of the window. This life he knew nothing about. This voice of his father, coming through the journal, a voice so familiar, or it had been years ago before the death of his mother. That's when the light went out of his father's eyes and the life out of his voice and the tensions developed between him and David. Prior to that there was always that hint of humour in the voice and an enthusiasm to embrace the colour of each day, rain or shine. But this other life - it was like opening a door into an unknown world.

*

September 20th. I saw her again ! (sounds like that line from the Mamas and Papas song) not across a crowded room but across a crowded sea. It was the start of the Morant Cays race and our boat, Coral Queen, was jockeying for position with six other boats at the starting line just off the small island of Lime Cay. We'd sailed out of the harbour the previous afternoon and anchored just beyond the Palisadoes. It was as we were manoeuvring to get a good starting position that I saw her. Not this time in an evening dress and holding a violin but pulling on a sail rope (sorry Carl, a sail 'sheet') in cut off denim shorts and a white bikini top. Wow, talk about a teenage crush! Those long ebony legs and arms, the slender neck and short wavy hair - it was her all right, just for a second and then as we tacked so I lost her in the rip and snatch of the canvas of the sails. Didn't manage to spot the name of her boat but watched it moving away, dipping into the swell. Then Carl shouted at me to sort the jib and that was it. She was gone. The sailing was full of mini dramas. We nearly lost the spinnaker under the boat at one point and then later we had to outrun a squall and I was a bit unnerved watching Ben, one of the crew, unclipping the main jib to clip on the storm jib. He was holding on to the forestay as the boat lifted and dipped against these onrushing walls of water. I feared we'd lose him overboard but we weathered the squall and arrived at the Morant Cays late the next afternoon. They're a small group of islands about 60 miles south-east of Jamaica only visited by fishermen and there are a couple of small shacks on the largest cay. We anchored near the other boats and there was much banter between the crews - paddling the dinghies across to share drinks. I was hoping to find her boat but failed and settled for a rather boozy night on a boat called Island Gypsy which was moored close by Coral Queen.

It was the following morning that my luck changed. Carl suggested I have a go at diving for lobster. The water is shallow near the reefs, you only need a snorkel and mask and the lobster are there for the taking. They sit in the sunlight and are a gift for someone with a good eye and a spear gun. So I'm swimming along the surface, spotting lobster, diving and spearing some beauties when I spot another diver. Unmistakeable! She was even more stunning under the water. She saw me and I motioned for her to go ahead and collect the lobster I'd been eyeing. She gave me the thumbs up, dived and, using only a short pole with a barbed end, pinioned a lobster by its tail but then struggled to get it into the bag she was carrying. I swam down and helped and then we surfaced. And there we were - finally face to face. I'll never forget that moment or that face - beads of water streaming over her dark skin, the smile, the pearly teeth, the open mouth, the eyes, the laughter. 'Thank you,' she said, gasping a little. 'I nearly lost him. Which boat are you off?' 'Coral Queen,' I replied. 'I'm Will Pearson.' 'Nice to meet you Will, I'm Maya.' 'I know, you're that great violinist.' She shook her head, blinked, frowned. 'I was at the concert. You were great. Loved that Shostakovich.' 'Well thank you

Will Pearson,' she said. We trod water for a while getting our breath and then she said, 'There's another concert in a couple of weeks - brilliant Cuban guitarist. You might enjoy it.' Then she waved and was gone with a 'See you later'.

So that was it, David nodded to himself. It was the same person - Maya. And then he remembered that moment in the care home. His father sobbing, but he had shouted out something - something like 'My..oh..my..' But maybe it was her name 'Maya'. And then the heart-rending 'She's gone, she's gone.' And when his father was sinking in the estuary mud and repeating 'She's gone,' David had assumed he was referring to Beth, his mother. But maybe that wasn't so. And maybe the obsession with sitting for hours on the end of the pier looking westwards was a yearning for something and someone David hadn't known about. He felt for his phone, scrolled through his playlist and found the Andante again. He listened to the soft lilt of this exquisite melody but now listened for the sound of the strings - tried to picture this young violinist who had so captivated his father. She would probably be in her sixties or even seventies now, if she was still alive.

October 12th.   Was hoping to see Maya again at the concert but it was cancelled as the theatre's been flooded by the torrential rain we've had. The island's been side-swiped by the tail of Hurricane Carmen. Never seen rain like it. Hope Road was like a brown swirling river. Car broke down half-way home. Had to abandon it and battle through knee high torrents. Local kids were sailing makeshift boats down the gutters. Terrible landslides in the Blue Mountains - whole hillsides gashed with mud slides over the roads and people's homes washed away. Every day grey clouds - reminds me of Hengland. I was telling Eveline that this is English weather. She said 'me don't kyar bout de wedder- it de ol' mudder country an me like see where de Queen live dem'.

Been doing a little detective work - quizzing Carl about Maya. He says she often crews on a boat called Blue Lady owned by a Texan named RJ. More importantly, found out Maya works at the Jamaican Embassy. I sometimes drive past in the afternoon, hoping to spot her. So far, no luck.

October 14th. The rains have scuppered things at the project. Foundations are flooded and no building work is possible. So I've had some forced leave. Drove to the west end of the island with Jim and a couple of the other guys from work, Don and Larry. Don's from Alabama, talks with this hillbilly type sing-song accent - it's amusing at first until you get used to it. Larry's from upstate New York. Quite different. A little earnest and kinda formal. We stayed in this amazing old guest house near Negril called Saxham Grange. It's an old plantation house owned by the feisty Mrs Delaney. From the balconies you look out on to acres of coconut palms and sugar cane. Had visions of the colonial grandeur of the past until old Mrs Delaney put me right. Not much 'grandeur' apparently. Lots of sickness and brutality. She pointed me to her small library and suggested I 'heducate yourself' about the reality of the plantation system during the slavery period. My knowledge of Jamaican history is pretty thin. So I've been reading 'To Be A Slave' by Julius Lester which documents the experiences of ex-slaves from capture in Africa, to being auctioned in America and the West Indies and then the grim realities of life on the cotton and sugar plantations. So much for my notion of 'colonial grandeur'. Mrs Delaney certainly scotched that delusion! But that doesn't alter the fact of the incredible beauty of this island. The coastline with its offshore reefs and small sandy bays lapped by crystal clear waters is just a slice of paradise. We dived off the high rocks at Negril - Don is a brilliant swimmer and does these amazing swallow dives from cliffs that I wouldn't venture up. But he goes through the water like a dolphin. He had a spell in the marines and is in great shape.

October 15th. Had an interesting evening with Don, Larry and Jim. Opened my eyes kind of. We were drinking at a beach bar at a little bay near Savannah La Mar, just down the coast from Negril.
The talk became political. Seems there's a concern about the current government flirting with Castro. They talked of Jamaicans travelling to Cuba to be trained in what they called 'brigadistas' - military camps where they teach about guerrilla warfare. Don reckoned there's going to be civil war in Jamaica soon. They were saying what a good guy the Opposition Leader, Edward Seaga is - that America is backing him to take down the Manley government sometime in the future.
I had no opinion on all this. It was all news to me. But it's intriguing hearing what's going on behind the scenes.

And was there ever a civil war in Jamaica? David wondered. He decided he needed to check out this period when his father was in the country.

He searched Wikipedia on his laptop. In the late Seventies there was certainly a lot of blood spilt between the rival parties of the governing PNP and the JLP, Edward Seaga's party. Bob Marley had been shot and wounded in 1976 in a house on Hope Road, the very road his father had mentioned. Marley fled to England but was persuaded to return in 1978 for the 'One Love' concert in which the 'king of reggae' had brought the two leaders together on stage in a gesture of truce.

And had his father witnessed all this? But he couldn't have - his parents were married in 1978? So he must have left the island sometime earlier.

October 27th. It's weird being made aware of your skin colour - being for the first time in a racial minority. Never thought about it before. Always been surrounded by white faces in England. Can't recall ever having spoken to anyone who wasn't white. Where we lived in England, where I went to school, university, work, there were few faces that weren't white. And now, suddenly I'm surrounded by black faces. At first they all looked the same to me, and then this strange process of individual faces - like Eveline, like Jerome on the gate at the project, like Richard, one of the other architects and of course, like Maya - it's like they emerge out of this dark morass, distilled almost and I'm seeing individual features and there's recognition.

And then the other day, driving up into the Blue Mountains for the first time, some kid yelling at me 'White pork!' as I drove through his village. White pork? Set me thinking. Never thought about my whiteness being significant, but it was to that little boy.

Lots of excitement about the release of the new Bob Marley album - 'Natty Dread'. Keep hearing the track 'No Woman, No Cry' played on RJR. It's really haunting. Getting ready for the Hallowe'en party at the yacht club. Not sure they mark Hallowe'en much in Jamaica, but at the yacht club there are so many Americans - and they make a big thing of it. Hoping Maya might be there.

November 6th. I suppose it would have been Guy Fawkes' Night at home last night. Here nobody's really bothered about some English rebel who tried to blow up Parliament. And that's another thing. At home what happens in the UK is all consuming, it's the centre of your world. Over here England could have disappeared beneath the waves and it wouldn't really affect much. Certainly disturbs where my centre of gravity is. I suppose it's that old illusion that our geography perpetuates when we look at a map of the world where Mercator placed Europe right in the centre. Gives you a sense that we're at the centre of everything. From here Britain's round the other side of the globe, out of sight and almost out of mind. Disconcerting!

25

But the Hallowe'en party was a blast. It's noticeable that it's a very light-skinned place, the yacht club. You don't see many black faces apart from the bar staff, the car park valets, and the guys serving the buffet. Jim mentioned this little saying he'd heard - 'If you're white you're all right, if you're brown stick around, if you're black stand back'. And it certainly applies at the club. Apart from Maya! She looked amazing in a turquoise jumpsuit. Among the white faces she stood out like a beacon, and boy, was she turning heads. Didn't think she'd remember me, but she did.

'Hey, it's my lobster buddy,' she said as she was about to move past me. And she stopped, smiled, eyes dancing with the light. I was a little tongue-tied. 'What a memory,' I said. 'How are you?'

She frowned for a moment, 'Will, wasn't it?'

I nodded: 'Pity about the concert being cancelled.'

She shrugged: 'These things happen this time of year. Always a lot of rain. But at least we didn't get the full weight of Carmen like Cuba did.'

'Wasn't the guitarist from Cuba?'

She was sipping from a fruit cocktail and I had time to take in her face again - the high cheek bones, the tight, wavy hair, hooped gold earrings. 'Yes, Juan Giminez, I know him quite well, and he was going to play the Concerto de Aranjuez.'

'Rodrigo?'

'You know it?'

I nodded. 'Yes, I love that piece.'

'Yes, I love playing it. It's rescheduled for December. You could catch it then.'

She asked me whether I'd explored much of the island. Mentioned that a group from the orchestra was planning a hike up in the Blue Mountains just before Christmas to a place called Cinchona where there were some gardens. Did I want to join them?

No hesitation! Didn't want to appear too eager but said I'd like that. So it's fixed that I'll see her again, although

it'll be a group thing. No matter. Something to look forward to.
But that face, those eyes, that alluring black skin. She bewitches me in a way I can't explain.

David closed the journal. Turned again to his computer. He did a search on Google Earth for *Cinchona, Jamaica,* watched the globe spinning then the fast zoom into the Caribbean and the island of Jamaica and yes, there it was, *Cinchona*, way up in the Blue Mountains at 5000feet and not far from Blue Mountain Peak. There were some photos of the gardens - pine trees and eucalyptus and rhododendrons. It looked more European than tropical, apart from the mountains sheering away down into the clouds, steep green slopes clothed in grass and stands of bamboo. It had been established in 1868 by Sir John Peter Grant, a past governor of Jamaica. David tried to picture his father as a young man, sitting on the grass, looking out at the view, with the intriguing Maya at his side.

*

'What else have you found out, dad?' It was the weekend and Joe and his dad were back clearing out Pops' house. 'I was telling mum about the diary and Pops being in Jamaica. She said a friend at work went on holiday there and what a great time she had.'

David wondered how much to tell. 'Well, seems that your Pops was working as an architect there in   the mid Seventies.'

'Wasn't that when Bob Marley was famous?'

'Not sure that he was that famous when Pops first got there.'

'But he was shot there, right?'

'Yes, in 1976, December I think.'

'Did Pops write about it in his book?'

'I haven't got that far yet. I've only got to his first Christmas in 1974.'

'Oh, yeah, dad, forgot to show you something else I found in the workshop.' He went into the hall and came back holding up the wooden name board from Pops' yacht - *Jamaya*. 'Found it on a shelf. It's kind of like the name Jamaica, isn't it.'

But David noticed something much more obvious - 'maya'. So each time his dad went sailing he was reminded of Jamaica and Maya. He wondered if his mother ever understood the significance of the name. He doubted it, considering how this part of his father's life had never been mentioned.

November 18th. Some weird events going on at the project. At a meeting chaired by the CEO some union guy pulled a gun and laid it on the table. According to Jim, Maxim went ballistic and ordered the guy out. A dangerous move considering the unions are very powerful and contracts are normally given on the basis of 'back-handers' and are underwritten by one of the two main political parties. So there's rivalry for the contracts and pulling a gun was meant to seal the deal. Maxim's trying to stay neutral but Jim reckons he's on a loser. These guys are ruthless and we're hoping things don't deteriorate.
On the plus side, I'm getting a taste for Jamaican patties. There's a small stall just outside the main gate at work. It's run by Flora, a local lady, with her little boy, James. James is always there with his rag and his bucket begging to 'Clean yuh window for a ten cent, nah mon!' So I often stop after work and while James cleans the car windows I buy one of Flora's patties. They're like a small pasty but the pastry is thinner and the meat is quite spicy. But I'm getting a taste for the heat, although Flora asked me:'Yuh not try Scotch Bonnet yet, Mr William?' Apparently Scotch Bonnet is at the top of the hot chilli league, so I'm giving that a miss at present. But I've tried paw paw and star apple and these little round fruits called guineps.

Flora sells them in bunches. You peel the hard skin and then suck on the soft pulp which surrounds the stone. They're kind of sour but nice on a hot afternoon after work. Flora says she aims to 'heducate you in arl tings Jamaican, Mr William.'

December 2nd. The weather's cooling down a little. Much less humidity than when I arrived and we don't get the build up of rain clouds and the torrential downpours in the afternoon so much now, so the building work is progressing well. Up to first floor level. They say this is the best time of year. Looking forward to the hike to Cinchona next weekend. Haven't seen Maya for almost a month.

December 12th. Someone reckoned there were 150 bends in the 12 mile drive up to the army camp at Newcastle. Certainly felt like it. But what a road. It's like a switch-back snaking up into the mountains from the top of Hope Road. You pass gullies and streams of rushing crystal clear water, and then the road gets steeper and the shacks of the locals cling to the hillside on little terraces where they grow their crops and tether their cows and donkeys. It's a different world up there away from the heat and tensions of the Kingston streets. Kingston dissolves into the clouds and you enter a world away in time and space. There are small settlements with rustic rum bars, maybe a school and a church. At Newcastle the road crosses the parade ground of the army camp which was built in the 1840s by the British to get away from the mosquitoes and yellow fever down in Kingston. And the Blue Mountains are so green, even up to Blue Mountain Peak at over 7000ft. You see the ridge and the peak from Cinchona and the name comes from the blue haze which filters the light off the mountains.
We travelled in two cars - there were 8 of us - 5 who play in the orchestra with Maya - Jonathan, Courtney, Charles, Lloyd and Marianne, and a Cuban guy called

Diego, a friend of Jonathan's. Marianne studied music at the University of Miami with Maya and they all clearly live for their music. All the way up the mountain we listened to a mix of some new reggae from The Wailers but also Motown and Cuban salsa which they all seem to love - I was introduced to the voice of Celia Cruz, the queen of Cuban salsa.

Arrived late morning at the lodge where we were staying. It's on the old Clydesdale coffee estate. Up there at 5000 feet it's a different Jamaica - pine trees, rhododendrons, roses, wild strawberries, eucalyptus - cool breezes and cloud curling over Blue Mountain Ridge. And the mountains fall away into space, down towards the distant valleys and Kingston lost in a haze.
In the evening we made a log fire and while Diego cooked chicken and ribs on the barbecue, the others set up their small ensemble and played some amazing music. Some classical but they're great at busking in various styles.

I must mention this strange skin factor which constantly squirms under the surface in my mind. When I first met them all I was aware I was the only white face among 7 black faces - so much seems woven into the surface of that black skin - so much is lodged deep in my subconscious - primitive stereotypes and myths, deep rooted assumptions - where it all comes from - who knows? But it's always there just for a while until the individual features and personality of the person distil themselves out of the veneer of skin blackness. And so quickly have these folks banished all those assumptions with their wit and their amazing musical virtuosity. But it still disturbs me that my mind is so tainted by hauntings over which I seem to have no control.

David sat back frowning. He had no experience of living in a multi-racial community and this 'skin factor' and the reference to 'primitive stereotypes and myths' was puzzling. He didn't really get this notion of 'hauntings' which his father had mentioned. He shook his head and read on:

After an evening of music, much Red Stripe, Appleton rum and laughter I slept heavily. But I was awoken early. It was the faint sound of a single violin, light on the air, distant. The others were sleeping as I went out into a dew soaked morning; the pines silvered with moisture, the grass wet against my feet and the valleys below filled with mist. I followed the sound which rose and fell gently on the air. Down from the lodge there were a series of terraces used for drying the coffee beans, and then a grassy sitting area fronted by a terrace wall. I stood for a while watching. It was Maya playing in the way I'd first seen her play at the theatre - lost in the music, eyes closed, the bow stroking the air, the music rising in a series of upward cadences. I waited, watched, entranced, not wishing to intrude and break the spell.

Finally she made the last stroke of the bow, held the gesture for a moment before dropping her head. I continued to wait until the moment was past and she set the violin down at her side.

'That was exquisite,' I said. She looked round, a little embarrassed and I felt guilty that I'd intruded. 'What was it? I know it from somewhere.'

'An English composer - Vaughan Williams - The Lark Ascending,' she said. 'I first heard it at the college in Miami. Seemed to capture my mood this morning.'

'Have you ever seen a lark ascending?'

She shook her head.

'As they rise through the air they seem to almost dribble this watery song down through the air, their little wings fluttering madly.'

She smiled and lifted her head. 'Maybe one day I'll see one.'

Later we hiked up to Cinchona where there are botanical gardens. Quite a long haul which involved wading across some torrents swelled by the recent rains. But it was misty and cool so few mosquitoes. It's a rather run down place - some ivy covered estate buildings, raised beds laid out for planting but mostly overgrown. It was set up in the mid 19thC for growing the cinchona trees from which they got quinine for treating malaria which was rife down in Kingston. A couple of estate workers oversee the place. We gazed out over the space below which was filling with dense cloud moving up the valleys. Humming birds were busy around some feeding stations - the small bee humming birds like tiny jet aircraft zooming and hovering, wings beating so fast you could barely see them. The more elegant doctor birds with their long black paired tail feathers glistened an iridescent green and hovered in the air sipping the sugar juice from the feeding tubes which hung from the branches of the trees. It was a magical lost world kind of a place.

The descent back to Clydesdale was quicker but I spent time keeping close to Maya. I wanted to get beneath the surface of her outer vivacity, to get beyond my schoolboy crush to something more real.
I asked about her music career. She had gained a scholarship to the Conservatoire at the University of Miami and was sponsored by her uncle Ned, who owns a small coffee farm near Port Antonio on the north coast. She has an older brother, Edward, who is a lawyer in Montego Bay. Both her parents are dead and she shares a house with Marianne. Now she works at the Jamaican Embassy dealing mainly with visa applications. Then she turned and looked across at me: 'And what about you, Will, tell me about your life in England.' And as we walked on, now and then our arms brushed together, maybe just for a second, but skin to skin - it was electrifying. Whether it was the same for her I don't know but I felt a kind of intoxication being close to her.

Probably talked too much out of nervousness, but finally,
as we arrived back at the lodge so she touched me lightly
on the shoulder and said: 'It's been nice getting to know
you, Will. I'm so glad you came.'
What to make of that comment? How much weight of
expectation to load it with? I didn't give away my real
feelings but simply smiled and nodded and replied:
'Thanks for asking me. It's been a great weekend.'

David opened up his laptop and again Googled
Cinchona and *Clydesdale*. Amazingly, someone had
posted on You Tube a short video of a visit to Cinchona.
He called Joe to come and see. 'Look at this, Joe. I've
just been reading about Pops visiting this place called
Cinchona and here it is.'

Joe settled down beside David and they watched
the grainy images on the screen. There was the winding
road up to Newcastle, the green slopes of the Blue
Mountains plunging into cloud and mist, a road running
alongside a flooded river, then the gravel track up to
Cinchona, with a battered sign which read '*Cinchona,
Botanic Garden.*' There were decaying estate buildings
which nature was reclaiming, some overgrown flower
beds, a wide lawned terrace and then the steep, green
mountainside plunging into the valley below. And David
pictured Maya, sitting there in the early morning, playing
her violin with his father watching from a distance.

'But why don't we know anything about this?'
asked Joe. 'Has it been kept a secret? D'you think Nan
knew?'

David shook his head: 'I don't know, son, I really
have no idea.'

'Remember we listened to those old Bob Marley
albums with Pops and he talked about when he got shot.
That was a clue.'

'Well maybe, but then my dad liked all sorts of
music. How were we to know that reggae was special for
him for other reasons.'

'Will you tell me when you find out more things? It's like solving a mystery.'

'I'll let you know when there's something new.'

But David knew he would choose what to reveal, especially about Maya. Joe didn't need to know about Will's attraction for the young woman. Not yet, anyway.

*

December 20th. The Rodrigo Concerto was wonderful - such an emotional evening for me - not only does that Adagio by itself always move me to tears but watching Maya playing alongside this brilliant Cuban guitarist was almost overwhelming. And when I saw her in the foyer afterwards I couldn't help myself - but hugged her and said how much it had moved me. I then regretted the impulse in case it was a step too far but she didn't pull back, only smiled and nodded her thanks and said she too found the experience of playing the concerto utterly inspiring. I joined her and most of the Cinchona ensemble for drinks afterwards at the Terra Nova. They seem to have accepted me into their little group and I don't feel quite the outsider anymore even though I'm one white face among six black faces. Don't know whether they're just taking pity on this solitary Englishman or that they like my company. However, it didn't end there. I'm invited to join them on a Christmas trip to Mexico. They're playing at a small venue in Merida. It's somewhere in the east in what's called the Yucatan Peninsula. Couldn't believe it when Maya said: 'Why don't you join us, Will? You'd love Mexico, and the Mexicans really appreciate our music. We've played there once before.'

So I can't believe my luck. Christmas in Mexico with Maya! Doesn't get much better.

December 22nd. There's tension in the air at work. Maxim gave a drinks party before we left for the holiday but there were more murmurings about the workers being threatened by some outside bully boys. Since Maxim threw the union guy out of that meeting last month there's been a change in the atmosphere at the site. On the approach road to the gate there are these four guys in Toyota pickups who sit watching us go by. Jim reckons they're armed and are from one of the political groups. They wear these 'tams' - big woolly hats covering a mass of what are called 'dreadlocks' - long plaited hair - which normally defines those of the Ras Tafarian religion - but there's nothing religious about these guys as far as I can tell. Very intimidating!

January 4th 1975. What a trip that was! What a mind-bending, emotion-tilting trip. Flying into Merida you drop into an entirely different culture. Short, black-haired, bronze-skinned people. The Indians predominate but alongside are what they call the Mestizos - the people of Spanish origin who sometimes have reddish hair and paler skin. And Merida is a classic Spanish style city - beautiful main square with winding paths, fountains and cathedral at one end, cloister type walkways along the side of the square and then the grand civic buildings facing the cathedral. And it buzzes with street life. The Indian women wear white cotton dresses, embroidered with stunning patterns of flowers around the neckline. The men have white cotton shirts and trousers and wide brimmed straw hats. Along the roadside women bake tortillas on charcoal heated metal domes and there are stalls selling freshly squeezed juice from the oranges which grow everywhere here. They use an ingenious device for peeling the oranges - it's like a small lathe - the orange held between small metal centres and then as a handle is turned a small cutter moves round the profile of the orange taking off the skin - I was intrigued. Then they press the peeled oranges and the taste of the juice is amazing.

This time there were just 7 of us - Diego didn't come on this trip. Their first concert was in the church of Santo Domingo the night before Christmas Eve. Religion dominates here - it's an interesting mix of Roman Catholicism and some ancestor/nature worship. Flowers are strewn down the aisle and the church is decked with decorated pine branches. The little church was full of families dressed up for the occasion. They seemed to love the music. I didn't know Maya was so fluent in Spanish - she never fails to surprise me - she spoke to the congregation before they started and explained the pieces they were playing. I just love watching her - such effortless charm and warmth and she looked so elegant in a red dress trimmed with black. Afterwards the priests and the congregation applauded and more flowers were thrown before we were taken into a small side room for food and drink. I have to get used to the hot spice in Mexican food and the colour too. We had enchiladas - tortillas filled with spiced meat and vegetables and then 'cochinita pibil' which is slow-roasted pork. Some dishes are almost black from the use of chocolate. I've never come across chocolate being used like this - it isn't sweet like we get at home but dark and made into a thick sauce - chocolate 'al natural'- I'm told.

And then out into the flickering streets - a soft warm glow from the kerosene lamps and candles which light the little street stalls - the air balmy, a starlit sky with a bright half moon. And as we strolled through the square, past the splash of the water in the fountains so Maya had linked her arm in mine - it was so unexpected that I flinched a little - and she had looked up and asked: 'Are you okay?' I took the liberty of patting the back of her hand and letting mine rest on hers for just a moment. 'Never better,' I replied. 'Just wasn't expecting that.' 'D'you mind?' she had asked. I squeezed her hand and shook my head: 'How could I mind? You're a delight to be with. I just love your company - feel privileged to even be here with you all.' We were walking behind the others who were a little way ahead. Just for a moment Maya had leaned her head against my shoulder and I felt the gentle squeeze of her hand against mine - it was like an electrical charge which ran right through me. She lifted her head and we walked on, but something had happened in that moment which we both had acknowledged. Or so I hoped.

David closed the journal. He smoothed the cover with his hand. This felt like prying into something very private and intimate and he questioned whether he should continue reading. Should he not just destroy the notebook and let this unknown life of his father be laid to rest with him? But then he wondered whether the dementia had been hastened only by his mother's death. Maybe his father had been troubled by something else in his past. And David could not forget that mournful cry, 'She's gone, she's gone,' and the sobbing which followed. He rubbed his eyes and glanced at his watch. It was after midnight and there was the school run in the morning. He closed the journal and slid it into the drawer of his desk. Mexico and Maya would have to wait.

*

The next day we were taken by minibus an hour's drive east of Merida to the Mayan ruins at Chichen Itza. We passed fields of henequen, a spiky cactus plant crushed and dried to produce sisal for rope-making. So much history here that I had no knowledge of. The Mayans were great astronomers and there was a circular observatory on one side of the site. But more intriguing was how they applied their cosmic knowledge to the architecture of the temples. We climbed the pyramid called El Castillo which houses the Temple of Kukulcan and counted 9 levels on each of the 4 sides, supporting 10 steps on each level. Then up another 4 sided tier to the top most level which supports the temple building. This adds up to a total of 365 - the days in the year!! The pyramid is decorated with carved stone images of plumed serpents, skulls and other figures and from the top there is a great view across the flat scrubby landscape of the Yucatan.

All morning I was recalling the touch of Maya's arm in mine, the momentary press of her fingers, her head leaning for a while against my shoulder. Maybe it was just a passing thing brought on by the mellow mood of that evening, walking the streets in the moonlight, the romance of being in a strange and exotic place. But I treasured the memory nevertheless.

That day I found myself sitting at the top of the temple with Marianne. I could see Maya on the far side of the site at another temple taking photographs - a small figure dressed in cut off denims and a lemon coloured shirt knotted at the waist. Wherever she goes she turns heads. There are few black faces in this part of Mexico and she cuts a striking figure as she strides along the narrow side streets in Merida.

I asked Marianne where she and Maya had met. 'Maya' was a pet name, Marianne explained - shortened from Mahalia. Maya's father was a lover of American music and Maya was named after the gospel singer Mahalia Jackson. She and Maya had been at high school together and both won scholarships to the music college at the University of Miami. 'You seem to have bonded with her,' said Marianne. 'She's such a lovely person,' I replied. Marianne nodded: 'A bit fragile at the moment. On the rebound from an old relationship. Take care with her.'

Was that an implied invitation to develop my friendship with Maya? I couldn't tell, but I hoped it was.

*

It was the following Saturday morning that David drove into Carlisle to do some shopping while Joe was at his karate class. As he was passing Waterstones bookshop he saw in the window a photo of the Man Booker prize winner, Marlon James, alongside his book, *A Brief History of Seven Killings* - described as *A dramatic account of a dark period in recent Jamaican history.* He found a copy of the book on a display shelf inside. It was a hefty piece of work, almost seven hundred pages and he took it upstairs to the coffee shop. Curiously, it was set at the same time his father had been in Jamaica. It seemed the story was woven around the attempted murder of Bob Marley in 1976. David settled down with his coffee and leafed through the book. The list of characters alone was impressive - numbering about sixty. The list gave an impression of the dramatic scope of the book - there were CIA operatives, gang leaders, gang members, drug dealers, 'enforcers'. It sounded like a cauldron of violence and high drama. But then it only confirmed what he'd read from the Gleaner online. Jamaica in the Seventies was a hot-bed of gun-toting violence. David wondered whether his father had ever been caught up in any of it. He took the book to the cashier and checked his watch. Joe would be finished soon and they had to get a move on. There was the football game at Brunton Park and Joe would not forgive him if they were late for the kick-off.

*

February 10th. Drove past the Gun Court for the first time. It was opened last year but I don't have cause to go to that part of Kingston. It was one of Manley's ideas to combat the rise in shootings. It's meant to be pretty intimidating, and it is - painted deep red, there are armed guards in high turrets at each corner and coiled barbed wire topping the fencing. Looks like a POW camp from the last war.
Haven't seen Maya in over a month and it's left me feeling empty. The Mexico trip seemed to promise so much. She phoned me last week. Is preparing for an

orchestra trip to Cuba. Michael Manley is backing it with lots of publicity. Fidel Castro's his close buddy, it seems, although the Americans are dead against it. Larry was sounding off at work that things are going to have to change. Not sure what he means, but then Larry's full of hot air and talk of Armageddon.

February 24th. Been busy at work. Maxim wants to extend the project which requires some plans for a whole new complex of warehouses and offices. He certainly is ambitious, riding on the feeling of optimism that the Manley government tries to generate. Manley upset the Americans and the IMF by raising the bauxite levy - he doesn't want so much money going to foreign countries but that doesn't earn him any friends in high places abroad.
Spent another weekend in the west of the island with Jim. There's a long straight section of road as you approach Negril and we're driving along listening to Jimmy Cliff on RJR when a light aircraft swoops down over our heads and lands on the road some way ahead. We stop and watch as a truck pulls out of a track and some guys are throwing sacks through the open door of the plane which is still moving. Then they're back in the truck, off in a cloud of dust and the plane takes off. Jim and I look at each other amazed. That's how the ganja trade works, apparently !!

March 6th. Read the report in the Gleaner about the orchestral concert in Cuba. Manley hailed it as a great cultural achievement for Jamaica. There's to be a return tour by a Cuban dance troupe later in the year. Seems my so-called 'bonding' with Maya was something of a delusion.

March 10th. Maya phoned - out of the blue! Asked if I'd been to the beach at Hellshire, just round the bay on the west side of Kingston. It's a favourite place for a Sunday morning swim, she said. She thought I'd like it. I expected the usual posse from the orchestra but it was only her and Marianne. We met in the car park of the Sheraton and then I rode in her car. I felt a distance between us again, like when we first met. She seemed distracted but it was great to see her. She always looks attractive and I find it hard to take my eyes off her. But I tried to act casual and relaxed.

The beach at Hellshire is unspoilt by any development - just a few wooden shelters behind a white sand beach where local women cook fish and cassava bread they call 'bammies'. A short distance off shore there's a reef and always a line of surf breaking. The swimming is glorious.

After we'd swum and glanced at the Sunday Gleaner, Marianne walked away down the beach. It was then that Maya questioned me about Maxim. How much did I know about him? It seems some requests had come to the embassy to the department where Maya works - requests for visas for some Cuban workers. And then she asked about Larry although she used his full name 'Lawrence Newsom'. I said that he was the most outspoken critic of the Manley government and she seemed surprised at that. I asked her why she was quizzing me. She smiled and touched me lightly on my arm - 'Sorry, it was just a coincidence that the name of where you worked came across my desk and I wondered how things were going with your work. It also reminded me that I hadn't seen you for quite a while and I so enjoyed the Mexico trip.'

How should I read this? I wondered. Would she have called if Maxim's visa requests hadn't landed on her desk?

But then we swam out to the reef and she was playful and fun and she held on to my arm when the swell was threatening to push us against the coral on the reef. Ended up with a bad graze on my back and it wasn't until we came out of the water that I realised it was bleeding so badly. Maya cleaned it with some tissues and I have to say I delighted in all this attention, the softness of her

41

touch, her closeness and then finally and unexpectedly the light touch of her lips against my shoulder as she said: 'There, you'll live.'
What do I make of it all? Just go with the flow? as they say.

March 20th. Got a call from a guy who calls himself RJ - an American who owns beachfront land near Port Antonio. Wants me to look at his ideas for some resort complex and draw up some plans. Said he'd heard of my work from a friend. Could be lucrative. Going to drive over this weekend.

March 28th. What a surprise! Turns out RJ's friend was Maya and he owns the yacht Maya crews on. When she heard about his project she thought of me. How good is that! And she was there when I arrived. Seems her uncle Ned's coffee farm is not far from RJ's property. RJ's a big gum-chewing Texan. Has this great piece of beachfront real estate called Zion Hill, near the famous Blue Lagoon and San San Bay east of Port Antonio. Wants me to draw him some plans for a resort of small guest houses grouped round a central hospitality area and a new dock. He's from Houston but lives for half the year in Jamaica. Says he met Maya when she was studying music in Miami. What a great challenge for me - a bit more creative than designing warehouses and office blocks.

Maya then took me to meet her uncle Ned. His farm is a few miles inland in the hills. He's Maya's mother's brother. What a character. He'd be mid 50s. Smokes an old bent Meerschaum pipe which he stokes with tobacco he grows on the farm.
He showed me over part of the property which stands high above the coast with an amazing view of the coastline. He grows coffee and bananas, a little sugar cane and coconut palms. Several streams run through the property and Maya led me to her favourite place higher

up in the hills. It's where a river drops in a waterfall from a height of about 20 feet into an amazing deep plunge pool. She didn't hesitate to strip off to her bikini and challenge me to do the jump from the top of the waterfall. She jumped first and I watched her dark body swimming under the water to the side of the pool. She emerged, face glistening, her wide smile, the beads of water like so many tiny diamonds caught in the waves of her hair. It was one of those moments which imprints itself indelibly.

'C'mon, chicken,' she taunted. So I jumped, hit the water in a flurry of bubbles and then sank into the deeper blue of the pool. I swam underwater until I saw the shape of her legs near the side and pulled her under. We chased in and out of the waterfall like a couple of kids and then for a moment we both emerged inside the curtain of water where there was an echoing stillness. She was panting and laughing and for a moment her expression changed and she stared at me with a slight frown before duck-diving under the waterfall again. It was a curious look, as if a cloud had passed across the sun momentarily. I watched her as she climbed out of the pool, the water glistening on her skin, outlining the curves of her body. I'll never forget that moment.

I had fully intended to drive back that evening, even though the road from Kingston is pretty tortuous. But Maya invited me to use the small cottage which stands on the hillside below Ned's house. It's a small wooden cabin with a pitched roof and wooden deck which looks down on the bay of San San. A touch of paradise and a world away from Kingston. This is 'Island in the Sun' territory.

Maya barbecued chicken and made what they call 'rice and peas' and then cut slices of paw paw she picked from a tree at the back of the house. And although there's a kind of bliss about being with her, there's always something getting in the way. Like that look when we were swimming, a momentary closeness and then she pulls back and I'm left wondering how to make the next move. I didn't know how this evening would end until she

43

got up, kissed me on my head and said: 'Thanks for a nice evening. I'll be down early to take you for a swim,' and she was off up the hill to Ned's place.

The following morning she took me down to see the famous Blue Lagoon. They say it's 'fathomless' but it's really a collapsed limestone sink hole - very deep which makes the water an intense dark blue. Nearby is San San Bay. Now this really is a bit of paradise - a curving sandy beach fringed with palm trees, an offshore reef a short distance from the shore and an island - Nina Khan's island - named for the wife of the Aga Khan who owns it. The swimming is fabulous and I'm looking forward to regular visits here while I'm working on the plans for RJ.

Maya was staying on a couple of days with her uncle so I set off mid-morning, took the mountain road over the Blue Mountain Ridge back to Kingston, rather than the longer route via Annotto Bay which I'd driven the previous day.

The drive was steep, narrow at times with stunning views over the valleys and across the mountain ridges. My mind was not on the views, however, but on the puzzle that was Maya. I didn't know how to play this 'friendship'. At times she seemed to want to get more intimate but then she would become more distant. And in any case, I felt I was in very strange territory - a white Englishman falling for a black Jamaican - there was a kind of double vision operating all the while I was with her - always the enigma of her black presence - the old colonial myths of slavery, white dominance and exploitation dancing on the surface of her skin. But then there was the person that was Maya - this vivacious, beautiful young woman with her many talents - her musicianship, her humour, her sensuality, her intellect, the joy of just being with her. I didn't know the rules of this game - how to read the signs. It was a bit like treading water and I needed help.

Again, David noted the reference to Maya's skin colour and that curious phrase - 'the enigma of her black presence'. What did his father mean by this? He lodged the question away at the back of his mind while he turned to his computer and Googled *Blue Lagoon* and *San San*.

It looked like a really attractive coastline east of Port Antonio - small bays, rocky headlands, an island called *Monkey Island*. Then he traced the road from Annotto Bay to Kingston and the other road his father had taken from Buff Bay over the Blue Mountain Ridge - that switchback road that passed the turning for Cinchona just north of Newcastle. He wondered about the location of Ned's farm but there was nothing to give him a fix on where it might be. Most frustrating was that he had no surname for Maya. So each time he did a search he would get numerous references to 'Maya Angelou' or the 'Maya' civilisation in Mexico. And 'Mahalia' only threw up references to Mahalia Jackson, the gospel singer. He was also struggling with the Marlon James novel. Many of the chapters were narrated by some gangster or 'enforcer' using a strong Jamaican patois which was difficult to follow. And the book presented a tapestry of casual violence and corruption; there were gangster turf wars and clandestine machinations with CIA agents working the streets and bars for 'intelligence' on the latest plots in the political cauldron that was 1970s Kingston. It was anything but uplifting. The novel painted Jamaica in the Seventies as a pretty sordid place which was quite different from the impression he was getting from his father's journal. Where the true reality lay was anyone's guess.

*

April 10th. When I was buying my patties after work yesterday, Flora said a curious thing. I was handing over my money and she held my arm for a moment and said: 'Be careful, Mr William, ob dem bad people in dem truck.' And she was pointing to the guys who sit in the

Toyota trucks just down the street from the main gate of the project. They're there each day, not doing very much just watching what's going on. They don't seem to bother or approach anybody but Flora was clearly concerned. I asked who they were and she just sucked her teeth (they do that over here when they're annoyed) and repeated 'Bad people, tek care.'

Some new guys arrived on site today - six Cubans. Not sure what they're here for but Larry was showing them round and then at the end of the day drove them off in a minibus. It was then I remembered Maya asking me about Larry and the visa applications - these must be the Cuban guys she was talking about.

Been working on my plans for RJ's little resort. Using the photographs I took, it's interesting trying to work the landscape and the vegetation into the plans so that the guest houses sit naturally in their surroundings. Very different from my usual work where there's an empty space to start with. I'm finding it really creative. Going to drive over next weekend and see what RJ thinks of my proposals. This weekend going with Jim and a group from work to the north coast - a place called Mammee Bay, near Ocho Rios. Another new one for me. Haven't heard from Maya for a while. Missing her.

*

Joe sat on his bed with his guitar. He was trying to pick out the melody of that piece his dad kept playing - the classical piece mentioned in Pops' journal. His dad had played it so often it was like an ear worm lodged in Joe's head. The guitar had become like a close friend since Pops had died. It sat in the corner of his bedroom in his dad's house on its special stand and Joe couldn't resist picking it up each time he went into his room. When he was at his mum's house he missed having the guitar but she had a piano and he sometimes tried to work out tunes that way. But it wasn't the same as the guitar.

It was Pops who had encouraged him to have lessons and he had played at a couple of school concerts in a little band he had formed with a couple of his friends. Pops had come and watched and he remembered him nodding and winking as he clapped at the end. Joe had felt a shiver of warmth inside and realised for the first time what feeling proud was like. But it was the acoustic rather than the electric that he really liked. He remembered Pops playing at Christmas when he was little. He would dance around to 'Jingle Bells' and 'Rudolph' and when he was seven, Pops gave him his first guitar for his birthday and showed him some basic chords. That's when he started to finger the strings and work out simple tunes.

He put down the guitar and went across to the chest of drawers where he had placed the wooden name plate off Pops' yacht, *Jamaya*. How he had loved that boat. He remembered catching mackerel one morning off the little island near Gatehouse in Scotland. He couldn't believe how many they caught. They were using lines cast out from the back of the boat, lines with lots of hooks with small coloured feathers attached. Joe never understood why you would use feathers to catch fish. It didn't make sense. But it worked anyway. The feel of the tug on the line sent shivers through your body and when you pulled in the line you could see the silver sides of the fish shimmering deep down in the water. The most he ever pulled out on one line was seven but Pops had to help him as the pull of the line was so strong. And, when they lay flopping on the floor of the boat, Joe felt a bit sad and wanted to throw them back. They had sort of silvery rainbow colours in stripes which caught the sunlight. But Pops had said you had to eat what you caught and even though they fried them later for tea, Joe didn't like the bones and the grey flesh and felt guilty that he had pulled the poor fish out of the water.

There was a knock on his bedroom door and his dad's head appeared: 'Found a bit of video on Jamaica you might find interesting. A place called Blue Lagoon on the north coast where your grandad worked on designing some cottages near a fabulous beach. Want to come and see?'

'Might we go to Jamaica, dad? We could see some of the places Pops writes about.'

'Not sure, yet, son, it sounds a bit of a wild place from what I'm reading.' He was remembering scenes from the Marlon James book - the lawlessness, the casual violence. 'We'll see.'

*

April 29th. Making real progress on RJ's beachfront project. Stayed over at Ned's cottage again. Sadly no sign of Maya this time. Ned tells me she's like a 'peenie wallie' - a firefly - 'Me never know when she here and when she gone. She like a peenie wallie - here and dere - a likkle flash of brightness and den she gone again.' I agreed with him that I never knew when I would see her from one week to the next. Clearly Ned's not keen on RJ. 'Him full of gas man. Big belly and big talk.'
Can't say he's my type but he's paying me well and he likes the designs I've done. Wants the dock and boathouse started first within the next week or so. I doubted that was possible with the 'Soon come' mentality of Jamaicans where no-one seems in a hurry to get things done. But RJ said, 'We'll bypass that, you'll see'. Not sure what he meant but   certainly the dock will allow materials to be brought in by boat rather than by road over the mountains which makes sense. However, my enthusiasm for the project was somewhat clouded by a meeting I had with Maxim last week. He'd heard about the project with RJ, said he couldn't stop me doing extra work out of hours, quizzed me about what I was designing and, when I showed him some plans, he said he liked my ideas. But then said a strange thing: 'Watch your back, Will, I would

be wary of that guy.' And when I asked why, he just repeated: 'Just watch your back. That's all I'll say.'

The talk at work is all pretty paranoid - gossip about what they're calling 'foreign agents' infiltrating the country to destabilise Manley's government. I just keep my head down, do my work and look forward to heading to the north coast at the weekends to manage my Zion Hill project. Can't do with politics.

May 6th. RJ doesn't hang around. When I arrived I was surprised to see the progress on the dock. He's brought in some American workers to dredge out the dock area and they've already sunk the piles and put in the concrete foundations for the dock side. At this rate the dock will be operational within a couple of weeks. That'll mean we can bring in more materials by boat and I can focus on the guest houses. Stayed over again in Ned's cottage. Didn't see much of Ned and no word from Maya. But I love this little retreat. I'd bought paw-paw and mangoes from a road-side stall and barbecued chicken and plantain. Washed it down with Red Stripe and some Appleton rum and then craved Maya's company. Think I might get myself a guitar to wile away the evenings. I sit on the little terrace and watch the fishing boats with their kerosene stern lights moving along the coast. Noticed some big motor yacht anchored just offshore this time. Ned says they come in from Miami. Reckons it's some mafia boss up to no good - he likes to spin his little fantasies. I just nod and play along.

On Sunday I drove down the coast to Boston Bay. It's a great beach with surfing rollers tumbling in on this wide stretch of sand. The local guys cook what's called 'jerk pork' in earth pits under the trees. The meat is marinated with some secret spicy concoction which they won't divulge and then stretched over the fire on cedar poles. They also roast breadfruit in the charcoal embers. The scent in the air is amazing. They serve it all on banana leaves and the meat just falls off the bone in moist

49

chunks. The hot spice hits your throat and makes your eyes stream at first but a cold beer soothes the hit and you gradually get used to the spicy flavours.

*

David put down his coffee cup and closed the journal. He was sitting at a window seat in the corner of his new favourite retreat - the Cakes & Ale Cafe. It had opened the previous year at the back of an antiquarian bookshop not far from his office. He liked its quirky ambience - stripped wooden floors, distressed paintwork, old books, artwork on the walls by local artists, 1940s jazz classics playing on an old record player. It served great food and more importantly coffee with that edgy bitterness he loved. Mid afternoon it was always pretty quiet before the offices closed and he often walked to take a break there before Joe came out of school.

He read a little more of the Marlon James novel. It was still a tough read but he was getting through it. It painted a grim picture of life in downtown Kingston in the mid Seventies. But he was not fully concentrating. His mind was adrift elsewhere, still musing on the journal. And now he did something he'd resisted so far - he picked up the journal and flipped to the end, to the final entry:

July 12th 1976. Gotta get out. Too dangerous. Feel utterly betrayed.

Nothing else. He turned the remaining blank pages. No more writing but there was a small piece of paper lodged between two of the pages. It was a shopping receipt from a local supermarket. He read the date - June 2006, a month after his mother had died. So his father had been re-reading the journal. But why? He closed the book. And what on earth had happened to him back in 1976?

He became aware of someone standing at the side of the table. Then a voice: 'How are you finding it?' He looked round. She was tall, black braided hair, ebony skin, hooped gold earrings, a tailored blue trouser suit. And absently, he said: 'Maya?'

'Sorry?' she said, tilting her head a fraction.

David turned round to face her: 'I'm sorry, just confused. You came in on a muddle of thoughts.'

'No, I should be the one apologising, for barging in on your privacy. I just noticed you're reading Marlon James. Wondered how you were getting on with it. It's a bit of a challenge, don't you think. None of my friends have managed it.'

'Will you join me?' said David, half rising and pulling out the chair next to him.

'Are you sure?'

'Of course.'

She sat down. David was intrigued by this stranger. Not many black faces in Carlisle.

'It's such an unusual book,' she continued. 'How it won the Booker I'll never know. And I should be able to follow the language - my parents are Jamaican and I've grown up with hearing the accent, but this is one helluva read.' She placed a khaki canvas bag on the table and extended her hand: 'Sorry, I'm Gina Harvey.'

David noted a slight foreign lilt to the home counties accent. He nodded, taking her hand: 'David Pearson.'

'You called me 'Maya' ?'

'Sorry, you came in on a train of thought, a coincidence, it's a long story.'

'And it's the end of a working day?'

'Something like that. Would you like a coffee?'

'It's okay, I've got a smoothie on its way,' she said adjusting her hands in her lap and sitting back in her chair.

David breathed for the first time, but the phrase *'Feel utterly betrayed'* still buzzed in the back of his head. 'D'you know Jamaica well? You said your parents…'

Gina shook her head: 'It's another long story. They came over in the late Sixties, not exactly the Windrush lot, sometime after. Dad was twenty two, he met momma on the boat. They lived in London for forty years, and dreamed of retiring back 'home' as they called it.'

'And did they go back?'

'Briefly. But it didn't work out. They weren't welcomed by the locals and they missed England. Ironical isn't it?'

'Dreams versus realities,' said David. 'So often we kid ourselves.'

'Or we're misled.'

'Did you go over?'

Gina nodded: 'When I finished uni. They'd just gone back. I went to check out how things were going. But it was sort of tragic. They were unhappy. So what's your interest in Jamaica, then?'

'Have you got a week? Long story. I just discovered my father lived in Jamaica as a young man, back in the mid Seventies.'

'Hence, the Marlon James.'

David nodded: 'Yes, he was there around the time the events in the book take place. So I thought it would give me some background.'

'Not the easiest way in,' added Gina.

David took a sip of his coffee, trying to collect his thoughts. 'D'you work here in Carlisle?' he said.

She nodded: 'I'm a lawyer, and you?'

'I'm a designer, often work from home but have a small office near the cathedral.'

'What kind of design?'

'Interiors, office spaces, renovations of old properties. It's pick and mix really.'

'Sounds interesting. Not like legal work which can be stultifying at times.' She turned as a young waitress arrived with her drink. 'Thanks, Emily,' she said.

'You're a regular here are you? Surprised I've never seen you before,' commented David.

'I work away quite a lot, but when I'm back, yes, I'm a regular.'

David nodded and took a moment to study her as she took a sip from a dark green smoothie. Bright, sharp, confident, very striking - not unlike Maya. This was almost history repeating itself in an odd sort of way - his father's infatuation with Maya and now here was Gina suddenly arriving in his life.

She had grown up in London, studied for her degree and law qualifications there and then practised for some years in Winchester before moving north.

'So why Carlisle?' asked David.

She ran her hand over the braids of her hair fingering the fine rills and smoothing the coils. Her hair was an intriguing work of art. And then her eyes, looking first down into her drink and then across at him - deep brown, a snatch of humour skating on their moist surface. 'Oh, it was an old boyfriend who was into mountain-biking and wanted to drag me up to this place called The Lake District. I'd hardly been north of Watford. And the North was of course that place of dark primitive practices - you know, pigeon-fancying, whippets and northern grit. Well that's what my parents told me, anyway. They had certainly never been north of Watford.'

'So you ventured up here.'

She smiled and nodded: 'I've been doing consultancy work for clients developing solar and wind farms in the north of England and Scotland. And I love it. Fell out of love with the boyfriend but fell in love with getting away from London. Must have been the Blue Mountains of Jamaica calling to my soul. We stood on a hill called Latrigg and looked down the valley towards the mountains. That view down Derwentwater was like something I'd only seen in books. I felt I'd come home in a curious way. If I had to choose a place to die, that would be it.'

'I think I know the spot. I camped there once and my father used to take me sailing on the lake.'

'This is the father who was in Jamaica?'

David nodded. 'I only found out recently after he'd died. Came across an old journal he'd written in the Seventies. I'm in the process of working through it.'

Gina nodded and continued to stare across the table at David: 'Sounds like you've embarked on something intriguing. Will there be skeletons in the cupboard?'

'I've a feeling there might be.'

She was easy company, this young woman, and the fact that she knew Jamaica was a bonus.

'Will you go and visit?' she asked.

David shrugged: 'My son, Joe, is keen for us to go but I'm not sure. Reading Marlon James doesn't really inspire me but then reading my father's journal makes the place sound fascinating.'

'It's like so many places,' said Gina. 'I wouldn't choose to spend time in certain parts of England but there are other places that I love. Jamaica's just the same. I'll have to devise an itinerary for you.'

'That would be helpful,' said David. He glanced at his watch. 'Uh oh. School run calls. It was nice meeting you, Gina. Hope to catch you here again.'

'Yes, I'm sure I'll see you sometime. Take care now.'

*

May 20th. Amazing weekend sailing. Met a new guy, Ted, from Wales, who's big into dinghy sailing. Took me out in his GP14 on Kingston harbour. Had me out on a trapeze - this was a first for me - and the sense of speed was incredible. We capsized a couple of times when I hit the water and was launched across the boat into the mainsail! But what an experience. You get a very different view of Kingston from the water. The Blue

Mountains look magical veiled in mist, and the city seems to be floating on a raft amid the greenery of the hills. Sailed close to that motor yacht I'd seen off the north coast a couple of weeks ago. It was anchored just off the dock area and there was a Jamaica Defence Force launch moored alongside with police on the deck of the yacht. Not sure what was going on but the police waved us away when we sailed in close to take a look. Always the feeling there's something dodgy going on but what it is, is anyone's guess.

Bumped into Carl Da Costa in the yacht club. Asked him if he'd seen anything of Maya. He'd heard she was in the US with her embassy work.

May 29th. She's back and she called me. Said she would be going to stay at Ned's this weekend. Sounded keen to see me. Can't wait to get away from work early Friday. My stomach's in knots!!

June 5th. Don't know where to begin. This young woman never fails to surprise me.

Arrived early afternoon at RJ's to check progress on the project. The dock's functioning and the boathouse is almost complete so they're able to bring in materials by sea now which has really speeded things up. Since talking to Maxim, I'm more wary of RJ. He's brash, bombastic, obnoxious when things aren't going well. He rarely invites me into his house which stands on a high bluff above the beach. Normally we meet at the small office by the dock and this time there were several other guys there huddled over some maps in a back room.

Then who should appear but Maya. She seemed a little nervous as if she wasn't expecting to see me there. And yet she'd phoned me earlier and said she'd be coming. RJ gave me an envelope with an interim payment for my work and then Maya breezed out, took my arm and told me we were going swimming at Frenchman's Cove. I'd heard about this place, the playground of celebrities for decades.

A short drive along the coast past the Blue Lagoon and San San Bay and then we turned off down a drive overarched with almond trees and palms and arrived at this little sandy cove, hedged in by two wooded headlands. The sea surges in and fans out onto a widening beach and meets a freshwater stream which flows in along a shaded channel and keeps the water chilled. Where it meets the seawater the contrast in water temperatures is quite a shock. Maya pulled me in to feel this curious phenomenon. We splashed around for a while before lying out on the sand. She asked me how I was getting on with RJ and mentioned the great job I'd done with the design of the dock and boathouse. I asked her how she knew him and she said she met him way back when she was at college in Miami. I asked her about the other guys who were there. She just said 'business associates' she'd met through the embassy and then changed the subject.

That evening up at Ned's cottage we barbecued while the sun was setting and then dragged the small settee out on to the deck. We threw some logs onto the barbecue and got a decent fire going. Maya produced a bottle of Appleton and a blanket and that's how it started. It was the first time I'd kissed a black girl and I found my head swimming with a swirl of strange phantoms. I was both in the moment and not in the moment. My white skin on her black skin sent a rush to my senses. I was taking my cue from her and it was clear she was setting limits. She would pull back and re-establish a little distance between us. Asked me about my work and what I knew about Maxim. I found this a little weird bringing Maxim into what I'd thought was a developing intimacy. I quizzed her as to why was she asking about Maxim? 'Just curious over some recent visa applications,' she replied.

So there was no headlong rushing into bed, it was all fairly innocent - just some gentle touching, and a feeling that we'd crossed a line. She returned to Ned's house to sleep leaving me floundering in a sea of tangled emotions.

The next morning she knocked on the door early and we went down to San San Bay and swam out to the island. It's a small knoll covered in coconut palms and we climbed to the top and looked down on the reef which is just beyond the seaward side of the island. The water changes from the clear pearly aquamarine on the bay side to a dark blue on the outer side of the reef where the water goes suddenly deep. The reef is etched on the water by a line of white surf breaking on the coral.

When we were back on the beach I asked her about her trip to the States. 'How did you know about that?' she asked, frowning. I said that Carl at the yacht club had told me. She nodded slowly and fingered some circular patterns in the sand before looking up and saying: 'I have to tell you Will, that in my work at the embassy we're coming across some weird things happening which we're not sure about. I could use some help from you.' I was surprised by this. 'How can I help?' I asked. She said that they needed information about Maxim, about any unusual things happening at the project, any unusual deliveries into the warehouse, that type of thing. 'So you're asking me to spy on Maxim?' I said. 'I can't do that. He's a good employer and a good man. He supports the government and what Manley's trying to do for the poor. And I agree with that, don't you?' She shook her head: 'Things aren't what they seem, Will. There's a lot going on.'

Then she did an unexpected thing - leaned over and kissed me on the shoulder and then full on the lips. 'I hope I haven't spoilt the morning and upset you,' she said. 'You couldn't upset me, Maya - ever,' I replied. 'That's good,' she said.

And that was the end of a rather strange exchange. It left me unsettled during the drive back to Kingston although the memory of her last kiss and her touching soon eclipsed the other stuff. We seem to have moved to a good place in our relationship.

David closed the journal and tapped his fingers on the desk. He was remembering an early section of the Marlon James book when the CIA chief in Kingston is talking about the way the Agency, or what he calls 'The Company', operates to undermine left-leaning governments in different parts of the world. It appeared that this was happening in Jamaica in the Seventies when his father was there. Could this Maya woman be involved in any of that type of thing? His father was clearly infatuated with her and here she was trying to get him to do some spying on the guy, Maxim. Thankfully his father had resisted and stuck to his principles. But for how long?

He heard Joe's footsteps along the hall then his face appeared round the door of David's office. 'Hey dad, did you know that if Usain Bolt wins the 100 metres, he'll be the first athlete to win three golds at an Olympics?'

Joe's performance in school athletics had improved dramatically this year. He'd grown a lot and seemed to be wearing his new height quite comfortably. David had noticed Joe's legs growing by the way his jeans appeared to be shrinking. With the Rio Olympics only a month away, Joe was eagerly poring over schedules for the various events. 'August 9th, dad, that's when he's running.'

Since discovering about Pops being in Jamaica, the country was now firmly on Joe's radar. Usain Bolt had become the latest icon to be posted on Joe's bedroom wall alongside Bob Marley. The thump of reggae often shook the house coming from the speakers in Joe's bedroom as well as Joe's attempts to master the strange snatch of the reggae rhythm on his guitar.

'He could pick up three golds if he wins the 100, 200 and the relay,' added David. 'They call it the 'triple-

triple' - that's when you win three golds in three consecutive Olympics. He could do that.'

'No kidding,' said Joe. 'That would be awesome!'

*

June 20th. Despite trying to avoid it, you do get sucked into politics in this country. I'm still disturbed by Maya's pressure on me to spy on Maxim. Maxim seems a solidly good guy. He's a friend of the PNP, speaks highly of Michael Manley who he knows personally and applauds what he's trying to do - trying to help Jamaica stand on its own feet and not be in the pocket of America. I drove down Spanish Town Road last week and there's the evidence - Manley's Impact Program is there for all to see - a program to help the poor - you see gangs of them cleaning the roads, sweeping, collecting litter and stuff - it may be low level work but at least it's money in their pockets and gives a measure of dignity and purpose. And yet Manley's being attacked daily for his ideology of Democratic Socialism which to me seems to have all the right values. I'm not religious but it seems very Christian in its concern for the little guy and the downtrodden or 'downpressed' as they say here.

July 4th. Wasn't sure how I'd be greeted at the yacht club today, being British - there was a big party for American Independence Day - a lot of back slapping and jokes at my expense but it was all good humoured. Maya was there with some people from the American embassy. Seems the two embassies work closely together. She's off to Cuba again soon with the orchestra. Michael Manley is again personally endorsing the trip as part of his links with the Castro regime. I asked her how it felt going to the country which was America's Bogeyman. She smiled and said simply: 'Music is the language which unites us - and that's why I go.' Since our last meeting at the cottage

59

I feel closer to her but she still remains what Ned calls a 'peenie wallie'. She's there but not there. Her quintet is playing at Devon House next week. She said she'd like me to come. Haven't seen any of them for weeks and I always feel comfortable with Marianne. Easy to talk to. Looking forward to it.

July 11th. Asked Jim Suarez what he thought about Manley's policies. He just said that Manley's out of his depth. Doesn't realise what's coming at him. That you can't play games with the IMF like Manley's trying to do. They'll screw him and then the country's sunk. Said there were rumours that Kissinger is coming to put the screws on Manley to stop him supporting Cuban troops going to Angola to fight against apartheid in South Africa. And Henry Kissinger's heavyweight, he was Nixon's Secretary of State, now Gerald Ford's. 'He's a tough cookie,' said Jim, 'the toughest!'

July 13th
Went to the concert at Devon House. It was quite magical. After the intense heat of the day and the dust and dirt of the project, here the cool shade with the lights in the trees was a welcome relief - the audience in evening finery, colourful outfits, sparkling jewellery, and the music itself - Bach, Brahms and Mozart and my Maya, centre stage introducing the programme — how I love to watch her, the sensuality of the way she moves, her expression when she's playing, that intense emotional absorption in the music. And then I remember her lips and the touch of her skin against mine. And it all seems like a dream I've dreamed. Marianne came and sat with me during the interval. Surprised me when she asked me how I thought Maya was doing. 'Why?' I asked. Marianne looked across to where Maya was chatting to a group of people: 'She's juggling a lot of pressure at present, pressure at work. I worry about her.'

I asked: 'What kind of pressure?' Marianne just looked straight at me and said: 'She'll tell you sometime. But just tread carefully with her. She's not as strong as she seems.'

*

In the first week of Joe's summer holidays he and David drove to the west coast of Scotland and pitched their tent at Camusdarach, just south of Mallaig and the 'silver sands of Morar', a place David had come to as a child. In his memory it was a magical place of white sand beaches and sea coves. He was desperate to revive some of those cherished memories of good times with his father to try to eclipse the fallout they had had during his father's latter years.

They launched their canoe at the little harbour at Arisaig and paddled down the seaward channel to some small sandy islands where the sea lapped pearly white onto the sand.

'Let's pull in here,' said David. 'I can't believe the colour of the water.'

'D'you think this is what Jamaica's like?' asked Joe.

'Could be,' replied David. He stepped out of the canoe and steadied it while Joe used his paddle to ease himself out onto the sand - although it wasn't exactly sand but small white shells which crackled under their bare feet. Out at sea David spotted the familiar shapes of the islands of Rhum and Eigg. He recalled it clearly - all those years ago - they had sailed out from Arisaig harbour in the little wooden dinghy and now he remembered that his dad had said: 'This is what the Caribbean's like, clear aquamarine water, coral beaches.'

He remembered the strangeness of the word 'Caribbean' which he'd never heard before. And he had asked: 'Have you ever been there?'

And his dad had replied: 'Before I met your mother I did some work out there.'

If this was a place of magic for David, so it was for Joe, too. Growing up reading his library of Harry Potter books, he couldn't contain his excitement when David told him where they were going. In the stories the train to the school of Hogwarts passes over the viaduct at Glenfinnan just south of Arisaig and Joe was enthralled with the idea that they were here in Hogwarts territory. The previous day they had been in Mallaig when the *Hogwarts Express* had arrived in the small station. Hordes of kids dressed in Hogwarts uniforms or wizards' cloaks had tumbled out of the train onto the small platform followed by their parents and then crammed the cafes and chip shops for two hours until the whistle blew and the train chugged its way out of the station to return to Glasgow. Joe watched the puffs of steam rising above the trees long after the train was gone from view until the sound of the engine finally faded. Part of him wished he had been on the train dressed in a Hogwarts uniform and waving a wizard's wand.

But later, as they sat on the beach near the campsite, toasting marshmallows on sticks over a driftwood campfire and watching a brilliant blood-red sunset, he thought maybe the Hogwarts thing was kids' stuff and being here with his dad just staring into the flames was much more him.

'I can still see Pops' face, dad, but I can't remember Nan,' said Joe.

'You were a baby when she died. You were only one.'

'What was she like?'

David stared into the fire and reeled in some memories: 'She loved plants. We lived in a small terraced house when I was little. It had a tiny back garden and I remember picking garden peas from the vegetable plot and digging up potatoes. It was like hunting for buried gold. Your Nan loved sowing seeds and in the spring the window sills would be lined with seed trays with tiny green shoots poking up above the soil. She said it was her 'veggie family' and she tended all her plants as if they were like so much treasure. When we moved to the Solway house she had a big veggie plot in the garden and a greenhouse for growing all sorts of things.'

'Was she fun, like Pops? Did she do daft things and tell jokes?'

'She was fun, but in a different way. She was a great story teller. She could just make up stories on the spot. We played this game where I had to choose an object and she would make up a story about that object. Where those stories came from I don't know. But something about her voice, the way she moved her hands and her eyes as she spoke - it kind of hypnotised me.'

Joe prodded his stick into the fire and stirred the embers. 'Shame people have to die. I hope I die before you do, dad.'

'I remember having that same thought, Joe, when I was about your age. Don't worry, we have lots of years ahead of us yet.'

*

July 30th. Left a message for RJ that I'd come over on Saturday morning, but then decided to drive over Friday to be there early. Ned's left me a key to get into the cottage so I'm a free agent in that sense. But wasn't expecting what I found. It was dark when I got to the cottage around 10pm. Helluva drive through the mountains but at least with the headlights you can see something coming round the next bend. From the deck of the cottage I could see down the coast to RJ's and there was a large sailboat anchored just off shore. Through the binoculars I could see two small boats going out and coming back. Curiosity got the better of me. There's a gully below the cottage which brings you out onto the road about half a mile from RJ's. As I got closer I could see lights and movement down by the new dock and boat house. Thought it might just be some social gathering that RJ was hosting using my new dock and boathouse but after what Maxim had warned I had my doubts. They were off-loading some cargo - long, narrow crates - heavy because it took 4 guys to lift them from the boat to the dock. Could have been domestic stuff for RJ's private use but when I went down in the morning the larger boat had gone and there was no sign of the crates. RJ quizzed me about when I'd arrived and I lied and said I'd driven over that morning. He seemed unusually sociable, gave me a cold Red Stripe and then said he was putting the project on hold for a while so that I didn't need to be driving over so often. He was pleased the dock and the boathouse were finished and said he was looking forward to using them. Didn't mention the previous night's activities and there was no sign of whatever had been off-loaded. Paid me some more of what I'm owed and said the rest would follow. He made it clear that there was no need for me to hang around as he had to go into Port Antonio. It all seemed rather weird, something didn't feel quite right somehow. I'd thought he'd want the guest houses completed for the winter tourist season. That'd been the original plan. Obviously something's changed. I'll have to check with Maya when she gets back from her Cuba trip.

August 5th. The heat, the humidity and the bugs are pretty unbearable this time of year but I've found somewhere new to escape to. A friend of Maxim's has a small cottage in the Blue Mountains, an hour out of Kingston. Little place called Bermuda Mount. It's just a wooden cabin but cool and shaded by tall stands of bamboo and eucalyptus trees which have this strange peeling bark and leaves which catch the slightest breeze. No mosquitoes, no bars on the windows and doors and the country people have this old world charm so different from the hustlers on the Kingston streets. There's a small terrace and a barbecue pit and humming birds fly to the feeders which you fill with sugar juice. I love it and want to bring Maya up here but haven't heard from her yet.

*

David closed the journal and opened his lap-top. He put in a search for *Zion Beach Resort, Port Antonio*. Google Earth never failed to intrigue him with its slowly turning globe and then the zooming in to the landscape of Jamaica. He saw the curve of the coastline east of Port Antonio, homed in on the crescent bay of San San with its small island which he remembered his dad had swum to with Maya; further east to Blue Lagoon and the headland of Dragon Bay and finally, there it was, *Zion Beach Resort*, the resort which his dad had designed for the Texan guy, RJ. No doubt it had changed over the years, but it thrilled David to be looking down on the reality of what his father had described in the journal. Then he moved the landscape on the screen, travelling south over the ridge of the Blue Mountains to find this new place, *Bermuda Mount.* It was off the road to Newcastle, where his father had described how the road crossed the parade ground of the army camp. He found the settlement of Irish Town - a cluster of small red roofed houses. And he marvelled at how the technology allowed him to hover over the landscape of his father's earlier life. It was almost like time travel, reading the journal and then being able to hang like a spying drone over the places where the ghost of his father as a young man had walked.

A few moments later, Joe came into the room: 'What have you found, dad, anything new?'

'Just looking at this beach resort that Pops designed and some place he went to in the mountains to get away from the heat.'

'We've just gotta go, dad. We've gotta go and check out these places. It would be brilliant.'

'Not as simple as that,' said David.

'Why not?'

'Expensive, for one thing. And they say Jamaica's a tricky place to travel in. Can be dangerous.' He was remembering something Gina had mentioned in the cafe.

'But mum's friend said it was great when she went. And we've gotta go for Pops' sake, go for the adventure. It would be like a pilgrimage. We did about pilgrimages in R.E. at school. So this could be our pilgrimage.'

'Maybe,' said David. 'We'll have to see what else his journal tells us.'

'Don't forget Bolt's running this afternoon. Can't miss that.'

And later that afternoon they sat glued to the television watching the magic of this phenomenon which was Usain Bolt - six feet five inches of athletic grace cruising to win the gold medal in the 100 metres. They watched him working the crowd draped in the Jamaican flag, the gold, green and black colours massed in the stadium with Jamaicans dancing and whooping at the joy of his win.

'Can I get a Jamaican shirt, dad? I just love those colours,' exclaimed Joe. 'And don't the Jamaicans look like fun people. Pity Pops couldn't be here to see this. He'd be cheering for Bolt along with the Jamaicans. It must have been great for him to spend time in the country all those years ago. But can I get a shirt dad, please!'

'I'm sure, that if he wins the triple, there'll be Jamaican shirts in every sports shop.'

*

The next time David had seen Gina was at an 'Open Mic' night at the cafe. These were held every month to raise money for local charities. Aspiring poets, writers and musicians would turn up and take turns at the mic. The standard of offerings was variable but all the efforts were greeted with great enthusiasm by the audience and David always enjoyed the boisterous buzz of chatter and laughter. He was sitting with Mike, an old school buddy whom he often met at Brunton Park on a Saturday when he and Joe went to cheer on the Carlisle United team.

Gina was sitting with a group of friends in the corner of the cafe. David spotted her immediately but didn't catch her eye until the interval when he went up to the bar to get a drink. She waved and came across to him.

'Hey, I was hoping to catch you,' she said, 'but I didn't have your number. I've been checking up on the Marlon James book, you know, Seventies Jamaica? That was the time when your father was there, wasn't it?'

David nodded: 'Yes, that's right.'

Gina continued: 'Well maybe we could meet. I've found some stuff which you might find interesting.'

'Take down my number,' said David, 'and text me. Late afternoons are usually a good time. Be interesting to hear what you've found out.'

'What else did the diary throw up?' asked Gina.

'All sorts, too much to tell you now. I'll save it for when we meet.'

Gina noted David's number on her phone and glanced up at him: 'Great, I'll get back to you.' She smiled, waved and made her way back through the crowd to the table where her friends were sitting.

When David sat back at his table, Mike was giving a wry smile. He nudged David's arm: 'Going over to the dark side are you?'

'Don't be so bloody crass, Mike. You sound like some dinosaur from my parents' generation.' He took a sip of his beer. 'Smart lady is Gina, she's a lawyer. Just met her a few weeks ago in here. She's interesting.'

'I'll bet she is,' replied Mike, with another smirk.

David didn't respond.

And a few weeks later, not long after the excitement of the Olympics had subsided a little, Gina came over to the table where David was sitting and placed her coffee and a package on the table. 'I was hoping to catch you again. Thought your boy might like one of these, after what happened in Rio. Did you see my brother knocking them dead. A triple triple or what! Proud of my old country, I can tell you.'

'How did you know?' said David. 'Joe was desperate for a Jamaican shirt after watching the 100 metre race. And then came the 200 and the relay - well, I couldn't stop him dancing and he keeps appearing at the door doing his Bolt arrow impression.'

Gina smiled and sat down: 'I remembered you talking about your son, Joe. Thought I'd spread a little of the Jamaica vibe.'

'You're very kind,' said David nodding. 'Thanks.'

'No problem,' replied Gina. 'And I have more for you. I've been doing some research on that period in Jamaica when your father was there. Have you come across Operation Werewolf?'

'No, what's that?'

Gina took a sip from her coffee and went on: 'Seems that after Henry Kissinger came - you know, he was the US Secretary of State - well after his visit in September of 1975 when he tried and failed to stop the Manley government supporting Castro, the CIA launched a major campaign of destabilisation, running guns into the country, disrupting government projects, fire bombing and violent gangland shootouts. It was linked to a couple of the Opposition politicians and some key gang bosses in Trenchtown. But not before there'd been close on civil war in parts of the country. It was named Operation Werewolf. I got you a copy of an original leaflet.' She handed over a brown envelope.

'Thanks. Sounds like some of what Marlon James is writing about in his book,' said David. 'There's this constant undercurrent of corruption and subversion. And there are hints of it in my dad's journal. Nothing specific but just a few hints of things that he's noticing.'

'Well I'll be interested to hear whether any of this impacted on your father's life.'

'At first he seems oblivious of anything political going on. He was just getting used to the novelty of the place. But the last few entries seem to hint that he's picking up that things aren't what they seem.'

Gina nodded: 'You've really sparked my interest in that period, which I knew nothing about really. I knew about the Bob Marley shooting from my parents and now from the Marlon James book but beyond that I know very little. So I'll keep digging and pestering you for your latest revelations if that's not too much of a cheek.'

'No, it's good to have someone to bounce ideas off. It's all news to me as well. And the fact that my dad was dropped into the middle of it all is intriguing. So yes, I'll keep you posted.'

*

September 20th. Lots of publicity and news stories about the Kissinger visit. Photos in the paper of a big reception at Jamaica House. But the gloss masks what's going on behind the scenes. People talk of his 'crocodile smile'. No doubt Maya will have the inside story.

October 6th. The papers are saying Kissinger was furious with Manley when he left after his visit. He was trying to get Manley to stop supporting Castro sending Cuban troops to Angola. Manley refused to co-operate and is openly applauding Castro. And now the US is imposing sanctions on us. What effect this will have is not clear but there are bound to be shortages in the shops and I was stuck in a queue at the gas station on Windward Road for half an hour this week.

Maya seemed troubled when I met her for a drink at Devon House. She'd not long returned from Cuba herself and they'd been busy at the embassy with the Kissinger visit. She didn't give much away when I tried to question her about what was happening, but she'd lost her usual verve and seemed distant and tense. She relaxed a little when I told her about my new hideaway at Bermuda Mount and I took the plunge and invited her up for the weekend. Didn't expect her to agree to come but she nodded slowly and said: 'Yes, I think I'd like that, Will.' Couldn't believe what I'd heard and found it hard to contain my delight. And then she added: 'I might need somewhere to escape to.' Wasn't sure what to read into that but then recalled Marianne's comment about her vulnerability. Anyway she's coming and that's amazing. I told her about RJ putting a stop to my work at Zion Hill and casually asked what his plans were for the place. I didn't mention what I'd seen going on there. She flashed a look at me and then her drink was all over the table and there was lots of fussing with napkins before she composed herself again and asked me what the question was. Then she kind of shrugged and said RJ was an odd guy, very impulsive and always changing his mind about things. So I didn't get any sort of an answer. Maya's clearly not herself at the moment.

October 19th 10pm.
Bermuda Mount. I'm sitting on the terrace, trying to collect my feelings about this weekend. Maya's just left and driven back to Kingston. Don't know what I feel. This place is a world away. We've been floating above the clouds which have sunk into the valleys. There's a stillness to the air and the darkness is thick, pricked only by the glow of lights from the cabins further down the valley. Yesterday we hiked to Catherine's Peak - just across the valley. From the top you get a great view down

over the ridges to the haze of Kingston. It was while we were sitting contemplating the view that Maya said : 'I wish that place down there was all a bad dream and I could wake up in a place like this every morning.' She said I was one of the few people she could talk to about things - there was so much going on and you didn't know who to trust. She felt her poor country was being ripped apart and she was caught in the middle of it all. She didn't agree with the US sanctions and the pressures coming from America. She couldn't go into details but was scared about the direction things were going.

That evening, while I tended the barbecue, Maya played her violin. Her feelings always come out through her music and this evening she was playing something by a French composer called Satie. It was sad, whimsical and the notes floated away across the darkness of the valley. The flicker of the candle light caught the moistness in her dark eyes. She wasn't shedding tears exactly but not far from it. I tried to lift the mood by picking out some chords on my new guitar. We attempted a kind of duetting around some simple folk songs and Maya's mood brightened. After we'd eaten and drunk quite a lot of red wine, I stoked up the fire in the barbecue and we pulled out the bed settee and lay together looking up at the stars. There was something childlike about her need to be held but then nothing childlike about the way we made love. And now I'm trying to make sense of it all - a mix of agony and ecstasy. And I don't know where it's all leading....

David drove to his father's house to carry on sorting things out. Joe was at his mother's so he had plenty of time to get things done. But he was keen to read the details about Operation Werewolf that Gina had given him. He made a coffee and settled down in the sitting room facing the window which gave a view of the estuary. He took Gina's envelope from his bag. Inside was a photocopy of a leaflet published by the 'Agency for Public Information'. It was headed:

PLOT TO OVERTHROW GOVERNMENT
Jamaicans, Know Your Enemies And Be On Guard

It outlined a plot linked to a couple of Opposition politicians and cited the Saint Ann's area on the north coast where there was reputedly a cell of: *22 trained men, 100 ideologically indoctrinated with supplies of 200 rifles, 100 sub-machine guns, 2 barrels of gun powder and 50,000 anti-government pamphlets.* Pamphlets had been found in a brief case which stated: *Michael Manley and his Government are dedicated Communists and we intend to destroy them at all costs.* The pamphlet spoke about: *WEREWOLF - A MILITANT UNDERGROUND MOVEMENT* which was *willing to take up arms against this communist regime and purge them from our shores.*

David placed the leaflet alongside the journal on his father's desk. No wonder Maya was troubled if she was working at the embassy and the CIA was fuelling an attempt to overthrow the government. Where did that leave her, a young Jamaican trying to steer a course through an increasingly complicated situation? And what about his dad? David could see him being sucked into a situation which was dangerously messy. Apart from the copy of the leaflet, Gina had given him some additional information. In June of 1976 Manley had declared a State of Emergency and detained five hundred people including prominent members of the Opposition party. There had been tanks on the streets, road blocks, shoot-outs between rival gangs in western Kingston. David remembered much of this being woven into the Marlon James novel.

He got up and put on his jacket. He needed to clear his head and a walk might help. He walked to the footpath which followed the course of the old railway and then cut down to the shoreline of the Solway. It was early evening. The lights of Annan across the estuary winked in the twilight. He passed a fisherman standing in the shallows, slowly winding in his line. If only he, himself, could cast a line back in time and warn his father of impending events. It was a silly idea but he felt his young father was heading for something where he'd be out of his depth. It was still October 1975 in the journal but events were certainly heading into uncharted territory.

*

October 29th. Making love to someone crosses a line. I was never one for casual sex. Even though I've grown up surrounded by the free love communes and hippie ethos, I never signed on to that notion. There's something special about sex but making love to a black girl carries extra significance. It crosses several lines, breaks taboos. In the moment, up there in the clouds of Bermuda Mount, it seemed the most natural thing to do. Now, in the full glare of sunlight my white skin on her black skin raises a bundle of concerns in my suburban English mind. How would my parents and friends react if I turned up at home with Maya? How would my work colleagues here feel about it? It smacks of that old colonial stereotype of the black concubine, a kind of 'blaxploitation' - a word I came across in a film magazine the other day. Is that how it would be seen? But then do I care? Do I care what people will think? Am I foolish anyway to assume this relationship is going anywhere long term? But then I do care about Maya. In her there is something rare - I see it especially when she's lost in her music and I want to be in that place with her, a place which is removed from the chatter of petty prejudices about skin colour. That song from West Side Story comes to mind - 'There's a Place For Us'. But in the film their romantic delusions ended in tragedy. Am I similarly deluded?

November 6th. Maxim's home was broken into last night. There was a lot of damage but at least it wasn't fire-bombed. He reckons it's political and that they were looking for his safe. Luckily he and his wife were out or they might not have survived the attack. His support for Manley has been constant and one newspaper described him as a 'Castro groupie'. He called us all to a meeting - talked about 'tightening security' which for us means more guys with dreadlocks and guns in Toyotas posted in various locations around the plant. Seems we're all smeared with the same left-wing label if we work for Maxim. And I find myself checking my rear view mirror more often when I'm out in the car.

Tried to phone Maya but with no success. I'm desperate to find out the state of our relationship after the weekend at Bermuda Mount. There's a yacht race this weekend so hopefully I'll see her then and maybe get the rest of my money from RJ.

*

Joe's eyes moved slowly along the line of stones, the stones from the bag in Pops' workshop. He had placed them along the window sill in his bedroom and now he was about to add another, one he'd picked up on the beach at Morar. He was going to write the word 'Morar' in some white paint he'd bought from the art shop in town and then maybe draw a seagull flying over a beach. How great it would be to add some stones from Jamaica. That would really make his collection special - to have some stones from the very place where Pops had lived as a young man and the same place where Usain Bolt was from - yes that would be extra special.

He unscrewed the lid of the bottle of white paint and picked a thin paint brush from the tin on his desk which was crammed with pencils and paint brushes. He dipped the tip of the brush into the paint and carefully brushed off the excess like Pops had shown him when they had been painting some stones. He remembered the last one they had done together, picked up the stone from 'Tayvallich' and remembered the little bay on Loch Sween, the bay where Pops anchored *Jamaya*.

It was the first time Joe had seen a grown up cry. Well, it wasn't really crying but a tear ran down Pops' cheek and he wiped it away quickly. They had been talking about Nana Beth and how she loved to be on the boat and Joe heard something change in Pops' voice, a sort of cough and when he looked up there was the tear running down Pops' cheek. Pops laughed it away but Joe felt a weird flutter of something in his stomach and knew that Pops was upset. Pops had blown his nose on the crumpled white handkerchief he kept in his pocket and hugged Joe before he went on painting the word 'Tayvallich' onto the piece of flat blue-grey stone. Joe smoothed his finger across the word and placed the stone back in line with the other stones. And he made up his mind that a stone from Jamaica just had to go into his collection. He was sure Pops would have been pleased.

*

November 20th. Yacht race cancelled thanks to a tropical storm which caused some minor chaos across the island. Got a message from RJ about needing to do some reinforcing to the dock which has been damaged. Says he wants it properly engineered so that it's reliable. Not sure if this is a criticism of my original design or the shoddy workmanship of the guys who built it. Finally got through to Maya - she sounded in good spirits and said she'd drive over with me at the weekend as she needs to see RJ about some business matter. Something to do with visas for the workers he's employing. I'm hoping she'll stay over at Ned's cottage.

November 24th. We're back on track! RJ was pleased with my suggestions for modifying and strengthening the dock and he's paid me what he owes, plus a bonus which I wasn't expecting. But I don't like the way he treats Maya. At times he speaks to her as if she's a skivvy - seems to have some hold over her as she's not so confident when she's around him. I mentioned this later when we were back at the cottage but she just said he's not easy but he has a lot of influence so she has to respect that.

I told her about the hit on Maxim's place and she pressed me about the details - was any evidence found as to who had carried out the attack? What was taken? Were the police investigating? Was Maxim hurt? I was surprised at her interest but then she's asked me before about Maxim. When I commented she just said: 'He's a prominent person on the island - close to the government. So it's something to take note of.'

As night fell and the peenie wallies winked at us in the darkness, so politics was set aside and we enjoyed another night of great food, drink and wondrous love-making. Something hauntingly beautiful about our naked bodies bathed in soft moonlight. Unforgettable.

*

Once again, David felt embarrassed reading about these intimacies. Seeing his father as a lover did not sit comfortably. Reading about this close intimacy with Maya was like voyeurism - spying on a world which should have been closed to him. Looking down the telescope of time was unsettling, especially when it was your own father. He had always wondered about his parents when they were younger, what they thought and felt. Now he was finding out, it didn't feel right, somehow. And yet he sensed his young father was being drawn into events which were not going to end well and he had to read on to find out.

There was a ping on his phone - a message from Gina - to meet him at the cafe the following day. *Some new info. for you. xx*

As usual she looked striking. Today a black pin-striped trouser suit with a vivid red scarf at the neck.
She greeted him with a quick touch on his shoulder as she went behind him to take the seat in the corner. 'How're you doing?' she said. 'I just left work and I could murder a coffee.'

David stood at the counter waiting to place the order. This new acquaintance with Gina was so welcome. Where it was going he had no idea but he loved her energy and she lifted his spirits. On his own with Joe was fine at times but he'd lost contact with friends since spending so much time looking after his dad. Then there was his father's death, the clearing of the house and now the new burden of knowledge coming from the journal. It was all weighing heavily on him.

'You look tired,' she said.

He nodded: 'Yes, this Jamaica thing is wheeling round my head, day and night. I'm having weird dreams about all sorts of odd-balls from this journal I'm reading.'

'What's the latest?' asked Gina as she sipped her coffee.

'Well, my father's boss, Maxim - his house has been ransacked and they've tightened security at the plant. Seems they're expecting some sort of trouble. Maxim's a PNP supporter so he's something of a target.'

'What about your father's relationship with this Maya person? Did you say she works at the Jamaican Embassy?'

'Seems they're now lovers.'

Gina shook her head slowly: 'I'm not sure about this young lady.'

'What d'you mean?' asked David.

'Not sure. Just my lawyer's instinct picking up something odd about her.'

'How so?'

'Well she's this talented musician who travels to Cuba and she's working at the embassy. Didn't you say she asked your father to spy on Maxim?'

'It was something to do with visas for some Cuban workers.'

Gina continued nodding and then shrugged: 'It's just a feeling. She doesn't quite add up. And you say they're lovers.'

'Yes, I'm not finding it easy reading about my dad's sex life.'

'I can imagine,' said Gina.

'It's weird,' said David, 'but I'm worrying about him. I feel he's getting out of his depth.'

'Yes, that must be odd, being the son but feeling like a parent.' She handed a wad of papers across the table. 'I've been doing some digging. It's what we do as lawyers every day. Came across this ex-CIA agent called Philip Agee. He published this book 'Inside The Company' in 1975 which was all about his work for the CIA in central and south America in the Sixties. But I also dredged up this expose on Jamaica he wrote in the Seventies and the way the CIA set about destabilising the PNP government. It's what Marlon James touches on in his novel.'

David leafed through the papers, shaking his head. 'Frightening - the way the Americans meddle in global politics, bring down democratically elected governments, spread corruption and subversion. I hate it. And now there's Trump in the White House. Heaven knows what mayhem he's going to spread.' He looked across the table: 'Thanks for these.'

Gina smiled: 'No problem. I'm finding it interesting. Didn't know anything about these events. Of course my parents were over here during the Seventies and they didn't really keep up with Jamaican politics, they were too preoccupied with surviving in north

London, which wasn't always a great place to be back then if you were black.'

'How are they now?' asked David.

Gina nodded: 'Better since they came back and finally abandoned the romantic dream of 'going home'. They've realised that there's lots they like about England and that today's Jamaica is not like they'd imagined.'

'Painful for them, though,' said David.

Gina nodded: 'My mum cried a lot when they came back here, but she's over it now. Just seems to curse more and suck her teeth. But then her new hero is, of course, Usain Bolt. He's her brown-eyed boy. Has his picture in pride of place on her dresser.'

'Yes, Joe and I watched his amazing performance in Rio. What a guy.'

Gina nodded, 'Yeah, makes me feel proud to have the connection with that little island in the sun. But I have no illusions about the place. It seems constantly bent on self destruction.'

'Joe keeps pestering me to go there, check out these places that my dad mentions in the journal. But I'm not sure.'

'How much does he know about what you're finding out?'

'Very little. Just knows his 'Pops' worked there as an architect when he was young and that he travelled round various parts of the island. I haven't mentioned anything about the politics or this relationship with Maya.'

Gina nodded: 'Probably best to keep it simple.'

'Yes but I don't think it's turning out to be very simple. That's the problem.'

*

December 5th. It's Mexico again for Christmas! Maya's organising another trip. Six of us. Two concerts in Merida again but then she wants to explore the Caribbean coast south of a place called Cancun. It's just developing as a tourist destination and she wants to check it out. And there's an interesting Mayan site at Tulum. This is just what I need. To get away from the tensions in this place. Now there are curfews after 9 in the evening. Seems, since the Kissinger visit, Manley has really upset the Americans. There's talk of a CIA backed plot to unseat him. There's always paranoid gossip, but this time the newspapers are raising the heat. This week the Daily News headed with 'Secret Arms Cache Discovered in Portland'. At night helicopters drone overhead with their eerie searchlights piercing the darkness. More shootings and whereas they were confined to downtown, it seems the uptown area is the new hunting ground for gunmen. Maxim called me in for a private meeting. Says he feels he's a target so wants to take some precautions. Seems to trust me as I'm an outsider. Wants what he calls a 'bunker room' built, with different exits. There'll be some extra reinforcement involved which he knows I've worked on before, back in UK. He doesn't want this project to be common knowledge. He fears there's a JLP mole in the place. For a long time I was kind of out of the loop, a bit like a tourist, wide-eyed and fascinated by everything. But it's all starting to feel pretty real now and I feel I'm being sucked in much closer.

December 12th. Asked Maya her views about what's happening, and about this CIA rumour. She offered very little. Thought she'd have her finger on the pulse, being at the embassy. Says she's just a lowly clerk dealing with visas. But there's a change in her. The light has gone out of her eyes, especially when we meet in Kingston. It's only when we're up at Bermuda Mount that she seems to relax and the tension goes out of her. One evening after we'd eaten we walked down the track and stood on the ridge which looks down towards Kingston and saw the helicopters hovering like malign insects. We're so far away, there's no sound just an eerie 'otherworld' quality to it. Maya pulled me away, said she wanted to forget it all for a while and then she opened up about her brother, Edward, the lawyer in Montego Bay. She doesn't see him often but got a letter last week and he's planning to leave for Miami. He's had enough. He was a PNP supporter back in '72 when Manley got elected. But he's become disillusioned and fears what's going to happen in the near future.

Maya still quizzes me about Maxim but I'm saying nothing, especially about the new project. But we're making progress on the bunker room. It's not easy as only me and the four Jamaican guys who are working on it know what's going on. That area of the site has been sealed off and only certain people are allowed in. Maxim has not let on to any of the Americans and Jim and Larry keep pressing me for information but Maxim has sworn me to secrecy 'On pain of death,' he said. 'And I'm not joking either!' he added. Two of the guys, Leonard and Marcus, are from western Kingston. They're great builders, very quick and skilful. During a lunch break, I got them to show me, on a map of the city, the JLP stronghold around Tivoli Gardens and the PNP area where they live. There are certain streets that are flashpoints where the opposing territories meet. That's where people get killed in the crossfire and children are often the victims. It sounds horrendous.

*

David sat staring at his computer screen. He was supposed to be working on a design for the renovation of an old Victorian industrial unit in Carlisle but his mind was anywhere but focused on the job. He still could not fathom why no-one had ever talked about his father's time in Jamaica. Why had it been kept a kind of secret? So, he'd been there during a period of political upheaval, he'd had a relationship with a young black Jamaican woman. Maybe in the Seventies that might still have caused tongues to wag but to keep it a secret for the whole of his life? It was not like his father or rather it was not like the father David thought he knew. And that was the crux. Maybe children never knew the truth about their parents. Things were withheld, or kept hidden in a locked room of memories. Would Joe ever know the truth of why his parents had separated? Why David's drinking and his obsession with work and building his business had led Anna to look for another companion? He had never tried to win points with Joe by bad mouthing Anna. He'd tried to explain the break up in terms that seven year old Joe would understand. But would he, in the future, ever admit to Joe that he, David, had caused the break up? Maybe, maybe not.

He reached for his phone. Found the music file and played again that haunting Shostakovich theme, all the time trying to picture the young Jamaican violinist, Maya, who had so bewitched his father. He had to admit the music was spell-binding and to a young white Englishman living in an exotic place in 1975, the forbidden fruit of a relationship with an alluring Jamaican girl was understandably irresistible. But then there was that final entry in the journal - '*Feel utterly betrayed*' - that was the real teaser.

*

December 20th. Had a curious encounter with RJ this week. He phoned me at the flat and said he was in town on business and could we meet. He specified a small bar called Chester Bridge on Stony Hill. I took the Constant Spring Road north out of the city, past the golf course and up a winding road into the hills. There are some smart homes up here perched on the hillside surrounded by lush gardens and greenery, with great views down over the city. RJ was already in the bar sitting at a table with two other men. One of them I had once seen at his beach house. As I came to the table so they got up and left.

There was something very strange about the meeting. RJ commended me on my work and handed over another envelope. He said it was a bonus for my 'commitment to the job'. And then he added that he didn't want me to talk about the work I was doing for him and tapped his hand against the envelope. He asked about Maxim and what work I was doing for him. I kept it vague and then I asked how he knew Maya. He was equally vague but said they went 'way back' to when she was in college in Miami and then later he knew her through her work at the embassy. Then he looked at his watch, nodded and got up. His parting words were: 'I'll let you know about the next phase of the project at the beach house but it's on hold at present. Enjoy Mexico.'

Driving back down the hill, I felt I was somehow being controlled - the extra money like a kind of bribe and it was unsettling that Maya was obviously in close touch with RJ - the fact that he knew about Mexico. But then I thought maybe I'm just being infected with the general paranoia that abounds at the moment. Maybe RJ's just a guy who wants to preserve his privacy and who's generous with his money. Or am I just too naive for words?

December 22nd. Eager to get off the island. Flying out tomorrow. Finished work on the bunker room. It has state-of-the-art electronic security and surveillance. Maxim's pleased but again swore me to secrecy about the work. I feel I'm caught in the middle between him and RJ but that there's no fence to sit on. I'm just hanging in some sort of confused space somewhere and nowhere. Hopefully I can put it out of my head for the coming week.

January 1976
A New Year! But what an amazing end to the previous one. Watching Maya playing her violin under the Mexican moon, lanterns threaded through the trees in the

square in Merida, the audience, like me, mesmerised by the music and all of us lapped in balmy evening warmth - it's a memory I will take to my grave. There have been moments, during this past week which were quite magical. Probably the relief of getting away from the tension of Jamaica into a land which is timeless. The local people, direct descendants of the Mayans, are steeped in the past - they carry with them ancient beliefs and practices - their reverence for ancestors, for nature, for ancient rituals - it seems to inform their every waking moment. The churches are strewn with flower petals, their vehicles are adorned with painted flowers and Christian symbols, their houses painted with bright murals of animals, birds, flowers. There is a delight in simplicity, none of the suppressed aggression and antagonism you get on the Kingston streets.

After three days around Merida, immersed in the Christmas festivities, we drove to the coast passing through the little town of Valladolid. A gem of a small Mexican town where Marianne bought some souvenirs from a road side stall and Courtney and Lloyd entertained the locals by playing an impromptu medley of folk songs. Some of the young Indian girls started dancing and before long the tequila and tortillas were being passed round and what was meant to be a brief stop turned into a three hour party. Maya was very pensive that day, she didn't join in the merry-making but remained distant. I asked her what it was but she just shook her head and remained inside herself. Got to the coast early evening just south of Tulum where there is an amazing Mayan temple perched right on the cliff next to the beach. We swam in the Gran Cenote, a limestone sinkhole of deep blue fresh water. They say it's where the Indians threw their sacrificial victims back in the time of the Aztecs. We found a small hotel called 'Jequina's', a few miles south where the coastline divides into a series of offshore sand bars and inshore lagoons. It's an untouched paradise of a place where the Caribbean nudges the sand with shades of pearl and aquamarine. After a long time of staring out to sea, Maya said: 'This is my kind of place, Will.'

She linked her arm in mine and we wandered along the beach to a secluded spot where there were some palm trees. I wanted to lie down to listen and watch the wind in the palm leaves but Maya laughed and said: 'Never sleep under a coconut palm, Will, you might never wake up. Coconuts can drop on you when you least expect it.' She had laughed for the first time that day and I was relieved. As the sun went down we swam naked in the sea and then made love under the stars - slow, coaxing love which had a tenderness which almost moved me to tears. Something has changed in Maya, there is a quiet sadness at times which I cannot fathom.

We spent two days there, enjoying the simple delights of Jequina's cooking, her family, her animals - her small son Sebastian entertaining us with his pet monkey and her daughter, Margarita, showing us her fine needlework, sewing exquisite flower patterns onto the white cotton fabric which the Indians wear. Maya bought a small scarf which Margarita embroidered specially for her, with the name 'Maya' edged with a red hibiscus flower and a small humming bird.

It was a week that we didn't want to end and when we arrived back in Kingston to curfews, a shootout at the Sheraton Hotel and the army manning roadblocks with tanks. It was like going from heaven to hell in the space of two hours!

David clicked on Google Maps to find Tulum on the Mexican coast. It was south of Cancun, which looked like a major tourist resort. Off the coast was the large island of Cozumel and further north a small island called Isla Mujeres. The Mayan temple at Tulum was striking in its position overlooking the sea and the Gran Cenote was described as a great place for snorkelling.

When Joe arrived back from staying at his mother's, David showed him the pictures of Mexico.

'Didn't you say Pops went there once before?'

'The previous Christmas, yes, with this music quartet to play some concerts.'

'So was Pops playing?'

'He was friends with the people in the group and they invited him along. I don't think he played.'

Joe scrolled through a selection of the photos. 'It looks amazing. We learnt about the Mayans and the Aztecs at school. It would be great to go there, follow in Pops' footsteps. Maybe when we've been to Jamaica we could go on to Mexico. What about that, dad?' said Joe. 'And to swim in that sinkhole looks awesome. And it says here it's where they threw people who were sacrificed. Now that's spooky!'

David nodded. The whole thing would be 'spooky', going back to these places haunted by his father's early life and love. He closed the laptop, got up and stretched. He and Joe were staying in Pops' house for a few days. As it was the school holidays it made sense not to keep driving back and forth to his own house and it meant the clearing of the house could proceed more quickly. He hadn't decided yet what to do about the house. Should he sell his own and move back here to the old family home? Or was it weighed down with too many memories? But then they were mostly good memories. He and his mum and dad would often cycle round the Cardurnock Peninsula. From here, there were great views to the south of the distant Lake District mountains, the Pennines to the east and the Scottish hills to the north. It was here that Pops had taught David and then Joe to sail the little wooden dinghy. And David had never tired of plotting the movement of the clouds, anticipating the weather patterns and breathing in the wide skyscapes which typified the Borderlands.

No, he would not make any decisions yet. There was too much to sort out and too much of the past to fathom before he could sleep easy.

*

January 15th. There are road blocks each day - soldiers with guns checking every vehicle on Hope Road. There have been arrests of a couple of Opposition politicians. The newspapers are full of stories about infiltration by 'Brigadistas' - Jamaicans trained in Cuba who return to form pro-government cells to subvert the Opposition, JLP. And this coincides with Seaga, their leader, launching a nationwide anti-government campaign. He's organising rallies and marches all over the country in a run up to the general election later this year. There's certainly more heat on the streets than usual. And I began wondering about the Cuban guys who started working at the project a few months ago. Were they part of this Brigadista thing? Is Maxim encouraging anti-JLP subversion and is this why he's become a target?

January 24th.
Maya phoned me to meet her at the same hotel bar on Stony Hill where I'd met RJ. I hadn't seen her since our return from Mexico and was reassured when I got her message. I'm never sure that this wonderful relationship is going to last. It all seems too good to be true. She's rarely showy in her affection when we're in a public place and I immediately felt there was a more serious undertone to this meeting. She wore large framed dark glasses which half covered her face and I felt unsettled that I couldn't see her eyes. We sat at a table in a shaded corner of the bar. She briefly touched my hand across the table and then spoke quickly. She said she wanted to warn me that as I was working for Maxim I, too, could become a target. 'He's on a hit list,' she said, her voice almost a whisper, 'and that includes anyone working with him. I shouldn't be meeting you really but I'm worried, Will.

Stuff is happening since the Kissinger visit, stuff that you don't want to know about. But I need to know if Maxim is bringing in any more people from Cuba. This brigadista development is really serious and I hear that people at the American embassy are out to kill it.' I told her that since those original guys came in, the ones she knew about, I'd not seen any new arrivals. She nodded and then asked me to keep her informed about any new developments. I thought about the bunker room that I'd worked on but decided not to mention it. When we parted I was eager to touch and hold her for a moment, but it was clear that she wouldn't permit that. 'What about Hellshire Beach, Sunday?' she said. 'Same place, 9.30?' I replied. She nodded, touched my arm and walked away. It felt that somehow the party was over and something sinister was taking its place.

February 4th. Things are certainly changing. Armoured cars on the streets, shortages in the shops, petrol rationing and prices going through the roof. There were queues at the gas station on Hope Road this morning. Tempers were very frayed and I kept looking over my shoulder after Maya's warning. The only light relief was a couple of 'likkle yout' setting up a portable sound system and doing a break dance routine along the line of cars begging for money. You have to credit the inventiveness of these kids who have to hustle every day to keep their bellies half full.
Met Maya at the beach as we arranged. She came with Marianne and they both seemed distracted. There was small talk about stuff but I never felt we really connected. Marianne asked me how long was my contract and would I stay on after it ended. And suddenly I was made to realise this strange dream I was living was finite and that it would end. I said the contract ran until September but that there might be more work. Marianne said it would be sensible to take a break as the next election was timed for December and it wouldn't be wise to be around in the run

up. 'Things will get nasty,' she said. And I looked across at Maya and wondered where that left our relationship. She was staring across the bay and said distantly, 'The mountains are really blue today. We should be up there in the cool of Bermuda Mount. We need to make the most of it.'

February 25th. There was a shootout at the Continental Restaurant in Kingston last night. It's the place Maxim dines at, along with government ministers and Jamaican celebs. Two gunmen were shot by one of the customers who had a semi-automatic weapon. It was over within seconds. But Maxim was a little shaken when he came into work this morning. 'They're getting closer by the day, Will,' he said. 'We all need to watch our backs.' The papers identified the dead men as gunmen from Tivoli Gardens, a JLP stronghold. Normally the shootouts are part of the turf wars in downtown Kingston but it seems uptown is becoming the new target area.

March 6th. Some semblance of normality again. I attended a dinner at the Sheraton for the Jamaican Institute of Architects. There are parallel universes on this island. Here we were, men in smarts suits and the females in their finery, dining on the best of Jamaican cuisine and who would have thought that a mile down the road was a curfew with tanks and armed police and gunmen shooting the hell out of each other! Maya couldn't attend as she was sick so I invited Marianne. Strange how little I know of her. She was in Miami with Maya as a student - her instrument is the viola - and after graduation she lived in Philadelphia for a while playing in the city's orchestra. She's different from Maya - lighter skinned - father is Chinese, mother Jamaican so she has this wonderful blend of the oriental with the African. Whereas Maya's hair is wavy, Marianne's is straight. She's normally less animated than Maya, there's a quiet composure about her which I enjoy. Maya is more unpredictable. She was easy company for the evening. She works as a nurse at a private clinic in Kingston. I asked her about Maya's connection with RJ, that he'd told me he first met Maya in Miami. At that point Marianne became quite unsettled. She shook her head and said she didn't know much about the man but I'd clearly struck a nerve and she quickly changed the subject. That was the only moment when the evening was slightly edgy. Otherwise Marianne's company was a delight. None of the sexual tension I feel when I'm with Maya. There's a serenity in Marianne which is very comforting.

*

Joe stepped off the ladder and stood on the floor of what was left of the tree house. It had been built on some thick branching limbs of the ash tree which overhung the wall at the end of Pops' garden. In a recent storm it had been badly damaged and now Pops was no longer there, it hadn't been repaired. It was the tree house which was built when his dad was young. Pops had improved it for Joe and put in new timbers where the old ones were getting rotten. It still gave a brilliant view down the Solway Firth and he remembered playing games of pirates with some boys from the village when he was younger. As he peered out through the tree house porthole he could see in the distance the rounded top of Criffel - it was clear today, the dark patches of heather contrasting the green of the moorland grass. Closer was the promontory which had carried the railway across to Scotland. It was a strongly built sandstone buttress which extended like a finger part way across the estuary matching the finger which came out from the Scottish side. Pops had shown Joe a picture of the old railway bridge. It had been damaged one winter years ago by ice crashing against the bridge supports. The railway had been closed for the bridge to be repaired but it had never reopened and the bridge was later demolished. All that was left was the sandstone promontory and a few of the original iron bridge supports.

Joe leaned against the wall of the tree house and looked back at Pops' house with its long garden, the winding path, the overgrown vegetable plot where they used to pick raspberries and strawberries in the summer and green beans in the autumn. Digging for potatoes was like searching for buried treasure and there were always those small sweet tomatoes hanging like little jewels in the greenhouse. But now it was all weeds and nettles, the lawn needed mowing and the flower beds were a jungle of the long prickly creeper Pops called 'sticky willy'. As kids they would throw it at each other so that it stuck to your clothes. But now the laughter was gone. The garden looked sad and unloved and Joe cried again for the Pops he missed so much.

When he got back to the house he found his dad still sorting papers. 'What's going to happen to this house, dad?'

'I don't know, Joe. It's a big question.'

'Couldn't you sell your house - come and live here?'

'There's a lot to think about.'

'What's the latest you've found out about Pops in Jamaica?'

'Well, I'm up to 1976 and there are curfews in parts of the city at night, that's when you're not allowed out of your house until the curfew's lifted. And there are road blocks on the streets because there are a lot of shootings. But Pops seems to be coping ok, he's been working on designing a beach resort for some American man and he went to Mexico for Christmas.'

'When did he come back to England?'

'Not sure but his contract ended in the summer of 1976. Haven't got to the end yet. But I'll let you know what happens.'

91

March 19th. Some of the guys at work are talking about leaving. It's mainly the Americans. Larry's booked his flight out and Jim is weighing up options. Went for a drink with them and we talked over what's happening. Larry reckons expats are targets and working for Maxim heightens the danger. There's talk of Manley declaring a State of Emergency and preventing money being taken out of the country. The country's finances are in such a dire state that Manley's had to accept a loan from the IMF but with it come some crippling restrictions. His welfare programs and literacy initiatives may have to be cut. All his good intentions are going belly up and the Opposition are feeding the unrest. More targeted shootings of prominent people. There were gunshots close to the street where I live last night although the curfew still doesn't extend above Half Way Tree, so we're able to come and go with caution. It's still spooky though seeing the helicopters hovering low, probing the street with their search lights. It's like something out of a dystopian movie. In other respects life continues strangely untouched. There's a yacht race to Morant Bay this weekend so it'll be good to breathe some sea air and see the wind in the sails again. Maya won't be there as she's going to Cuba to help organise some government sponsored music festival. I need to catch up with her as she's not been well these past weeks. Some stomach bug she reckons. We need a weekend up at Bermuda Mount. The weather is still cooler and there aren't the torrential rains yet. It's perfect weather for some high level hiking. We ought to do Blue Mountain Peak. I may suggest that.

March 26th. The yacht race was thrilling. We started late afternoon with a brisk easterly sending us surging across the harbour, bright coloured spinnakers ballooning out from each boat. Rounded Port Royal on to a thrusting port beat, the yachts heeling into the surf, waterlines exposed. It was really dramatic. We were close to RJ's boat at one point and tacked across his bow. He was not happy! Marianne was crewing with him and waved as we passed close on his starboard side.

Arrived at Bowden, Port Morant, late evening. Entertained at the home of one of Maxim's friends who has a plantation there - acres of coconuts, bananas, and sugar cane. There was suckling pig, roasted breadfruit and plantain, ackee and salt fish and mountains of rice and peas. And the Appleton rum flowed until the early hours. The old great house stands on a hill overlooking Port Morant. Ruins of the old estate buildings and slave quarters festooned with vines and creepers. Feeling of a place lost in time and slowly decaying but a world away from the curfews of Kingston. Saw Marianne briefly as we were embarking the following morning. She'd stayed over with a friend of RJ's. Talked about a hike up to Blue Mountain Peak. She liked the idea and said she'd mention it to Maya and the music crew.   Brilliant sail back on an easterly - again spinnakers sending us surfing the swell. Maxim was delighted that we came in second. He was more relaxed than I've seen him for months and no talk of politics for the 48 hours we were at sea!

Whenever David came across a new reference he did a quick Google search. It seemed Morant Bay was a place of real historical significance in Jamaican history. It was the place of a rebellion in 1865 when a local preacher, Paul Bogle, led a revolt against wide ranging injustices in the area. The rebellion was brutally suppressed by the Governor, Edward Eyre. Hundreds of men and women were arrested and executed. There was a picture of a statue of Paul Bogle, who was now a national hero.

'I'm learning quite a lot about Jamaican history,' David said when next he encountered Gina. She was sitting in the garden of the coffee shop when he called in one afternoon.

'What's the latest?' she asked.

'The Morant Bay Rebellion, 1865.'

'No, I meant the latest from the journal. I'm keen to know what happens to your father.'

David sat down at the table with his coffee. 'We're up to spring 1976 and things are heating up, politically.'

'That was the year of the Bob Marley shooting that Marlon James describes.'

'Yes, that was later in the year. We're not there yet. Seems some of the expats are getting the jitters and leaving.'

'Not only the expats - a lot of middle class Jamaicans left for America taking their money with them. That's what hastened the economic collapse. A lot of businesses folded.'

'Well, his employer, Maxim, seems to be in for the long haul. He's just had my dad overseeing the construction of what he calls a 'bunker room'.'

'Sounds pretty extreme.'

'Well, Maxim reckons he's a target.'

'And what news of the mysterious Maya?'

'Oh, she's off to Cuba again, organising another government sponsored music festival.'

Gina nodded and slowly sipped her drink. She fingered the petals of one of the flowers which were in a vase on the table. Then she looked up. 'D'you reckon she's involved in this Brigadista thing, you know, training Jamaicans as guerrilla fighters.'

David shook his head and smiled: 'C'mon, now who's getting carried away. Maya comes across as pretty feisty, but she's no Che Guevara.'

'Well, the music is sponsored by the government and they're working with the Cubans.'

'True,' said David. 'I think my dad left Jamaica later that same year but whether it was just the end of his contract or for other reasons I've yet to find out.'

'Well, get on with it then. Get the journal finished. I'm keen to know what happens,' urged Gina.

'Yes, miss, will do, miss,' smiled David, giving Gina a mock salute. 'As soon as I know, I'll give you a call and we'll meet for a meal or something. And all will be revealed.'

'I'll look forward to it,' said Gina, 'but don't take too long.'

David wondered again why he hadn't read the journal in one sitting. But he knew. It was too painful and too disconcerting. Painful, in the aftermath of his father's death, to be reading about this person that he didn't know - entering a world of intimate thoughts and revelations which did not sit comfortably with him. He felt a guilt at this voyeurism of a father whom he had so loved and admired over the years. And now he was being confronted by a different personality. His confidence about knowing what was real was being undermined every time he opened the journal. Had he been deceived all these years? Where was his real father in all this?

*

April 10th. Increasingly the need to get away from this cauldron which is Kingston. More tensions at the plant. Now Larry's gone, the pressure on Jim has increased and he's looking at options for leaving. I'm now designing another annexe for the processing machinery which is due to arrive next month. Maxim's hoping to get early production started by September. So the Blue Mountain trek was a welcome distraction.

We drove up to a place called Mavis Bank late afternoon on Friday and hiked up to a bunkhouse. The plan was to get up to the Peak to see the sunrise. This meant leaving the bunkhouse at 3.30a.m. for the two hour hike up to Blue Mountain Ridge which takes you to the Peak itself at 7,400ft. There was the music crew - Jonathan, Courtney, Charles and Diego plus Marianne and Maya. Maya was full of bonhomie but something didn't seem right. She was affectionate, held my hand now and then and when we had rest stops made a point of sitting close to me. She said the Cuban music festival had gone well and she'd had a handshake from Michael Manley at a reception at the Sheraton. At the bunkhouse we didn't really sleep much. Diego nudged us at around 3a.m. and we set off in the dark under a clear starlit sky. The darkness vibrated with night noises - cicadas, tree frogs but no mosquitoes, which was a blessing. The air was light and cool and the climb not too strenuous. Surprisingly Maya had to keep stopping to get her breath. She's normally so fit. She said she was getting over a chest cold she'd caught in Cuba. Not like her at all.

I'd expected the main ridge to be like the moorland fells in England, treeless and open but there was thick bush and tree cover even at the highest level. At the Peak you look down along the Blue Mountain Ridge, at the mist over the lower hills of Portland to the sea and watch the sun warming the darkness with pink light. As the first rays of the sun peeked over the cloud banks and we stood mesmerised by the magic of it, Maya linked her hands round my arm, put her lips close to my ear and whispered: 'We need some time at Bermuda Mount, just the two of us. There are things I need to tell you. But don't ask me now. Wait until then.' And when we came down from the mountain, were back in Kingston, and the group went their different ways, she looked at me, nodded and kissed me briefly on the cheek. 'See you soon,' she said.

April 25th. Haven't seen Maya since the Blue Mountain trip. Got a letter from her before she left for America - very brief, something to do with changes to policy at the embassy. No return date as yet. Not sure where our relationship is heading but I fear Ned was right when he described her like a 'peenie wallie' - my elusive firefly.

May 6th.. Still no word from Maya. Arranged to see Marianne at the Stony Hill Hotel. I hoped she had news of Maya. Saw RJ at his usual corner table with some guys I'd seen him with before. He waved but didn't make an effort to come over. Marianne said not to pressure Maya too much. I said I was confused about my relationship with her. She rested her hand on mine and said simply: 'Enjoy what you've had but don't expect too much, too quickly.' And then said: 'The time is out of joint, oh cursed spite that we can't put it right.' She smiled: 'I changed the last bit, but aren't you impressed with my bit of Shakespeare. Hamlet, you know. Learnt that in high school.'
Just like Marianne to lighten my mood. She was right, of course. Here I was, the young English adventurer, falling in love in one of the most exotic places on the planet and expecting what? A long term relationship? Marriage, children? Get real, I tried to tell myself, but my heart ached and I longed for Maya's touch.

May 15th. Maya's back . Got a brief message. 'Looking forward to Bermuda Mount. We need to escape! Will be in touch.'

July 1st. Haven't been able to put pen to paper. My world is shattered. Maya's been wounded in a shooting at Stony Hill Hotel. RJ was killed, Maya shot in the shoulder. Marianne phoned me. Told me to come to her clinic. Not to say a word to anyone. I was trembling as she let me in, squeezed my hand and hugged me. Led me into a small room. And there was Maya, looking small and lifeless, her skin bruised, tubes coming from her nose and her arm, a heart monitor registering her pulse, a bag of blood dripping a crimson stream down a tube into her arm,

97

bandages covering her eyes. I feared she was blind but Marianne shook her head. No, it was just a precaution. I asked what happened. All Marianne could tell me was she thought Maya had been at a meeting with RJ when gunmen came in and started shooting. It seemed the corner table was their target, where RJ always sat. Maya just happened to be in the line of fire. And the gunmen? I asked. They got away. It was over in seconds. I leaned over the bed and touched Maya's hand. It's me, Will, I whispered. There was a slight response from her hand as she pressed my fingers. Give her time, said Marianne. Call back in a couple of days.

July 3rd. The country's on fire. Manley's declared a State of Emergency. 500 people have been arrested including the Deputy Leader of the JLP, Pearnel Charles. He's in prison at the army camp downtown. Tanks on the streets again. Curfews uptown and downtown now. The papers talk of some CIA backed scheme supporting the JLP to bring down Manley's 'communist regime'. It's all happening as people predicted weeks ago. I should have listened and taken it more seriously.

July 7th. Maya's gone! Went to the clinic. Marianne wasn't there but the nurse said she didn't know anything about the patient who'd been shot only that the baby was unhurt! 'What baby?' I said. 'There wasn't a baby!' But the nurse nodded: 'The lady who was shot, was pregnant. The lady's name was Maya.'

July 9th. Finally got to see Marianne. In some ways I wish I hadn't. Maya's been secretly taken out of the country but Marianne can't tell me where, as Maya could be followed and murdered. Seems I've been deceived all along. Maya's a covert CIA operative and so was RJ. All these trips to Cuba as a musician were covers for Maya's CIA work getting information on the Brigadistas. RJ groomed Maya for the Agency when she was a student in

Miami. He tried it on with Marianne but she refused to get involved.

Then came the next bombshell. I've been used! Maya set me up with RJ to build his resort but really all he was after was a new dock to use to bring in weapons for the CIA campaign against the government. And I recalled Maxim's words when I told him about the project with RJ. 'Watch your back'. And of course Maya had tried getting me to spy on Maxim.

So was I just a pawn in the CIA strategy? Have all my encounters with her been carefully orchestrated? Were all the words of love and affection from Maya merely bait to trap me? It looks that way. And yet it doesn't feel that way. Surely I haven't misread it all? All those nights of us being together, laughing together, enjoying each other's company and loving each other? Or was that another grand delusion of mine, that there was anything of love? Was it only her clever calculation that I was easy prey? But then why has she kept the baby? Surely the baby would be an inconvenience to a female CIA agent!

And now it seems I'm a target. Marianne warned me that working for RJ sets me up as a target for the PNP gunmen. And working for Maxim I'm a target for the JLP. She urged me to get the next flight out. Gave me her contact address, hugged me and said: 'How I wish it could have been different for you.' 'Is it my child she's carrying?' I asked. Marianne nodded. 'It can only be yours. She told me so.'

I feel confused, angry and foolish. Can't think straight.

July 10th There's been a bomb explosion at the airport - luggage going on to a Cubana flight. More CIA activity?

July 12th
Gotta get out. Too dangerous. Feel utterly betrayed.

The final entry was on a new page. David had read it some weeks earlier but had not read the other entries leading up to it. He thumbed the remaining pages of the journal hoping for something more. Sadly - all blank. That was it then.

He closed the book. His fist was clenched against its cover. He thought of his father's hand doing the same - closing the book. Closing off that chapter of his life. And had he flown out in July of 1976? Flown out with a mind awash with so much confusion and disillusionment and with the knowledge that there was a child - his child? And had his whole life then been haunted by the memory of Maya and the child and the way she had betrayed him? And with Marianne's warning not to try to find her as she could be murdered, had he given up hope of ever searching for her? Maybe the CIA had given her a new identity and protected her or was she just a low level operative who was expendable?

He stared out of the window at the grey waters of the Solway and shook his head at the sadness of what his father had lived with for all these years, the torment of not knowing what had happened to Maya and the child; the pain of keeping it all locked away inside. And then David remembered that small piece of paper in the back of the journal, dated 'June 2006'. He pictured his father re-reading the journal after Beth had died. Was he then grieving not only for the loss of his wife, but also for Maya, his first love, and for his lost child?

And he recalled his impatience with his father, the rows they had had before the dementia was diagnosed. If only he had known what he knew now. It could have been so different between them.

There was only one thing to do. He had to go in search of the truth of what had happened and try to find Maya and the child - his half brother or sister.

*

'I said she was an enigma, didn't I?' Gina was nodding at David across the table as she once again thumbed through the journal. They had now met a couple of times since David handed over the journal to her so that she could read it for herself. There were yellow 'Post It' notes on various pages and Gina had a blue folder with other notes and information she had collected.

'And have you decided yet?'

'What about?'

'When you're going there - to Jamaica.'

David sighed: 'Joe's been pestering me for weeks now. He thinks it would be just a trip down memory lane. He doesn't realise the situation.'

'Are you going to tell him about what happened and about the baby?'

David shrugged: 'Not sure how much to divulge. He's only eleven.'

'He's old enough to understand about the underworld of spies and 'cloak and dagger' stuff. He's watched James Bond hasn't he?'

'I suppose so; yeah, he's watched Bond and Jason Bourne.'

'So you can say his Pops had a girl friend who turned out to be a secret agent and she disappeared. He'd find that really exciting.'

'And the baby?'

'You're probably never going to find out what happened to the baby or if it survived. In the trauma of the shooting and its aftermath she may have lost the baby. Just tell him you're going to see if you can find out what happened to the girl friend, see if anyone's still alive who remembers Will Pearson and of course visit the places he mentions in the journal.'

'I suppose so.'

'And what about Maya's friend, Marianne, didn't she give your father a contact address in Jamaica?'

'But he never wrote it in the journal. And she's probably dead by now.'

'Not necessarily. She'd be in her seventies, like Maya. People live to good ages in Jamaica - as long as they don't get shot!' Gina got up. 'Another coffee?'

David nodded: 'Thanks.'

There were not many people in the coffee shop as it was late afternoon. David felt thankful to have someone to confide in. Since finishing the journal and having time to think he found more questions than answers. There'd been times when Maya had hinted that she wanted to escape with Will, somewhere away from Kingston - to the mountains or Mexico. When Gina returned with the drinks, David voiced his thoughts. 'D'you reckon Maya wanted to get away somewhere with my dad? Was she genuinely fond of him, d'you think?'

Gina sprinkled some chocolate onto the milky surface of her coffee and shook her head slowly. 'I'm never sure about her. There are hints that she's not at ease with her job especially after the visit by Henry Kissinger in '75. She'd be under pressure to be closely involved in more of the tricky stuff. And did you pick up on the clues that she was pregnant?'

'What clues?'

'Well, there was the apparent sickness bug soon after the Mexico trip and her problems on the Blue Mountain climb. Your dad mentions she wasn't as fit as usual.'

'And you think that's to do with the pregnancy?'

'Could be.'

'But I still can't forgive her for what she did. She deliberately set my dad up as a CIA stooge. She put him in touch with the Texan guy, RJ, to build his dock so that he could bring in guns. That was calculated. She tried to get him spying on his boss, Maxim. And what about the original invitation to Mexico for Christmas? Surely that was just the start of 'grooming' him.'

'And he was a sucker for it,' said Gina. 'Hook, line and sinker - she had him in the bag from early. And she knew it. But then there's a hint that she was having a change of heart. She wanted to see him and confess something to him. She said that a couple of times.'

'But sadly it never happened.'

'So what's your plan of action?' asked Gina. 'You've got to ask yourself why you're going and what you're going to do when you get there? I can see you drifting around in an emotional haze not finding out very much. You need to make a list of people and places that might throw up some leads.'

David nodded: 'Good job I've got you keeping me focused. Yeah, I'll probably be quite emotional. I just feel so desperately sorry for my dad. He was just a pawn in a game he had no idea about.'

'There's a sadness about it. I suppose he was very naive, going to his 'island in the sun' - all very exciting but unaware about the underlying realities.'

David toyed with his coffee spoon for a moment. For weeks he had mulled over raising with Gina the question of what he called the 'skin factor' in the journal. It was like the proverbial 'elephant in the room'. If he raised it, would the issue of racial difference become an issue between himself and Gina? But he had to raise it. He wanted Gina's take on the question.

'What's wrong?' she said. 'You suddenly look troubled.'

David smiled and nodded: 'Yes I'm troubled,' he said. 'But I've hesitated to ask you about this.'

'About what?'

'These references my father constantly makes to Maya's colour, to the fact that she's black. At one point he writes as if she both attracts and repels him. I didn't understand what he meant.'

Gina nodded: 'Isn't that interesting. Those references which are scattered throughout the journal just leapt out at me. I've got Post-It notes on all the pages where you father refers to the issue of race. Wasn't sure whether to raise them but they're so prominent.'

'How did you react when you read them?' asked David.

Gina just shrugged: 'I wasn't surprised. Young white man, in the Seventies finds he's suddenly dropped into a country of black people - is it any wonder that all the myths that he's been brought up with suddenly come flooding to the surface. No I wasn't surprised.'

'What d'you mean by myths?'

Gina looked steadily across the table at David: 'Forgive me for being a bit blunt here but you did ask me and I hope this isn't going to sound like a sociology lecture. But being white in a mainly white society, you don't realise how privileged you are. You enter a room like this cafe and nearly everyone's white. The colour of your skin does not cross your mind as being significant. But for me entering this cafe, or a shop or a court of law, I am very aware that I'm viewed as different. My skin colour carries a host of associations, generally negative ones, in the minds of a lot of white people. They've been brought up on a diet of colonial history, the glory of the British Empire, images of slavery, white dominance, apartheid. And when the positive role models that people see in magazines and on the screen are nearly all white, is it any wonder that black is seen as alien and negative? So here's your father wrestling with opposing instincts - one the attraction for this beautiful and talented young Jamaican, but then the other instinct, borne of the culture he grew up in, to see her as inferior. Is it surprising that he's confused?'

David nodded slowly, trying to digest all this. 'I've never thought about it.'

'But you've never had to, that's the point I'm making. Being white confers privilege in a mainly white society,' said Gina. 'Now it'll be interesting if you go to Jamaica, how you'll feel.'

'Don't you think things have changed since the Seventies?'

Gina nodded: 'Yes, there are a few more black politicians, prominent celebrities, newsreaders and so on but how much that influences those deeply held myths I'm not sure. Look at all the trolling of black footballers on social media and threats to prominent people of colour. I used to feel quite comfortable in this country but the mood has changed recently since the Brexit referendum and with the rise of right wing political groups.'

'So how do you yourself deal with it?' asked David.

'I have to be smarter in my work, sharper in discussions and debates; I have to dress well in public, show confidence, be assertive without being seen as aggressive. Basically I have, all the time, to be conscious of trying to dispel people's preconceptions.'

'Wow,' said David, 'that's quite a challenge.'

Gina nodded: 'It certainly is. How am I doing?'

David smiled : 'Well I'm definitely impressed.'

'That's good.' She went on: 'You see, being black in London is one thing, it's more accepted there, but in the north of England it feels very different. When I go to remote areas of Cumbria or Scotland looking at wind farm sites and meeting local land owners or farmers they do a double and treble take when they first see me. They'll probably be wrestling with all those prejudices that your father was dealing with. But then they see that I know what I'm talking about and that I'm good humoured and generally the barriers come down and I'm hopeful that they see me, not so much as a black person but just a person, new to them, who's got a job to do. But who knows what's going on inside their heads? You just have to have faith that people can change.'

David nodded: 'Thanks. That's a lot to take in and I'm really grateful.'

'That's okay. Now back to the question of your trip,' said Gina.

'Yes, you asked why I'm going,' said David. 'You see, dad and I had a falling out during the last couple of years. I now realise it was the dementia, his grief over my mother's death and perhaps this yearning for Maya and the baby.'

'But you didn't know,' said Gina.

'I still want to put things right for the sake of his memory. I want to find out how much dad was being used; whether there was any love between him and Maya and for that I need to find her and find Marianne. And more importantly did that baby survive and if so where is he or she now? That's as important for Joe as for me. They'd be my half brother or sister. I suppose going is a kind of penance for the guilt I feel at not being more sympathetic when my father was suffering so much.'

Gina nodded: 'I see. But don't be too hard on yourself. Dementia is cruel for everyone concerned.' She looked hard at David for a moment, then she shifted the coffee cups and placed a folder in the middle of the table.

'I've been doing some digging and I hope it's going to be useful to you. Firstly, I found that your father's employer, Maxim Moreno, became a minister in the PNP government of Michael Manley in 1989. Going through some recent editions of the Daily Gleaner in their archives, I found a reference to him this year taking part in a yacht race. So it seems he's still alive. He's certainly one you need to visit.'

'That would probably put him in his eighties, then. I wonder if he's still living in that area called Beverly Hills. D'you remember in the journal, my dad went to a party there just after he arrived?'

'That's right,' added Gina. 'My parents still have relations living in Jamaica. I'll contact them and see if they can find the whereabouts of Maxim Moreno.'

David started jotting some reminders on a note pad. 'Maya had a brother, Edward, a lawyer living in Montego Bay but I remember my dad recording that he was leaving for America when all the violence kicked off in the Seventies.'

'Problem is,' Gina went on, 'you don't have a surname for Maya or her brother. Nowhere in the journal is their surname mentioned, which doesn't make things easy.'

'What I'll have to do is maybe find this place called The Little Theatre where the orchestra played and see if anyone there remembers a viola player called Marianne and a violinist called Maya.'

'And there's Maya's uncle Ned who had the farm near Port Antonio. How old would he be?'

David shook his head slowly: 'I think it mentions him being in his fifties back then, so it's doubtful he's still alive.'

'But someone might remember him and remember Maya. It's worth a trip out there.'

David nodded: 'I certainly intend doing that drive over to the north coast. I want to see what happened to that resort my dad was working on.'

'Didn't it belong to the Texan guy who was shot and killed when Maya was shot?'

'That's right. 'RJ' they called him. But again I've no idea what his proper name was.'

Gina tapped her pen on the table: 'You know I checked the Gleaner for any reference to that murder in July 1976 at a bar in Stony Hill.' She shrugged: 'Not a mention. You wonder whether, if he was CIA, it was hushed up. Now that would be worth following up at the newspaper offices. But remember, you've got to be careful. There's a saying in Jamaica that asking too many questions 'is a good way to get dead'.'

'Is that right?' said David, surprised.

Gina nodded: 'The arm of the CIA is long and they don't let go of things very quickly.' She tilted her head a little and looked straight across the table at David: 'And when are you going to be telling Joe about this trip?'

'I know, I know. Soon. I've got to work out how much I'm going to tell him.'

'You ought to go around Christmas time. That's the best time for Jamaican weather. It's a little cooler, the humidity's low and you won't get the torrential rain that comes later in the year.'

'Sounds good. But I'll have to clear that with Joe's mother.'

'Well, just do it. Then tell Joe and book your flights.' Gina wagged a finger at David. 'Don't dither, Mr Pearson. This is a case I'm keen for us to solve.'

'Yes ma'am,' said David, smiling. 'I'm on it.'

'But we need another meeting. And I have some movies of Jamaica that you and Joe could watch. Give you some impressions of the place. Why not come round and we can view them and I can meet Joe. I'll do you some genuine Jamaican food to get you in the mood. In the meantime, I'm going to see what I can dig up about CIA activities in Jamaica in the Seventies.'

*

That evening David phoned Anna. She knew of the discovery of the journal and some of the revelations about Jamaica that Joe had told her about. She knew of his excitement to visit the island so she wasn't surprised about David's request for them to go just after Christmas.

'A trip down your father's memory lane, then?' said Anna.

'Something like that,' replied David.

'I know Joe's very excited to go. Just keep him safe. Don't do anything foolish.'

'Of course not,' said David.

'A friend of mine went there. Said what a great place it was. Lovely beaches.'

'Yes,' said David. 'I think Joe will enjoy it.'

'Well I hope you manage to find your father's old friends. I assume that's part of the trip.'

'Yes, it's a long shot that they'll still be alive. But you never know.'

'I'll leave you to tell him then. It can be your surprise.'

'Thanks, Anna. I appreciate that.'

*

Joe picked up the binoculars from the table in Pops' conservatory. This was the place where they would watch the movement of the sea birds. It had a clear wide window looking out on the Solway Firth. There were always the wading birds - the stately white egrets and the curlews with their long beaks and their sad piping call. Pops said it sounded like they'd lost a friend the way their call fell in a curve down to the sand as they took to the air. Then there were the gangs of oystercatchers. They were the 'rude boys' as Pops called them. They were noisy and had a raucous call and they always flew in gangs. When they took off from the shoreline they showed off their jagged black and white markings. Pops said they were like those bikers on Harley Davidsons who wore black leather jackets with lots of badges and emblems. One of Joe's favourites were the little ring plovers who skittered along the shoreline in and out of the waves as they broke on the sand.

In the spring around late April they would look for the first swallows returning. They always nested in the hayloft of Pops' barn. He said it was like his lost family returning. They flew from wintering in South Africa and when they first appeared Pops said it was, for him, the first sign of real spring. 'My long lost family's back!' he would shout down the phone to Joe. 'The swallows are here and all's well with the world again.'

But Joe's favourite time was in autumn when the Barnacle Geese arrived. Pops said they had flown all the way from a place called Spitsbergen in the Arctic Circle, two thousand miles away. They flew in great V-shaped formations constantly calling. This was the first sign that winter was on its way.

Often, he and Pops would leave the house as the sun was going down over Criffel and make their way along the shoreline to the old railway promontory which jutted out into the water. It was here that they would sit and wait for the Whooper Swans. On a still night you would hear from far off their calling and the steady thump of their wing beats. Then they would appear and fly low over your head and out over the water. When it was windy and the noise of the waves lashed against the pier and the wind stole away their call, the Whoopers would suddenly be there without warning, pounding the air, honking to each other through the fading light and almost brushing your head with their wings. Then Joe would grip Pops' arm and shiver with the thrill of it all.

He put the binoculars to his eyes and adjusted the focus. He could see the iron pillars clearly on the end of the pier and some white surf churning in the centre of the estuary where the incoming tide was meeting the outward push of the river. Another month and the Barnacle Geese would be back and then the Whooper Swans; but sadly Pops wouldn't be around to share the joy of it all.

'Hey Joe, what's happening out there?' said David.

'Just thinking about the geese coming back and the swans. I used to look out for them with Pops.'

David came across the room and put his arms round Joe and looked out with him at the view across the Solway. 'How d'you feel about Christmas in Jamaica?'

Joe turned and looked up at David, eyes wide and a huge smile across his face: 'You mean it?'

'Well it might be just after Christmas. I've checked with your mother and it's okay with her.'

'And we'll visit all those places Pops wrote about?'

'We'll see what we can fit in. And there are some other things I need to explain about the trip. But first we ought to check out flight times.'

'Wow, dad, this could be one of the best Christmases ever!'

David nodded: 'Maybe, son - maybe.'

*

A couple of weeks later Gina opened her door to David and Joe. 'Welcome, welcome,' she beamed and extended her hand to greet Joe. 'And you must be Joe. Your father has often talked about you.'

Joe watched his dad greeting this tall, glamorous stranger. They didn't kiss, there was just a touch on his arm from her. His dad had said she was a friend, a lawyer who was helping him sort out some of Pops' stuff - papers and that. But she knew Jamaica well and was helping with the arrangements for the trip. His dad had also said that when they got there they were going to do some detective work and search for an old girl friend of Pops who was mentioned in the journal. Her name was Maya and Pops had been very close to her but had lost contact with her.

Gina led them along the hall into the kitchen. 'So, Joe, as you're off to my home country, I thought I should cook you some Jamaican food. I was in London last week so went to see my parents who live there and we bought a load of stuff from the market in Brixton - that's where a lot of people from Jamaica settled when they came to England. It's a bit different from Carlisle - it's full of all kinds of people from different countries - black, white, light skinned, dark-skinned like me - just like you're going to see in Jamaica. And I bought some food you probably haven't seen before. Now, I know we're not in school but bear with me while we do a quick five-minute lesson on some of the things you'll see in the markets in Jamaica.'

111

Gina had set out on the work top a variety of fruits and vegetables. She explained about each in turn and how you cooked them and what they tasted like. There was callalloo, yam, plantain, soursop, jackfruit, paw-paw, breadfruit and she got him to pick them up, feel them and smell them.

Later when they sat down to eat she pointed out each in turn and urged him to try them. 'House rules, Joe. You don't have to like it but at least please try it and give me a verdict.'

Along with the fruit and vegetables there was chicken and what Gina called 'jerk pork' and some curried meat which she said he must try before she told him what it was. 'Any guesses?' she said. Joe chewed away and said it was a bit spicy. 'You'll see a lot of these when you go up country in Jamaica.'

'Is it goat?' asked Joe.

'Full marks,' smiled Gina, 'yes, curried goat, a Jamaican speciality.'

'I'm sure my father mentions eating 'jerk pork' in his journal,' added David, 'at a place called Boston Bay.'

Gina nodded: 'It's well known for some of the best jerk pork on the island.'

Joe had not said much, it was all a little overwhelming at first, but he liked his dad's new friend. 'Think I'm going to enjoy this trip,' he said nodding at Gina.

'You wait till you see the movies I'm going to show you. You'll love it. And you'll need a mask and snorkel - the underwater swimming is just a dream.'

At the end of the evening, as they were leaving, David leaned towards Gina and said: 'Thanks for a lovely evening. And thanks for making it special for Joe.'

Gina smiled: 'You have a great son, there. Take good care of him.'

On their way home, Joe said: 'Gina was fun. I liked her. Maybe she ought to be coming with us. She could be our guide.'

'She's a busy person,' said David. 'But what did you reckon to Jamaica then?'

'Looks amazing. Can't wait. And we need a mask and snorkel. That's for sure.'

***

PART TWO: The Tracing

The plane banked and Joe could see the outline of Kingston far below. He had studied the map many times and wondered how it would be landing on the end of the narrow spit of land they called The Palisadoes Peninsula. This was where the airport, the Norman Manley International Airport, was located, not far from Port Royal, the old home of those real pirates of the Caribbean. He had watched the original 'Pirates' film again recently with Jack Sparrow swashbuckling his way round Port Royal and the Spanish Main. Now he was over the actual place, the thin arm of land which twisted away from the city out to the airport. He nudged his father. 'Dad, don't miss this - Port Royal, where the pirates sailed out from.'

David leaned over: 'Didn't they call it 'The wickedest city in the world'?'

'Then the earthquake came and destroyed it,' added Joe.

It had been a long trip and David was tired and not a little apprehensive. The short flight down to Heathrow from Manchester had been fine but at Heathrow it was different. There was a two hour delay and people were getting irritable. And now he knew what Gina meant when she said London was different. In the departure lounge he and Joe were among the few white faces in a sea of noisy Jamaicans. The air bristled with raised voices: parents trying to control excited children who were dressed up for the Christmas holidays, mothers with new babies, young men in sharp jeans and hoodies elbowing each other in mock bravado, older couples standing resolutely in line waiting for the nod from the stewards that boarding was starting.

And then to the flight itself. When he made his way to the toilets at the rear of the plane he noted that the passengers were mainly black. And Gina had wondered how he would feel to be in a minority for the first time.

Yes it was odd, and disconcerting - this sudden awareness of his own skin colour being different. And it was noisy and boisterous but generally good humoured, a kind of party atmosphere. Not many tourists flew into Kingston, they went to Montego Bay; this was mainly Jamaicans - business people or 'returners', going to see family or retiring back to the old country.

Joe had the window seat next to David who was seated beside a smartly dressed lady called Violet. She'd been chatty during the flight and, when she heard it was their first visit to Jamaica, was anxious to recommend places to see. 'Now you mus' tek de boy to de Bob Marley Museum an' you mus' get ice cream at Devon House on de way. Just a likkle way up Hope Road.' She had leaned across to Joe: 'Yuh like reggae, young man? Cuz you cyarn get away from it.' She laughed. 'Oh lawd, reggae in the air we breathe in Kingston.' Violet was in the tourist business and managed a hotel in New Kingston. She passed a business card to David. 'Yuh have a hotel booking a'ready?'

David nodded.

'Cancel it. Come stay at my hotel. I give you a good rate and look after yuh.'

'Go with the flow,' Gina had said. 'Just let it wash over you...' and David found himself nodding, 'Okay, thanks, that's kind.'

'Violet, remember, Violet Hastings,' she nodded patting David's hand. 'People know me and I'll look after you, Mr David, and your boy Joe, don't you worry. Kingston can be a confusin' place at fust but you'll be fine. An' my brother is collectin' me so you can ride with us too, if you wish.'

'Thanks, we were going to get a taxi then pick up a hire car tomorrow.'

'Yuh don' need spend money on taxi. Dem tief yuh. Spen' money on ice cream for Joe and a Red Stripe for you.' She laughed again and smoothed her dress.

'Now when we land, we need to fight our way through arl of dese crazy Jamaicans.'

Just then the intercom crackled and the voice of Courtney, the tall flight attendant broke through the chatter. 'Now then Ladies and Gentlepersons, as they say in Kingston - Is yard we reach!' There was a whooping and a clapping and some people shooting imaginary guns in the air with a 'Brap, brap brap!'

Violet leaned over, 'Don' pay them no mind. He jus' mean we almost home.'

It was late afternoon, the sun still hot as they emerged from the Arrivals building into a blanket of heat. David shielded his eyes against the brightness and for the first time saw the white sweep of the city across the blue water of the harbour. And beyond, the humped shoulders of the mountains veiled in a blue haze. This is how it must have been, thought David, when dad got off the plane and looked at the city for the first time, forty years ago. Some things didn't change.

They waited a few moments and then a blue BMW pulled up nearby. 'Hey there, brother,' called Violet, waving. 'This here's my brother, Edmund. We have passengers, Ed. Can we fit?'

'Sure, no problem,' replied her brother. 'You Violet's friends from England?'

'We met on the plane,' replied Violet. 'David and his son, Joe. Their fust time here. They staying at the hotel.'

'Cool,' said Edmund. 'You know what BMW stand for Joe?'

Joe shook his head.

'Bob Marley and the Wailers.'

'Forgive my brother,' said Violet, 'he forever telling jokes.'

The drive from the airport took a while. First there was the winding road along the Palisadoes

Peninsula, the harbour and the city to the left and the open sea crashing on the beaches to the right. When they reached the intersection with the main coast road they turned left towards the city.

'This here's called Harbour View, and now we're about to pass somewhere you might know from the movies,' said Edmund.

'I know,' said Joe, 'it's that scene in James Bond, *Dr No*, at the start where there's a car chase round the cement works. We watched it a few weeks ago.'

'Right on, likkle Joe,' said Edmund, 'yes the Rockfort cement works, part of movie history. And you know most of that film shot around Jamaica?'

'My brother's crazy about movies,' said Violet.

'You see *The Harder They Come* yet?' said Edmund.

'We didn't manage to get that one,' replied David.

'Now that one you must see. That really tell the story of Jamaica. And the music - man, some classic tracks, me tell you.'

They turned on to the Windward Road and then up Mountain View Avenue at the base of Long Mountain. To the left the city was spread out below them.

Edmund pointed out the National Stadium: 'Dat's where Bob Marley perform his 'One Love' concert in '78 and try to bring the warring gangs together in peace.'

'Did it work?' asked David.

Edmund shook his head: 'Sadly, not for long.'

'Is there an area called Beverly Hills?' asked David.

'Jus' up here,' said Edmund pointing to the mountain on their right. 'You heard of it?'

'My father was here in the Seventies. He wrote about going to a party there.'

'It where the big people live, dem with arl the money. Some pretty houses up dere.'

David remembered from the journal the description of houses built out from the hillside and now he could see some of them - spectacular constructions with projecting balconies seeming to hang in space. Wasn't that where Maxim had lived? He needed to check back in the journal.

'Now, Joe,' said Violet, 'before we reach, would you mind if we divert to a likkle place call Devon House for some of de bes' ice cream in Jamaica - would you mind that?'

Joe smiled and nodded. He loved the warmth of this smiling lady as she put her arm around him and gave him a squeeze. He was beginning to get used to this new accent too although sometimes if was difficult to follow.

'One of the first places my dad came to when he arrived in Jamaica in '74 was Devon House,' said David, 'I wonder if it's changed a lot in forty years.'

They had turned on to a new main road and David checked the name 'Hope Road'. His father had driven up this road many times to his apartment near the University. There were white railings and soldiers at the gates of a long drive lined with tall palm trees leading up to a white house with columns at the entrance. Then a short distance away another impressive white mansion.

'A lot has changed, but some things jus' carry on,' put in Edmund. 'Now here yuh see all dis lawn and tree and ting, well dis is where our Governor General live. Yuh see dat big white house back dere, well dat's it, and then a likkle further along here is where the Prime Minister live. They call dem trees Royal Palm and yuh see those trees with the orange flowers, dem call Royal Poinciana trees or Flame of de Forest.'

'My brother thinkin' he a tourist guide,' laughed Violet.

'Shut up, sister. Let me speak nah. Dis is important for our guests.'

Violet nudged Joe and winked at him. 'Proceed brother,' she said.

'T'ank you,' said Edmund clearing his voice. 'Now let me tell you about this famous road, Hope Road. We seen the Governor General house, and the Prime Minister house, now we comin' to the most important house in Kingston.'

He slowed the car and pulled into the roadside. 'Dis was the home of Bob Marley, it call Island House and it now the Bob Marley Museum. Yuh see him gold statue dere, wid him arm raise. And dis de place where him shot an' almost killed in December 1976.'

For a moment David remembers the scene from the Marlon James novel - the gunmen arriving at the house, the frisson of forced bravado and panic, roaming the house firing at random, the blood, the maiming and then the chaotic getaway in the cars down narrow streets. He looks at the house now, brightly painted with murals and banners in the trees, tourist buses and white folks with cameras. Again the thread of time tangled in his head.

'That must have been soon after my father left Jamaica. He left around the summer of '76.'

Edmund nodded: 'Well de gunman drive in here and shoot up the place but Bob only wounded and yuh know wha' happen? Bob play at the big peace concert two days later with de bullet still inside him.'

'Not sure Joe need to hear about all this violence brother,' said Violet. 'Joe need ice cream, hey Joe?'

'Sorry, sorry,' said Edmund, 'but you mus' visit de museum while yuh here. It an important part of our culture. But so is ice cream, sorry sis. And here we are at the best place for it in Jamaica - Devon House.'

He pulled the car into a shaded drive and parked at the side of an old white plantation house. White railings framed the upper and lower balconies and at the front there were more Royal Palms and an elegant water fountain.

'First stop, ice cream,' said Violet and she led the way round to the *I Scream* ice cream parlour.

When they emerged with Joe clutching a mountainous cone of 'tropical fruit flavours' they sat under the trees in a little courtyard behind the plantation house. 'Yuh may think this was owned by some white slave owner, eh David?' said Edmund. 'But, let me tell yuh, dis was built for a black man, George Siebel, Jamaica's first black millionaire. Impressive, huh?'

David nodded. 'You're a great tourist guide, Edmund. I'm learning a lot this afternoon.'

But really he was caught in a strange twilight zone - thinking of his father here in 1974 with the young American - what was his name - Jim something? And now, here, eating ice cream forty two years later with a tide of memories washing over those years. He needed time to think.

There was a ping from his phone. He checked it and saw that it was now picking up the Jamaican mobile network and there was a new message from Gina:

Bet you're lost already. But I have Maxim's address and phone number. Blue Mahoe, Ocean View Road, Jack's Hill 876-361-8000. Have fun and keep safe. Gxx

*

The Balmoral Villa Hotel, like its name, was a quirky mixture of grand pretensions and modest accomplishment. The Chinese owners lived in Miami and Violet and Edmund were left to run the place with little interference from their employers. It was an old bungalow type building with fifteen rooms. Polished mahogany floors, bright painted walls and a courtyard of exotic colour and greenery - palms, hibiscus, orchids, bougainvillea - it was wonderfully homely and relaxed and David was glad he had accepted Violet's invitation to change his booking. There was a small staff, loyal retainers who had clearly been there for years: Bruce, the yard man, boney face, sinewy arms, a flat cap, constantly honing his machete which he proudly announced had been 'made in Birmingham, Hengland,' and he showed Joe the words on the blade to prove his point. Then there was Norah, the chef, who, assisted by a couple of youngsters in the kitchen, produced a feast of a meal on that first evening. And there was Patricia, the young receptionist, straight-faced, meticulously manicured and forever checking her face in her mirror and scanning the screen of her smart phone.

'So you lookin for what happen to this frien of your father?' said Violet.

She and David were sitting in the lounge after dinner. It was late and Joe had gone to bed, but David had stayed up to plan his next move. He was concerned that the purpose of this trip was not lost in enjoying the novelties of this new country. Edmund was arranging a hire car for the following morning and David was studying a local map. Priority was a visit to Maxim and then trying to locate if Marianne was still alive and in the country. She was the key to finding out about Maya and the child.

'And you say she was a musician in the Jamaica orchestra?'

David nodded: 'A violinist. He first saw her at a concert at a place called The Little Theatre.'

Violet clapped her hands: 'Me know it well. It not far; down on Tom Redcam Road. We often go see my niece, Louise, who's a dancer with the Jamaica Dance Company.'

'The thing is,' said David, 'I don't know her surname. I only know her as Maya and she had a friend called Marianne who played viola.'

'I'll call Louise and she can tek yuh down there and check it out. They may have some record of old programmes which might give you their names.'

'And there's my father's old employer, Maxim Moreno, who I want to see.'

'Him was a minister some years ago. Me remember the name,' said Violet.

'He lives at a place called Jack's Hill.'

Violet nodded: 'Rich people up dere. Nice, nice houses. Looks like you going to be busy on this holiday, David.'

'Looks that way,' David replied.

In the morning David phoned the number Gina had sent. There was no answer, just an invitation to leave a message. But at least it was the right number: 'Maxim and Lisa cannot take your call at present. Please leave your number and we will get back to you.' David left a short message saying who he was and that he was trying to contact friends of his father.

He looked at his note book. Nine more days was probably not long enough to do all that he had listed and he had to remember it was Joe's holiday too. There was The Little Theatre to visit and he wanted to do the drive over to Port Antonio and along the coast to see the resort at Zion Hill and maybe try to find Ned's farm.

'Mr David, come meet Louise, nah.' Violet, dressed in a smart trouser suit was standing in the entrance to the breakfast room where they had just finished breakfast. 'How yuh sleep, Joe, any mosquitoes last night?'

Joe shook his head: 'It was okay. And I had a swim in the pool this morning.'

'Wow, not too cold for you? It early for the sun to warm up the pool. You mus' be a hard man.'

Behind Violet there was a young woman in shorts and a running top, hair tied back with a peach coloured hair band. A small boy stood beside her. 'Dis here's my niece, Louise, and her likkle boy, Lloyd, who's my prince, aren't you, boyo?' She stroked the boy's head as she spoke. 'Dis here's Joe and David, from England. Now what I reckon is that Lloyd you show Joe all the animals we have here and maybe have another swim while your mommy tek David down to the theatre. What yuh think?'

David turned to Joe. 'I won't be away long. Just going see the place where Pops' friend used to work - see if we can look up where she might be now. Is that okay?'

'Don't be too long, will you,' replied Joe.

'Promise,' said David.

'Don't worry, Joe, auntie Violet will tek care of yuh while yuh daddy away. I got lots to show you on yuh fust real day in Jamaica.'

David followed the young woman outside to where a sporty blue Honda was parked. They drove out of the hotel entrance and on to the road signposted 'Barbican Road'.

'So you met my auntie Vi on the plane?'

David nodded: 'Kind of guardian angel. She took us under her wing.'

'And she says you're looking for an old friend of your father who he lost contact with?'

'It's a long story, but yes, I only know her as Maya, and that she used to be lead violinist in the Jamaican orchestra back in the mid-Seventies. My father died recently and I've only just discovered that he was in Jamaica and had this close friendship with her.'

'I'm sorry to hear that.'

They stopped at traffic lights and David recognised they were crossing Hope Road again.

'I hear my uncle Ed gave you his guided tour yesterday. Well this here's Matilda's Corner and we're just going down Old Hope Road. I'm not much of a tourist guide I'm afraid, David.'

She had hair braided like Gina's and wore small gold earrings and a sports watch on her wrist. The traffic was heavy at the intersection and there was lots of sounding of horns and the thumping pulse of bass speakers from in-car sound systems.

'Jamaicans don't go around quietly,' said Louise, 'you'll get used to it.'

'And you're a dancer, is that right?' asked David as they pulled across the intersection and joined a new line of traffic.

She nodded: 'I teach some dance at one of the high schools and I'm a member of the Jamaica Dance Company. Pity you're not here for long. You could see us perform. Pretty impressive, I tell you.'

They turned off Old Hope Road and on to Tom Redcam Road. 'This area's New Kingston. Across is The Pegasus, quite a famous hotel and here's The Little Theatre where your father's friend would have performed. Behind is the dance company theatre but we'll check in the office where they have the computer records,' said Louise.

They pulled up in front of a low white building. The logo 'Little Theatre' was prominent on the outer wall of the building. 'Now I do know a little about this place,' said Louise. 'Set up in the early Sixties by a Jamaican couple, Henry and Greta Fowler, who wanted to see good theatre in Jamaica. And now the place is buzzing, all sorts of drama and music and dance. It's kind of my second home.'

She led the way into the reception and spoke to the receptionist. Then she beckoned David through into the inner office where there were two more young women working.

'Julie, we want to look up the records for a music performance in 1974. We trying to find the name of two musicians who used to play in the orchestra. Is that possible?'

'One named Maya and the other Marianne,' added David, 'but I don't know their surnames.'

The young girl put in a search on the computer and scrolled through various files of scanned copies of old theatre programmes.

'I have the exact date,' said David and he checked in his notebook. 'Yes, here it is - September 12th 1974.' The day when Will had first laid eyes on Maya. He remembered how vivid was that early journal entry and the image of Maya on stage playing the violin.

David watched the girl scrolling through more files, watched the dates peeling back to 1974.

'This could be it,' she said.

'Does it mention a pianist, Calvin Richardson, playing a Shostakovich piano concerto?' David held his breath and leaned over the girl's shoulder to look at the screen.

'Yes,' nodded the girl, 'look here's a review, it talks about *the brilliance of the virtuoso pianist Calvin Richardson.....*'

'Now does it list the members of the orchestra - specifically a violinist named Maya and a viola player named Marianne?'

The girl scrolled onto another page and shook her head: 'I have a Mahalia Tennyson and a Marianne Chang, but no-one called Maya.'

'That's it, that's them,' said David, struggling to contain his excitement. He remembered Marianne had Chinese ancestry. Chang would be it. 'Maya was a pet name, I remember now, her father named her after Mahalia Jackson, the American gospel singer.' He turned to Louise: 'Wow, Louise, you've no idea how important this is.'

She smiled: 'I think I can tell.'

'Oh, another thing,' said David checking his notebook, 'there were some others who played with Maya in the orchestra, just a minute, I've got them here - yes, Jonathan, Courtney, Lloyd and Charles.'

The girl scrolled down the pages of names. 'There are four here with those names. If these are the same guys, they left the orchestra for America in December '76.'

'That was around the time of the Bob Marley shooting, wasn't it,' said Louise, 'wasn't there an election or something?'

'That's right,' said David. 'Julie, could you check if there's any contact address for Mahalia and Marianne.'

The girl put in another search and then scrolled through a couple of lists. Finally she nodded: 'I have an address and number for Marianne Chang. Says here she retired from the orchestra in 2006. It's an address in Barbican Heights, Plymouth Avenue.'

'That's not far from the hotel,' said Louise. 'We could go straight there.'

'But there's nothing for Mahalia Tennyson; it just says 'former Embassy employee.' She wrote down the information and handed it to David.

'Thank you so much. This is just amazing.'

'No problem,' said the girl.

'One last thing,' said David, turning to Louise. 'Any chance that I could see the auditorium of The Little Theatre?'

'Of course,' she replied. 'Follow me.'

He sat for several minutes in the empty theatre, staring at the stage. He pulled the journal from his backpack and found the entry and re-read it: *..mesmerised first by the music itself but then by one of the violinists - a young woman wearing a bright orange dress.....was held by the profile of her face, the lustre of her dark skin, the slender neck..... the curve of her back as she moved with the motion of the violin bow........'* and it was right here, he thought, right over there on that very stage. And now he had the names and he could renew the search. It didn't feel quite so hopeless after all.

Back in the car Louise waited before starting the engine. 'You got me curious about all this. So your father was here in the Seventies but you didn't know anything about it?'

'Until after he died and we found a journal in a box in his workshop,' said David.

'And he knew this Maya person and this Marianne?'

David nodded: 'There's more to it than that. He had a close relationship with Maya but it turned out she was a CIA operative and she was shot and wounded in a shoot-out in Stony Hill. And then she disappeared carrying his child, who he knew nothing about.'

Louise put her hand to her mouth: 'Oh my god, I had no idea it was this serious.'

'And it's Marianne who I reckon has all the answers,' said David.

'What was the address again?'

David checked his notebook: 'Plymouth Road, Barbican Heights. Number 16.'

'I think I know it,' said Louise.

As they were driving back up Old Hope Road David heard a ping from his phone. A text message: *Meet at Pegasus Hotel, 10.30am Tuesday 29th, Pool Bar. Maxim.*

The pulse in David's head quickened again. Tuesday was tomorrow. Wow, pieces of the jigsaw might be slotting into place quicker than he'd thought.

'Mustn't be too long, I don't want to leave Joe on his own on his first full day here.'

'Don't worry,' said Louise, 'Aunt Vi will look after him well.'

David turned to look at her again. 'Your accent is different from Violet's and Edmund's. How so?'

'Depends who I'm with,' she said. 'I spent several years in America and lost a lot of the Jamaican twang, but listen nah, me can switch it on mon, give yuh a likkle ob de ol' haccent, an' wave me han' an cuss de odder driver dem, lak a true Jamaican!' She looked sideways at David and smiled.

He nodded: 'I get it.'

They left the crowded streets, the lines of traffic on Hope Road and started climbing up through quieter suburbs of low bungalows sheltered behind lush garden foliage, some with high fences and barred gates, grilles on windows and front porches.

'This here is middle class Kingston,' said Louise, 'gates, grilles and guard dogs and lots of paranoia.'

'Is it justified?'

'To an extent. Yes, parts of Kingston are pretty violent and dangerous especially at night, but not up here.'

They turned up another steep hairpin and now, below them, the city was spreading out. David could see the distant ships in the dock area, the thin arm of the Palisadoes Peninsula and across the turquoise waters of the bay, the dark outline of some hills. 'What are those hills across the bay? It reminds me of somewhere,' asked David.

'That'll be Hellshire,' replied Louise.

'My dad wrote about that, going out there on a Sunday morning with Maya with the Sunday Gleaner and buying fish from the local women.'

'They're still there and people still go on a Sunday. And there's a guy who has horses who gives rides. Joe would like that, I'm sure.'

'Maybe we can fit that in. So much to do though in such a limited time.'

Louise slowed the car and pulled up in front of a small lemon coloured clapboard house set back from the road. There was a mass of purple bougainvillea cascading over a pergola in the garden, stands of thick bamboo to the rear. The house had a stunning view of the city below. 'This is it,' she said, 'number 16, Plymouth Road.'

Again, David felt his pulse quicken. 'Wish me luck,' he said.

There was no fence around the property but a grille across the porch and bars on the windows. He rang the bell and heard the growl of a dog inside. A shadow of someone moved behind the glass of the front door. A muffled voice saying 'Quiet, Bertie, quiet.' Then the door opened and a middle-aged lady wearing a colourful headscarf looked out round the edge of the door. 'Yes?' she said.

Too young, thought David. Marianne would be in her mid sixties. 'I'm looking for Marianne Chang? I was given this address.'

The lady shook her head. 'Miss Chang left years ago. She lives somewhere in Portland, I think.'

'D'you have a forwarding address?' asked David.

Again the lady shook her head: 'Only a Post Office box number. We don't get much mail for her now but that's where we send it. Port Antonio, I think it is. Just a minute,' and she disappeared inside again. The dog, some sort of terrier, ventured out and nosed up against the gate, giving a low growl.

'It's all right, Bertie, he's friendly,' said the lady and she handed a piece of paper through the bars of the gate.

'Thank you,' said David. 'You've been very helpful.'

'She played in the orchestra, you know. I heard her once. A fine musician.'

'I know,' replied David. 'I've read about her. Viola, I think.'

The lady nodded. 'Something like that. Goodbye.'

He returned to the car.

'Any luck?' asked Louise.

'Just this. A Post Office box number in Port Antonio.'

'Well, it's a start. And at least it sounds as if she's still alive.'

David's hopes weren't dashed exactly, but he was disappointed and Louise could see that.

'It is forty years ago, remember. People move on,' she said, 'things change. People forget.'

David nodded: 'I know, you're right, but what my dad wrote about is so vivid in my head, that I'm expecting to pick up the threads when probably those threads are broken, lost, gone forever.'

Louise leaned over, touched her hand on David's: 'C'mon now, you've got a lead, which you didn't have when you woke this morning, a lead that you can follow up. Where it'll take you is the big unknown. But just relive you father's memories, the places he visited. You may not find any of the answers but enjoy the confusion and beautiful chaos which is our Jamaica and, as Saint Bob sang, 'Everythin' gonna be all right'.' She tapped David's hand again, looked hard at him, smiled and then started the engine and drove back down the hill to the city.

*

Maxim Moreno was taller than David had expected. He walked with a stick and was accompanied by a young man, his driver. He had a slight limp but was very upright, white hair neatly combed, a red polo top, white linen trousers, white yachting shoes. David had gone early to The Pegasus with Joe. He'd bought a guest pass so that Joe could swim in the pool while he talked with Maxim. He wasn't sure whether Joe should listen in on the conversation.

Maxim extended a hand and shook David's firmly: 'I see your father in your face,' he said. 'And how is he?' Maxim sat down and his driver moved away and sat at another table.

'He died some time ago,' said David, 'after a long illness. When I was clearing his house I found the journal he wrote about his time in Jamaica. None of us knew he'd ever been here.'

'So you're here on your own?'

'No, with my son, Joe, he's over there in the pool.' He gestured to where Joe was jumping off the springboard into the pool. 'Joe was very close to his Pops, as he called my father. He wanted to come and see the places my father had written about in the journal.'

'So, it's a sight-seeing holiday? How nice that you thought to contact me. I was fond of your father and he was a good architect.'

'But that's not the only reason I came.'

A waiter arrived and took orders for drinks. Maxim ordered a Campari and soda, David ordered juices for him and Joe.

'There was a lot in the journal about the politics in the Seventies, and a close friendship he had with a young Jamaican musician called Mahalia Tennyson who worked at the Jamaican Embassy. But he lost contact with her and I was hoping to trace her.'

Maxim nodded: 'I heard something about that relationship from one of the guys who worked with Will.'

'But the journal finishes very abruptly in July '76 and it seems he left in a hurry, fearful about his safety.'

'We were all fearful about our safety during that time. After he'd left, my plant was fire-bombed. I only escaped by staying in this bunker room that your father had designed and helped me build. For that I am forever in his debt. It left me with this limp and this stick but at least I survived. Many didn't. And it got worse in the run up to the December election. My first wife was shot and killed by gunmen at our house. And of course they tried to kill Bob Marley. It was a terrible time.'

'I'm so sorry about your wife,' said David. 'My father described her when he came to a party at your house, soon after he arrived. Said what a wonderful hostess she was, made him feel very welcome.'

'Such memories,' said Maxim. 'She was a beautiful woman. I was lucky to have my years with her.'

'Something else I have to ask you,' continued David, 'd'you know anything about a shooting at Stony Hill, where an American called RJ was killed in July of

'76? He was the person my father had done some work for on the north coast.'

Maxim raised his eyebrows: 'You know about RJ?'

'I'm not sure what I know. The journal is unclear.'

'No-one really knows how it happened,' said Maxim. 'Lots of rumours circulated but there wasn't much in the papers. It seemed someone had hushed it all up. I knew of this man, he was big at the yacht club, brash, arrogant. I didn't like the sound of him. I never met him, just heard that he was close with Seaga and the JLP. And to us that meant one thing - he might be working with the CIA.'

'So nothing came out about who killed him. No-one was ever arrested?'

Maxim shrugged: 'It was one of many stories of shootings which were around at that time. We were all watching our backs, checking who was arriving at the plant or who was outside the gates of the house. There was one rumour that it was an inside job, that he'd been killed by an ex-CIA agent who'd been turned but there are always rumours being spread to divert attention from the truth.'

A waiter arrived with the drinks and David called Joe over: 'Joe, this is Mr Moreno, he's the person that Pops worked for when he was in Jamaica.'

Maxim smiled: 'Hello, young Joe. So Will was your granddaddy, or d'you call him Pops?'

Joe nodded and extended his hand: 'Pleased to meet you, sir, sorry about the wet hands.'

Maxim leaned forward: 'I was just telling your daddy what a great architect your granddad was. He helped me build my factory. It's not there anymore, so I can't show you, but I've built others since. I could have used young Will Pearson on other projects but he wanted to return to England. He was a fine young man, like your own daddy.'

Joe nodded, not sure what to say. He sipped his drink and Maxim said: 'It's okay Joe, you don't need to listen to boring adults talking. If you want to get back in the pool, go ahead. It's been great to meet you and shake your hand.'

Joe nodded, looked at David who gestured that, yes, it was okay to go. 'Nice to meet you,' said Joe, 'and I'm glad Pops did a good job for you.'

They watched him go, and Maxim said: 'What a fine young son you have, David.'

'I'm very lucky.'

'So you're trying to locate this young musician who Will was close to,' said Maxim. 'Have you tried the embassy where you say she worked?'

'Not yet. It's on my list.'

Maxim nodded. 'They don't give much away there but you might find out something.' He looked at his watch. 'How long are you here for?'

'Just over a week; not long enough for all the things I want to do.'

'And it's the holidays, so the embassy might well be closed into the New Year.'

'Oh, yes, I hadn't thought of that. But I'm also trying to trace another musical friend of my father; a woman called Marianne Chang. She used to live in Kingston but moved to Portland. So that's where we're headed next. But I wanted to see a place called Bermuda Mount. It's on the way to Newcastle and I think you had a friend with a place there. My father writes about staying there.'

'Yes, my friend sold it many years ago. But I can tell you where it's located.'

'Thank you,' said David. 'At least I could get a feel of the area which my father enjoyed so much.'

Maxim described the location and David jotted down the details. Finally he nodded: 'Well, I wish you luck, David. It's been great meeting you and renewing memories of your father.' He took a card from a wallet and handed it to David. 'Don't hesitate to get in touch if you're over again or if you need assistance while you're here. I still have a little influence in the country despite my creaking bones.' He nodded to the young driver who came over and helped him to his feet. And then he turned: 'Adios and keep safe.'

'Thanks,' said David, shaking his hand. 'And thanks for your help.'

Maxim waved, turned and walked away towards the hotel lobby.

David took out his phone. He wrote a quick text to Gina outlining his visit to The Little Theatre and his meeting with Maxim.

A short while later her reply came back : *Will try to trace Maya's brother, Edward Tennyson but feel Marianne holds the key. Keep up the good work. Don't forget to have some fun too xx*

*

Back in the shade of the courtyard at Balmoral Villa, David sat for a while sipping a cold beer and searching for guest houses in the Blue Mountains. His plan was to drive the route over Blue Mountain Ridge to Port Antonio, but to spend a night at Bermuda Mount, the place where his father had stayed several times with Maya.

Joe was out by the swimming pool playing with one of the puppies that Violet's retriever bitch had recently produced. On the drive back from The Pegasus Joe had asked: 'Why is it important that we find this friend of Pops, dad?' David had expected this question at some point but hadn't really thought how he would reply. He decided to come clean.

'What I haven't told you, Joe, is that Pops and this young Jamaican woman, Maya, became very close. You could say that Pops was in love with her. But it was complicated. It seems she was working for the American secret service, the CIA, and one afternoon she got shot and badly wounded by some gunmen who stormed into a hotel where she was in a meeting. Pops saw her briefly in the hospital and then she disappeared, probably out of the country. And judging from what he wrote in the journal, he never heard from her again.'

'Poor Pops,' said Joe. 'And he never spoke about it?'

'But that's not all,' David went on. 'It seems she was pregnant with Pops' baby.'

'Did the baby die when she was shot?'

'According to the journal the baby was not harmed.'

'So where is the baby now?'

'That's what we don't know. And of course, if the baby survived, that person, and we don't know if it was a boy or girl baby, that person would be about my age, just a little bit older.'

'And it would be your brother or sister?'

'Half brother or sister,' added David.

'Wow,' said Joe, 'and Pops never saw the baby. Maybe the baby died.'

'It's quite possible. And that's what we're trying to find out by going on this drive to the north coast tomorrow. There's a friend of Maya who we might be able to find and who might know what happened.'

A while later, Joe came across from the pool holding one of the pups. 'I was thinking,' he said, 'maybe there's stuff in Pops' house we haven't found yet, stuff which might tell us what did happen.'

'It's possible,' said David, 'but I'm thinking that maybe it's a time in Pops' life that he wanted to forget about.'

'Because it made him too sad?' said Joe.

David nodded: 'Probably.' He sat forward in his chair, and stroked the pup. 'Anyway, I thought that,

135

maybe later, we'd go see the Bob Marley Museum. Whad'ya reckon?'

'Really. Wow, dat shot!'

'What does that mean?'

'Means 'that's great'. Lloyd taught it me.'

'Go way, likkle bwoy,' said David smiling and tousling Joe's hair. 'Go way.'

*

The Bob Marley Museum was at 56, Hope Road. It had been a modest clapboard town house when Chris Blackwell, the founder of Island Records, had bought it in the early Seventies and then gifted it to Bob Marley in 1975, the year of Marley's great 'Natty Dread' album. Blackwell had named it 'Island House.' Now it was a tourist honey pot with a big car-park where tour buses would disgorge droves of tourists come to worship at the shrine of the 'King of Reggae'.

David and Joe walked under the arch which showed Bob Marley's smiling face and a couple of lions on either side. There was a gold statue of him holding his guitar and with his right arm raised and there were huge murals of Marley's family on one of the walls. They followed a tour guide through the house, the rooms decked with Marley memorabilia - his favourite guitar lying on his bed, gold discs on the walls, photos, flags, and everywhere the Rastafarian colours of red, gold and green: 'Red for the blood of African martyrs, gold for sunshine, freedom and the wealth of Africa and green for the lushness and fertility of the promised land of Ethiopia,' said the guide. It was said almost like an incantation. They saw the old recording studio of Tuff Gong records and the battered green Land Rover that Bob Marley used to drive. And they heard about the shooting, saw the marks of where the bullets hit the walls.

'Why did anyone want to kill Bob Marley?' Joe asked the guide.

'It was a kinda craziness,' nodded the young man. 'People jealous of Bob Marley success. Dem want to pull him down cos' him talk of freedom for de poor people and dat not what the rich people lak to hear.'

The guide moved on and ushered the group towards the souvenir shop and cafe. The shop was an emporium of all things 'Rasta' - key rings, pendants, scarves, woolly 'tams', 'Marley coffee'. Joe was eager to buy something but he couldn't decide. In the end he chose a tee shirt and 'Rasta' wrist band, something he could wear back in school and David bought a poster.

They had their photo taken in front of the gold statue and David noted a Marley quotation on one of the information boards: *One good thing about music, when it hits you, you feel no pain. Hit me with music….Hit me with music now.*

'So wha' you t'ink of the museum?' asked Violet, when they got back to the hotel.

'It was good,' said Joe. He showed Violet what he'd bought.

'Him a hero of the people and him bring in lots of tourists. Him good for business, eh David?'

'Seen,' said David.

And Violet snapped her fingers and laughed. 'Yuh catching the Jamaican vibe, nah mon?'

Edmund had organised a hire car for them, a 4x4 Honda, not quite the Beetle that David had hoped for in memory of his father but Edmund assured him this was what was needed: 'De road, deh mash up after de bad rain in October. Yuh might meet lan'slide and yuh sure to hit pot hole. Jamaican road dem bad, mon. Dis car, it de right one for yuh journey.'

'Thanks, Edmund, I appreciate that,' said David.

'No problem,' replied Edmund, 'go well and tek care, nuh.'

They set off in the early afternoon heading up Hope Road looking for a junction called the Cooperage where the mountain road up to Bermuda Mount branched off. They passed Mona, the area near the university where David's father's apartment had been located but he had no address for it. However, he did remember some reference to the market at Papine.

At the top of Old Hope Road just past the botanical gardens, they arrived at an open square where the buses turned and there were trucks and cars and boxes of produce piled next to a covered market. Goats nosed among the garbage and there was a low murmur of noise coming from inside.

'There are those soursop things we had at Gina's,' said Joe, eyes wide at the array of unusual produce on sale. 'And look, those are ackees, see them with the little eyeballs poking out.' He went across to one of the stalls and picked up one of the strange exotic fruits.

The lady behind the stall smiled: 'Hey nah bwoy, yuh like ackee?'

Joe shook his head: 'First time I ever see one up close,' he replied.

'Yuh from hengland, young mon?'

Joe nodded.

'An yuh never see ackee before?' She clapped her hands: 'Oh lawd, y'ever try guinep?'

Joe shook his head and the lady pointed to some bunches of small round fruits with hard green skins.

'Me show yuh, nuh,' said the lady. And she broke off one of the fruits, held it between her fingers and squeezed the sides together until the hard skin split and revealed a soft pale fruit inside. 'It a likkle sour but nice, nice when yuh mout' is dry. Try it nuh,' and she handed some across to Joe.

'I think Pops wrote about trying guineps in his book,' said David.

Joe was chewing and grimacing: 'Wow, it's a bit sour,' he said, 'but not bad. Can we buy some dad?'

They browsed the other fruits, checking the names of those they didn't recognise with the market lady. 'Dat's jackfruit,' she said as Joe held up a strange balloon shaped fruit covered with a nobbly green skin. Then she held up a round ball of a fruit with a purple skin: 'Listen, nuh, yuh try dis. Dis my favourite,' said the lady. 'It call star apple.' She took a knife and cut the fruit in half and showed them the inside. It had a shiny, moist texture, pearly white near the outer skin and blending to pink and purple in a star shaped pattern towards the centre. 'Yuh try it,' she said, handing Joe a spoon. 'Scoop it out, nuh.'

Joe scooped out a little of the soft jellylike fruit. He nodded and smiled: 'Now that's really good. You gotta try this dad,' he said handing the fruit and the spoon to David. 'Can we buy some?'

They ended up with a bag of bananas, oranges, guineps and star apples. The market lady showed them the different spices and peppers and pointed out the smallest. It was green and heart-shaped. 'Now dis one is de queen. She call Scotch Bonnet and yuh mus' tek care when yuh cut dis, don' touch near yuh eye. It very strong.'

Joe handed over some Jamaican dollars for the fruit and the lady nodded. 'Where yuh drivin' to?'

'Up into the mountains,' said Joe.

'It cool, cool up dere,' she said. 'Tek care, de road sometime mash up.'

'Thanks for your help,' said David, and the market lady waved as they went back out into the sunshine.

Before setting off, and while Joe had a go at opening one of the guineps, David pulled the journal from his bag. He re-read the entry for December 12th:

…..Someone reckoned there were 150 bends in the 12 mile road up to the army camp at Newcastle. Certainly felt like it. But what a road. It's like a switch-

back snaking up into the mountains from the top of Hope Road. You pass gullies and streams of rushing crystal clear water and then the road gets steeper and the shacks of the locals cling to the hillside on little terraces where they grow their crops and tether their cows and donkeys……

'Here we go then, Joe,' said David as he started the engine. 'Pops reckoned there are one hundred and fifty bends up to Newcastle. We're not going quite that far but pretty close. How was the guinep?'

Joe nodded, juice running down his chin: 'Good,' he said, 'a bit sour, but good.'

'And how are the mosquito bites?' They had both suffered the previous evening with the whine of the insects in the bedroom as they tried to get to sleep.

'Still itching,' said Joe.

'Fresh meat, I'm afraid,' said David. 'They say it happens to all new arrivals but it should be better in the mountains where it'll be cooler.'

'Hope so,' said Joe.

The road snaked its way alongside the Hope River for a few miles and then the hills started to close in. At a junction called the Cooperage there was a signpost indicating *B1 - Irish Town* and *Newcastle* to the left. 'This is our road,' said David, 'this is where the climb really starts.'

'What does Cooperage mean?' asked Joe.

'Coopers were the barrel makers who made barrels for storing coffee beans from the plantations here in the mountains. The guidebook says a lot of them were Irish and they gave their name to Irish Town where we're headed.'

And the road certainly was a 'switchback' of sharp hairpin bends rising quickly away from the lower valleys. There were smallholdings, bamboo fencing with goats and the odd cow tethered beside hillside huts. Small plots of corn, bananas, callaloo and yam teetered on the narrow terraces etched out of the steep hillsides. They passed modern bungalows sited where the land was flatter, often where a hairpin bend turned to make the next ascent. The mountainsides were green with tall grasses, thick bush, stands of bamboo and trees with overarching canopies.

'What are those, hanging down?' asked Joe, pointing to some trees shading the dirt yard of a smallholding.

'Look like mangoes,' said David.

He slowed the car and pulled off the road for a moment. The view was of a misty haze - valleys plunging away to the west and east and below was the drop into air and space and the shimmering frieze which was Kingston, the harbour and the distant shadow of the Hellshire Hills. Up here the air was cooler, lighter and there was the quietness which comes from being at such a height, just the odd cry of a goat, the tinkling of a goat bell and the lazy spiralling glide of the John Crows with their huge wingspan. David could see why the mountains had drawn his father. After Kingston this was another world entirely.

It took an hour to reach the plateau at Irish Town where there was a small settlement of ageing wooden shacks, newer concrete buildings - houses, a few small businesses and a handful of rum bars. There were cars parked and some men lounging in front of the 'Irish Town Emporium'.

David pulled up in the shade of a mango tree and switched off the engine. 'You okay?' he said.

Joe nodded: 'Are we here?'

'Just got to find this place we're staying at.' He pulled his notebook from the door pocket and read: '*The Humming Bird Guest House* run by a *Miss Olivia Bennett.* I'll just go and ask these guys for directions.'

The Humming Bird Guest House stood a little way off the road along a path which led to a low wooden building with a shingle roof and open balconies. There were valleys falling away on two sides and a narrow ridge extending eastwards. The rooms were simple with louvred windows, ceiling fans and polished hardwood floors. David noticed there were no bars on the windows. It was clean and welcoming and Miss Olivia Bennett was a lively hostess.

'An' yuh come arl dis way from hengland to stay in my likkle hotel. What joy. May the Lord be praise.' She smoothed her apron and extended her hand: 'Welcome Mr David and Master Joe. Let me get yuh a cold drink then yuh can tell me about yourselves.'

They sat at a table looking out over a valley towards the distant mountain peaks. Clouds were curling slowly over Blue Mountain Ridge and starting to seep down into the valleys. Miss Olivia appeared with glasses of lime and lemon juice, a sprig of mint sticking out from the rim.

David explained something of their quest. Miss Olivia listened intently, nodding. 'I know that place, Bermuda Mount. It not far. Yuh can walk it in the marnin. An' yuh say yuh father he was here in 1975? Dat would mek me about fifteen years old.'

'He drove a VW Beetle; he looked a bit like me.'

She shook her head: 'Sorry, I have no recollection but old Frank who live down the track to Bermuda Mount, he might remember. He look after the grounds of the place so yuh mus' hask him.'

That evening when Joe was sleeping David took out the journal and re-read the references to Bermuda Mount. Now he was here he began to realise what a significant place it had been for his father.

August 5th …… It's just a wooden cabin but cool and shaded by tall stands of bamboo and eucalyptus trees which have this strange peeling bark and leaves which catch the slightest breeze. No mosquitoes, no bars on the windows and doors and the country people have this old world charm so different from the hustlers on the Kingston streets. There's a small terrace and a barbecue pit and humming birds fly to the feeders which you fill with sugar juice……

And then when he first brought Maya to the place and she talked of wanting to escape from the nightmare that Kingston was becoming….

October 19th ...She said she felt her poor country was being ripped apart and that she was caught in the middle of it all..

There was the description of her playing her violin and his father playing his new guitar: *…while I tended the barbecue, Maya played her violin. Her feelings always come out through her music and this evening she was playing something by a French composer called Satie. It was sad, whimsical and the notes floated away across the darkness of the valley. The flicker of the candle light caught the moistness in her dark eyes. She wasn't shedding tears exactly but not far from it.*

After the Blue Mountain trek, in the entry for April 10th, she had said: *We need some time at Bermuda Mount, just the two of us. There are things I need to tell you. But don't ask me now. Wait until then.*

And there was a brief entry for May 15th: *Maya's back . Got a brief message. 'Looking forward to Bermuda Mount. We need to escape! I'll be in touch.'* But it never happened. Apart from seeing her in the hospital, it was the last time Will had ever seen Maya.

David put down the journal. For a while he watched the fireflies sparking the darkness - 'peenie wallies' - that's what Maya's uncle Ned had called her - here and then gone. And what were the things Maya needed to tell Will - a confession maybe that she had misled him? And did she really want to 'escape' with him

143

or was it all part of her deception? The questions hung in the air, hung in David's mind but he felt they were getting closer to finding answers. Maybe it was just being in the places his father had moved in all those years ago, a sense of his father's spirit here in the mountains. Or was this just more wishful thinking?

He sent a text to Gina giving her an update. Later, a reply came back:

The Blue Mountains sound wonderful. Hope you're getting close to solving a few of those teasing questions. Did some digging about Maya's brother Edward. Seems he died in mysterious circumstances in a boating accident off the Florida Keys in 1980. Another lead gone, I'm afraid. Enjoy the drive down to Port Antonio. Hope you find Marianne. Can't wait to hear.
G xx

David slept fitfully, dreams peopled by a bevy of ghosts. He woke a couple times to the sound of the cicadas and tree frogs and then the soft regular sound of Joe's breathing. He looked out through the louvres at the blue black sky, the stars and the dark ridges of the mountains. Images from the journal, memories, and this hunger to know, all stalking the darkness.

He was relieved when he awoke in the morning. There was bright sunlight in the room and the distant sound of someone singing. Looking out he saw the blue sky, the hazy blue-green of the mountains and wisps of white cloud folding over the peaks. He listened for a moment - it was a hymn and the voice was gentle on the folds of the music. He showered quickly and, when he emerged from the bathroom, Joe was up and standing by the balcony: 'Look, dad, the humming birds sipping from that feeding tube.'

David came across and looked out to see the long black tail and the iridescent green body of a Doctor Bird, its orange beak dipping into the juice of one of the feeders. Nearby were the smaller bee humming birds like little aircraft hovering and then moving jerkily from place to place, wings just a blur of movement. The Doctor Bird was more graceful in its movement, the curl of its long tail sweeping the air as it moved among the hibiscus flowers which formed a hedge along the pathway below.

Breakfast was served on the upper balcony - fresh peeled oranges skewered on forks, mangoes, small finger-sized bananas, boiled eggs, newly baked bread and freshly ground coffee.

Miss Olivia came in beaming: 'Yuh like yuh coffee, Mr David? Cos dis here is the world's best Blue Mountain, straight from our own bush. Mos' Blue Mountain go to Japan, so mek de mos' of your chance to get the real ting here.'

'Did I hear you singing this morning?'

'Oh Lawd, yuh ketch me dere. Me givin' praise for another fine marnin.'

'It was a nice sound to wake up to,' nodded David.

'Well bless you for dat.' She turned to Joe who was rubbing his eyes. 'Yuh lookin' still tired, Master Joe. Not sleep well?'

Joe nodded: 'Too much rice and peas and chicken last night.'

'Listen nuh, me squeeze yuh some fresh lime juice. You be fine. An where you goin' today, Mr David?'

'I want to find the house at Bermuda Mount and then we drive over to Port Antonio.'

'It a steep road dat, but pretty pretty. An' tek care wid truck and bus an ting. Dem drivers sometimes crazy yuh know!'

David felt his pulse quicken as he and Joe made their way back into the village and found the signpost 'Bermuda Mount Road.' It was a well beaten red earth track which sloped away from the main square. Miss

Olivia had said she thought she knew the cottage but said to look out for Frank, the old gardener.

Bermuda Mount itself was a narrow ridge sloping away steeply on both sides. David and Joe walked past a few modern bungalows tucked away behind screens of bougainvillea and hibiscus, some with steel fences, smart new cars parked in the driveways. Lower down the track there were the more traditional wooden cabins, smallholdings with goats and chickens, vegetable plots, trees with mangoes, lemons, limes and grapefruit, fences made from bamboo. The bamboo grew in thick stands twenty to thirty feet high, their green stems the thickness of your arm. And high up on the narrow hillside were the eucalyptus trees, the bark hanging off in strips of varied shades of bluey green.

An old man, wearing a battered leather cap sat on a stoop at the roadside sharpening a machete. He looked up as they approached.

'Is it Mr Frank?' said David.

He nodded: 'Dat's right. An' young man, yuh lookin' jus' like yuh father.'

David was thrown for a moment, hand to his mouth: 'You knew him?'

'Him come here with a lady - she a Jamaican, young and pretty. Miss Olivia tell me de story. I lookin' out for yuh.'

'Can you show us the house?'

The old man got up slowly, hand against his back. He waited for a moment, then nodded: 'Jus' up ere. Follow me.'

A short distance further down the track there was a driveway to the right and a wooden gate. A sign on the gate - *Bermuda Mount Cottage.*

This was the place then. In his father's footsteps again. Following the ghosts of Will and Maya. It was almost overwhelming. David had to stop and catch his breath, wipe the moistness in his eyes, swallow hard. Up some steps, through a gap in a low hedge and there it was, a small cabin painted white, a shingle roof, shaded porch, a terrace with a barbecue pit and a view across the valley; a backdrop of tall eucalyptus trees and clusters of thick bamboo, a small garden and then the hillside sloping down into woodland and tall grasses. Yes, this was the place.

The old man produced a key and opened the front door. Inside, a simple sitting room, small kitchen and bathroom and at the rear a single bedroom with floor to ceiling louvres opening on to a view across the valley.

There were some wicker chairs on the terrace and when David came back out the old man was sitting on one of the chairs next to a table. On the table was a paperback book. 'Yuh mus' sit down. I have someting for yuh,' he said. David sat down opposite him. Joe had wandered down the garden to where there was a chicken coop.

'After de las' time yuh father visit, he left dis book. Me expectin' him to return but him never come. When Miss Olivia tell me yuh comin' I find it and brung it for yuh. Dere's someting inside.'

He passed the book across to David - *The Aristos* by John Fowles. David had never heard of it or the writer. He opened it and saw some neat writing. *To Will, - a thinking person's book - love Maya xx Bermuda Mount, October 1975.* David moved his finger across the blue writing, where her fingers had touched. Then he flicked through the pages. In the middle - a photograph, an old Polaroid photograph, the colours slightly faded - a young man, tanned, wavy fair hair, his arm round the shoulders of a young black girl wearing a man's shirt, her legs bare. She was partly bent forward laughing openly and the young man was looking down at her and smiling. So this was Maya, the enigma. So many times he had tried to picture her from his father's journal entries, but always the images dissolved and shifted into transparency. But finally, here she was. Finally, the image could fix itself. On the back of the photo just the words *Maya and me - Cinchona.*

147

David looked up through moist eyes. 'Did you ever speak much to my father?'

The old man shook his head: 'Me jus' look after the garden and check de house when people stay.' He shrugged: 'Yuh father always kind to me, treat me nice. Me never forget dat. Me put de book in a drawer to give to Mr William next time him come but him never return. It stay dere all dis time until Miss Olivia tell me you comin'. Den I remember it.'

David looked at the photograph again, looked hard into it for some clues about this young woman. There was such life in her eyes and her smile. They were clearly having fun. And his father looked so happy.

When he looked up the old man had started to get up and make his way down the steps.

'Mr Frank,' called David. 'Many, many thanks.' He went forward and grasped the old man's arm and shook his hand. 'Thank you for your kindness to my father and to me.'

The old man nodded: 'Life is a strange journey, young man; we jus' have to go on each day an' do our best.' He turned, waved his machete in the air and carried on down the path and out of the gate.

David sat down, took up the photograph again. Where in all this was the real Maya? He looked at the beauty in her face, the laughter in her eyes and the look on his father's young face - he was infatuated, and David could understand why. The romance of this place, the cottage, the mountains and this vivacious young woman with her Caribbean charms. He, himself would have fallen for it all, he was sure.

Joe came back up the slope to the terrace. 'Dad, I saw some new chicks and some baby goats.' He looked around: 'Did Mr Frank go?'

David nodded: 'But he left this photo. It was inside a book that Pops had left behind the last time he was here. Mr Frank had kept it all this time expecting Pops to return.'

Joe looked closely at the photo: 'Is this Pops' girlfriend? Doesn't he look weird with all that hair. Is she the one who had the baby?'

David nodded: 'She's the one we're trying to find. And today I'm hoping we'll find Maya's friend, Marianne, who played with her in the orchestra. If anyone knows where Maya is living and if the baby survived, it's her.'

They returned to the guest house where Miss Olivia had packed a picnic for them.

'Now yuh tek care, Mr David and Master Joe, it a long road down to Buff Bay but I pack yuh some nice, nice treats for de trip.' She came forward and clasped David and hugged him. 'An me hope yuh find wha' yuh lookin' for, an' yuh find some peace in yuh heart cos I know yuh troubled by arl dis.'

David hadn't been mothered like this for such a long time. For a moment he felt that longing for someone to soothe away his troubles. But then he looked at Joe and clicked back into being the adult again. He sighed: 'Thank you Miss Olivia, you've been kindness itself. I will let you know how things turn out.'

She smiled: 'Come back and visit whenever yuh like. Tek care now.'

The air was cool and fresh today and there were clouds filling the valleys below. Kingston was lost in a grey haze and the sea and sky merged into a wash of pale blueness. The road quickly started to climb again, and as they turned the third hairpin, they could see high above them the red roofs of the army camp at Newcastle. David remembered that the journal described how the road went across the parade ground and it was a good stopping point to take in the views.

Now the vegetation started to change; the broad leafed tropical greenery of the lower mountain slopes was giving way to pine trees and more eucalyptus. Some of the gardens had roses growing and it felt almost as though they were in Scotland rather than the Caribbean. There was a scattering of guest houses, a sign for a mountain biking centre and a number of coffee farms.

The army camp was a cluster of neat red roofed buildings with cream coloured walls. The front part of the camp was set on a series of narrow terraces with neatly swept paths and trimmed grass separating the cluster of buildings. As the road took the final turn onto the wide terrace of the parade ground they could see the main buildings of the camp arranged in an orderly pattern stretching up the mountain side. David stopped the car by the wall of the parade ground where the slope dropped away into an airy view of mist and John Crows wheeling on the thermals off Blue Mountain Ridge. On the wall there were various insignia of the army regiments which had been posted at the camp.

'Why is it built up here, so far from the city?' asked Joe.

'I read that when it was under British rule a lot of the soldiers were dying from diseases down on the plain where Kingston is - yellow fever was one of them and it was swampy with lots of mosquitoes. So they decided to build it up here, away from all that. I think we're up at about four thousand feet here, that's the height of Ben Nevis.'

'Nice and cool, isn't it,' said Joe leaning on the wall and looking out, 'no wonder Pops liked coming up here. Maybe it reminded him of home.'

The parade ground was empty, save for a lone soldier who saluted as they passed through the open barrier and back onto the road. Another half hour and they were at the highest point on the road - Hardware Gap - where they drove through low cloud and felt the chill of the air and a feeling of being lost in space in a world that time forgot.

The descent to the north coast was quicker, the road still snaking round numerous bends and hairpins but gradually the landscape was changing. They were leaving the pine woods behind. Now there was a canopy of thick tropical trees and undergrowth, clusters of bamboo greenery, the odd coconut palm, stands of bananas and the start of riverside settlements which ran beside the road. *Buff Bay River* - a sign announced as they crossed a road bridge and passed through a small village.

Finally they could see the sea in the distance and the nerves started to zither in David's stomach as he tried to picture what a meeting with Marianne Chang might be like. She would be in her late sixties. Was she married with children? What sort of a life had she had since the turbulent Seventies? That was assuming they would actually find her. All David had was a post office box number in Port Antonio. Not much to go on.

They drove through the small town of Buff Bay, the sea breaking in shallow waves along the white sand beaches which bordered the road. There were plantations of coconut palms in places - iconic in their slender elegance, leaves combing the breeze which wafted in off the sea. The town was a place of traditional low rise buildings, a couple of churches, a school, general stores; it wasn't a busy place and David parked at the side of the road where narrow fishing boats draped in nets were pulled up on the beach. He checked the map while Joe ran down to the shoreline and paddled in the surf. It was a perfect place to stop for a swim but David was aware of time and the main purpose of their trip. And anyway, this evening they would be staying near the bay called San San that his father had raved about. Then there would be time to relax.

'We'll swim later, Joe, c'mon we need to press on,' shouted David. Joe was scampering through the surf which broke in wavelets onto the sand.

Joe trotted back to the car.

'Sorry, son, we'll swim later, I promise, but we need to reach Port Antonio by lunchtime.'

'The sea's so warm and clear,' said Joe, 'and there are incredible shells. Great for snorkelling. D'you remember, Gina said it would be.'

He thought of Gina - how she would have enjoyed this trip and what a great companion she'd have been. But then he dismissed that thought. No, he needed space in his head, not for anyone else but for dealing with what ever this trip threw at him. Seeing the cottage and the photograph had been enough to cope with already. There'd be more today, he was sure.

The post office in Port Antonio faced out on to East Harbour. David parked by the bus station and he and Joe walked along the foreshore. There were pelicans gliding close to the water, strange birds with their heavy sagging beaks and huge loping wing beats. The streets were busy with pavement market stalls and Joe watched a man with a drinks cart making snow-cones.

'Dad, can I get one of those?' he said pointing.

David nodded and Joe went across the road while David looked for the paper which showed the post office box number.

The man had a shaggy beard and wore a woolly tam in the Rasta colours. He looked up smiling: 'Peace and love likkle brother, you want snow cone? Wha' flavour? Me ave mango, strawberry, pineapple, or I can mix it for yuh?'

Joe nodded: 'Yes, a mixture, please.' He watched the man shaving flakes of ice off a block into a cone. Then he dribbled a variety of juices over the cone of ice flakes.

'Yuh soun like yuh from hengland.'

Joe nodded.

'Yuh on vacation?'

'Kind of,' said Joe. 'We're trying to find an old friend of my grandfather. He lived here back in the 1970s.'

'Wha' yuh friend name?'

'Marianne,' said Joe, 'Marianne Chang. She played the violin in the Jamaican orchestra.'

'An' she live in Port Antonio?'

'We're not sure. She has a post office box here.'

The man nodded: 'Maybe yuh try the police station just along the street. Dem p'raps tell yuh. Me never hear of her.' He handed the snow cone to Joe who held out some dollar notes.

'T'ank you likkle brother, an' good luck findin' yuh friend. Enjoy Jamaica, nuh.' He waved and nodded and Joe licked the ice cold juice which ran down the side of the snow cone.

David stood in line in the post office for ten minutes. The air was thick with heat and the paddle fans in the ceiling seemed to struggle to move the air. Finally he reached the counter, asked the girl if she knew of Marianne Chang who had the post office box number 348.

The girl shook her head and shrugged: 'We not permitted to give out personal information. Sorry.' She looked to the customer behind David, 'Next,' she said.

'But I've come all the way from England.'

'Sorry. Next,' she repeated.

David went out into the street where Joe was sitting on a low wall looking out across the harbour. 'Any luck?' said Joe.

David shook his head.

'The snow cone man said try at the police station just round the corner.'

'You asked him?'

Joe nodded: 'He hadn't heard of Marianne Chang.'

They wandered down the street, past the street vendors selling hats, drinks, cheap watches and jewellery and found the police station.

While David went to the counter, Joe noted the police uniforms - blue shirt, a red stripe down the navy trousers, the leather belt with its holster and gun and the peaked hat with its bright red band - quite different from the police at home.

'She used to play in the Jamaican orchestra some years ago. I thought she might be quite well known,' David explained.

'Portland's a big county,' said the officer. 'Lots of people tucked away in the bush livin' quiet lives. So we would never hear about them unless something happen to draw attention. You try Google her name a'ready?'

David shook his head: 'Nothing, I tried it.'

The officer shrugged: 'Fraid I can't help, then.'

They sat for a while on the edge of the harbour, David trying to think what to do next. He realised he'd been naive thinking that a post office box number would reveal all and that somehow the name of Marianne Chang would be well known. Seeing the town now he realised Port Antonio was no hicksville where everybody knew everyone else. And so many years had passed. Like the officer said, she was probably one of many tucked away in the bush living a quiet life.

'Where now?' said Joe. 'I really would like a swim in that sea.'

'Sorry, Joe,' said David. 'I'm forgetting this is your holiday. So now we're heading for a small guest house above the beach where Pops used to come and stay and where he worked on designing a beachfront resort for an American man - a place called Zion Hill. Be interesting to see what it's like now, but I remember him saying the beach was amazing and the snorkelling just great.'

They drove out of Port Antonio round the edge of East Harbour. On the promontory of the bay Joe pointed at an old ruined mansion - no roof, just the remnants of some stone built great house. 'What's that?' he asked.

'I think that's Folly Great House. Built by an American for his wife but it didn't last long. They say the builders used salt water in the concrete and that led to the place starting to crumble. Sad isn't it.'

Joe looked at the stone pillars and the stark grey skeleton of the house over grown and standing bleakly on the headland. 'Doesn't take long for things to fade away,' said Joe.

'Certain things,' replied David. 'Memories can last a long time.'

'Suppose so,' murmured Joe.

The road hugged the shoreline for much of the way, curving past rocky headlands and round small secluded bays. David could see why his father had so loved this part of the island. It was small scale, intimate, lush with its greenery cascading down the mountainside, swathes of bougainvillea and poinsettia along the roadside and festooning the gardens of houses, palm trees catching the sea breeze and always the aching blueness of the Caribbean folding in waves of milky pearl along the shoreline. It was truly exquisite. No wonder the American, RJ, had wanted to buy land and build a resort here. Who wouldn't if they had the money?

They rounded another small bay and then there was a sign - *Frenchman's Cove* and David remembered. He turned off down a wooded drive which led to a cluster of low buildings. This was the place his father had come with Maya, where there was a river running into the sea.

He parked in the shade of some trees and saw a small bay and the surf furling in up the beach. The river flowed in from the left and when they waded in they felt the contrast between the cold river water and the warmer sea water. 'Pops describes this in his journal. He and Maya came here when Pops was working on the dock for the resort further along the coast.'

'Can we go and see it?' asked Joe.

'That's where we're heading but I just wanted to check out this place. Thought you'd like to see it.'

Back at the car David pulled the journal from his bag. 'Here it is,' he said to Joe, 'June 5th, he wrote:

…we turned off down a drive overarched with almond trees and palms and arrived at this stunning little sandy cove, hedged in by two wooded headlands. The sea surges in and fans out onto a widening beach and meets a freshwater stream which flows in along a shaded channel which keeps the water chilled. And where it meets the seawater the contrast in water temperatures is quite a shock. Maya pulled me in to feel this curious phenomenon. We splashed around for a while before lying out on the sand....'

'Maybe Pops should have been a writer,' said Joe. 'He describes it well. And where were they staying, him and Maya?'

'I think just along the coast and a bit inland is where Maya's uncle Ned had a farm. There was a cottage there where Pops used to stay when he worked on this building project. We'll try to find it later as he described a great swimming spot with a waterfall. The cottage may have gone but the waterfall should still be there and maybe the farm, too.'

'So would her uncle Ned know where Maya is now?'

'I think Ned was quite old back then, so I don't think he'll still be alive.'

A short distance along the coast and here was San San, another jewel of a place - a crescent bay with waves breaking over a reef some way off shore and an island. In the journal Will had called it 'Nina Khan's Island' but the map showed it as 'Pellew' or 'Monkey Island'. He and Maya had swum out to it and snorkelled along the reef.

As Joe changed into his swimming gear and found his mask and snorkel, David re-read the description:

'*..and we went down to San San Bay and swam out to the island. It's a small knoll covered in coconut palms and we climbed to the top and looked down on the reef which is just beyond the seaward side of the island. The water changes from the clear pearly aquamarine on*

the bay side to this dark blue on the outer side of the reef
where the water goes suddenly deep. The reef is etched on
the water by a line of white surf breaking on the
coral……'

And that feeling again of seeing his father's and
Maya's footprints in the sand, watching them swim out to
the island where Joe was swimming now. That thread
through time linking past with present. These moments
when he felt he was so close to finding out what had
happened and finding a link to Maya. Sadly, he felt the
leads he had placed so much faith in were leading
nowhere. Finding Marianne had been the key but now
that didn't seem likely.

David joined Joe in the water and they swam
across the bay to the reef. Here the water was deep,
maybe forty feet or so and the reef rose up from the sea-
bed like a cliff-face. They both duck-dived. Joe was quick
and swam down below David. There were shoals of
small striped fish in and out of the coral, delicate coral
fronds like fern leaves combing the movement of the
water; larger fish, cobalt blue edged with yellow - it was
utterly magical.

Joe broke the surface with a gasp and a frown:
'Think I saw a barracuda, just down near the bottom, just
hanging around - long jaw and striped body.'

'Well don't go and annoy it and hopefully it'll
stay down there.'

They swam to the island, left their masks on the
sand and climbed the path to the top of the rise where
there was a clear view of the open sea and the surface of
the reef. In father's footsteps again, thought David.

Back at the beach they bought drinks from the
small beach bar and ate some of the picnic Miss Olivia
had packed for them. It was mid-afternoon and they
needed to find the guest house before too long.

'We'll just head along the coast a little to find this
resort Pops worked on then we'll look for the…,' David

checked on his phone, 'here it is.. *The Pink Flamingo Guest House.'*

It was a short drive along the coast, before they saw a sign, *Zion Hill Resort,* with a driveway leading down from the road to a small collection of wooden cottages. Was this it then? Could this be the place?

David parked the car and wandered through the garden to the waterfront. Joe went down to the dockside where some small dinghies were moored; there were paddle-boards leaning against some dwarf palm trees, a power boat rocking on its mooring. This might be the very dock that his father had worked on. 'Take care Joe, don't fall in,' called David.

'Can I help you?' A young man, smartly dressed in black trousers and a short-sleeved cream shirt stood on the path.

'I hope so,' replied David. 'I'm on a sort of trip down memory lane. You see my father was an architect working in Jamaica forty years ago and I'm sure this was the resort he designed back in 1975. Can you tell me anything about the history of the place?'

'I'm quite new here, but I'm sure Mrs Gonzales can tell you something. Come this way.'

He led the way along a tunnel of hibiscus and bougainvillea which arched over a wooden trellis, and on into the foyer. 'Mrs G, a young man to see you.'

A woman in her fifties came out from behind the counter. She was dressed in a brightly patterned cotton trouser suit. She held out her hand, smiling: 'I'm Rosa Gonzales. How can I help you, young sir?'

David explained something of the background.

'Come and take a seat, and Christopher,' she said turning to the young assistant, 'could you bring some lemonade for our guests? Thank you.' She turned back to David. 'Is that your son, down by the dock? He will be careful won't he.'

David checked on Joe who was now down on the beach in front of one of the cottages. 'He's fine,' said David.

He sat down and Rosa continued: 'My father took over this place back in the Seventies. It followed some tragedy, as I recall. The previous owner was killed somewhere in Kingston. They say those were bad times in Jamaica, lots of political problems. I have to say things are better now.'

David nodded: 'Do you remember the name of the man who was shot?'

Rosa shook her head: 'The only thing I remember was that he was American.'

'Sounds like the man who contracted my father to design Zion Hill. But only the dock was finished while he was here. A pity, he never saw it completed. It looks so lovely.'

'Yes, he did a pretty good job if this was his design. We love the way the guest cottages are grouped around this little bay. My father fell in love with the place all those years ago. Sadly he's no longer with us.'

'I'm sorry to hear that. It would have been interesting to ask him about the development of the place,' said David. He took a sip of his lemonade. 'There's another thing. I'm trying to trace a friend of my father's, well two friends really - Maya Tennyson and Marianne Chang. Maya's uncle Ned had a farm near here. And my father wrote about a waterfall and a plunge pool somewhere behind the farm.' He reached into his backpack and pulled out the journal. 'Just a moment, let me find it; you see he wrote this journal about his time in Jamaica and we only found it recently after he died.'

'How interesting,' said Rosa.

'Ah yes, here it is…*March 28th….the property.. stands high above the coast with a stunning view of the coastline. He grows coffee and bananas, a little sugar cane and coconut palms. Several streams run through the property and Maya led me to her favourite place higher*

159

up in the hills. It's where a river drops in a waterfall from a height of about 20 feet into an amazing deep plunge pool....' David looked up: 'Any ideas where this place might be?'

Rosa nodded: 'I knew old Ned Tennyson. When I was a child I would go and play there with a boy who worked on the farm. He showed me that swimming place. I can tell you how to find it. Sadly Ned died some years ago when I was away in America at college. But I've never heard of Ned's niece, Maya. Haven't been near the place in years so I don't know who's living there now.' She got up out of her chair. 'But let me show you around, show you something of the vision that maybe your father had for this place.'

'Thank you,' said David, 'that would be great.' He went out and called to Joe: 'Joe, over here, come and see.'

The resort nestled round a small sandy bay. There were six cottages, each surrounded by small gardens landscaped with rocks and planted with a variety of exotic flowers and shrubbery.

'I love these little gardens,' commented David.

Rosa turned: 'Flowers are my passion,' she said, stopping by one of the gardens. 'This little hedge is of crotons.' She gently fingered the leaves of a low bush with bright yellow, red and green variegated leaves. 'And these are one of my favourite.' She was pointing to a shrub with tall paddle shaped green leaves and curious red claw shaped bracts.

'They're like crab claws,' said Joe.

'You're close there,' said Rosa. 'This is the Lobster Claw Heliconia.'

'And are those baby bananas?' asked Joe. He was standing next to a tall plant with a thick trunk, a canopy of broad green leaves and a huge stem which hung down and ended in a purple beak-shaped flower. Behind the flower were clusters of finger sized bananas.

Rosa nodded: 'You're right, Joe. Yes those are bananas, and these are what I think you buy at Christmas in England.' She was pointing to a bush of long bending stems which ended in brilliant crimson leaves.

'Poinsettia?' asked David.

Rosa nodded: 'And of course you know azalea and hibiscus and you see there, Joe, that one like the head of a bird, that's a Bird of Paradise.' The flower stem ended in a point with a comb of bright orange petals projecting from its top.

'It looks like plastic,' said Joe.

'Don't say that, Joe. These are God's wonderful creations. Different, I reckon, from what you see in England, eh?'

They meandered down to the beach with its wooden boardwalk across the sand. Small pearly waves rushed onto the foreshore.

'I wish my father could have seen this. It's just fabulous,' said David.

'Let me point out where I think Ned Tennyson's place is,' said Rosa and she led them back out to the road. 'You see up there, that white roof top, well that's a small cottage in front of Ned's place.'

David remembered the reference to the cottage - the place where his father used to stay.

'And just along the road there is a track up to that waterfall place you spoke of. I remember swimming there on a number of occasions.'

'Thank you so much, Rosa,' said David. 'You've been very helpful.'

'Well, being nice to people costs nothing, does it? And I hope you find your father's friends. Bye Joe. Have a great trip and try out that swimming place your granddaddy wrote about. You'll love it.'

David remembered from the journal that one evening his father had walked down a track from the cottage to RJ's place and seen cargo being offloaded at the dock. He wondered if they might find the same track up to the cottage. He looked again for the white roof as they walked down the road. To the right there was a well beaten path which looked as though it might head up the hill in the right direction. At first it wound up through a small banana plantation and then over some fallen rocks through the gap in a wall and along a tunnel of overgrown bush. Ahead, the bush gave way to more open grassland and there were signs of cultivation - sugar cane, a plot of peppers and callalloo, cocoa yams and some dwarf palms with coconuts clustered under an umbrella of pointed leaves.

'Did you hear that?' said Joe, suddenly stopping.

'What was it?' asked David.

'Sounded like a piano.'

'A piano?'

Joe nodded: 'I'm sure, just wait. Listen now.'

The breeze was making the coconut palm leaves knock together and David strained to listen.

'There it is again,' said Joe and this time David heard it faintly, coming from further up the hill.

They continued up the steep path getting higher with the view behind them widening to take in the curve of the bay and wide sweep of the sea. The roofs of the cottages at Zion Hill were barely visible among their surrounding greenery. And now the path branched off to the left where there was the shingle roof of a small cottage. This could well be the cottage his father described, where he and Maya had met. It certainly had the view his father had described and there was a small terrace and fire pit. No wonder his father had loved coming here. Like Bermuda Mount, it was another piece of paradise.

They went back onto the main path and continued uphill. And now the sound of the piano was clearer. It was halting, with wrong notes, like a child would play.

They came to a low wall with a gate and David was about to open it when an old man appeared; he had a curved pipe between his lips, wore shabby working clothes and he was carrying a machete: 'Wha' yuh want, nuh?' he said.

'I'm trying to find an old friend. She was Ned Tennyson's niece, her name was Maya.'

The old man shook his head: 'Me not see Miss Maya since she a young girl, dat was many year ago.'

'So did you work for Ned?'

The old man nodded: 'Until he die a while back.'

'So who lives here now? Who is playing the piano?'

'Dat Miss Mary grandson. Him call Simon.'

'And is Miss Mary in? Could I speak with her for a moment.'

David's mind was turning in spirals. A grandmother called Mary?

The old man nodded: 'Come dis way, nuh.'

He led them on to a drive way. There was a car parked and a motor bike. The house was two storey, clapboard walls, a shingle roof, a balcony on both upper and lower floors and louvres floor to ceiling either side of some open French windows. It was through the open windows that the sound of the piano was filtering.

The old man went up the steps, onto the lower balcony and into the house. David waited, breath almost held. After a few minutes the old man emerged. He nodded: 'Miss Mary, she soon come. She say to tek a seat nuh,' and he indicated some garden chairs in front of the house.

'Who lives here?' asked Joe.

'I don't know, but it's where Pops used to come and stay when he was working on the project at Zion Hill.'

The piano playing had stopped and a small boy stepped out on the balcony. He didn't stay but retreated inside. A few minutes later an older woman appeared, light brown skin, grey hair tied back, spectacles hanging from a gold lanyard round her neck. She wore a loose tie-dye kaftan dress and walked with a stick.

She stopped for a moment holding on to the rail of the balcony and looked down at David who stood up. 'Tom said we have a visitor from England....' For a moment she seemed to stagger and gripped the rail more tightly.

David started forward: 'Hallo, I hope you don't mind but we heard the piano music…'

The woman continued gripping the rail and staring. Then she started shaking her head: 'I thought you were someone I once knew,' she said, 'the voice, your face. I'm sorry, foolish of me.'

David was just a few feet away now and he could see the shape of her eyes, the pallor of her skin, the obvious oriental features. 'It's not Marianne, is it?'

She stared, stared down the years, saw the young English man who had fallen in love with her closest friend. 'Will?' she murmured.

'David,' he replied, 'Will's son. I came looking for you. It is you, isn't it, Marianne Chang?'

She nodded slowly: 'Please get me a chair.'

David fetched a chair and held her arm as she sat down.

'Sorry,' she said, 'this is something of a shock and my new hip is not quite part of me yet.' Then she looked again at David and frowned: 'Are you really Will's son? David did you say? After all this time..'

'Forty years ago it was, that my father was here.'

'Is he with you?'

David shook his head: 'He died not long ago.'

'I'm so sorry, he was such a fine young man, your father. We became very close.'

'I know.'

'Did he talk about me?'

'I think I need to explain,' said David.

'And who is this young man?' said Marianne, looking across at Joe. 'He looks about the age of my Simon.'

'This is my son, Joe.'

'Will's grandson,' nodded Marianne. 'How wonderful. He deserved to have a family.'

'I have so many questions, you've no idea,' said David.

She held up her hand: 'Just a minute, let's get the boys sorted. Would you like to go swimming, Joe?'

'Yes please,' said Joe, 'but I don't have my swimming gear up here. It's in the car.'

'Don't worry, Simon has some you can borrow and towels. He'll show you. Simon, come here nuh, and take Joe swimming. Is that okay with you, David? We have a great swimming spot just up the hill.'

The young boy reappeared; he was a similar height to Joe, light brown skin, short black curly hair. 'Simon, this is Joe from England. He's visiting with his daddy. Now take him up to the swimming place and we'll come up later. Off you go boys. And Simon, no foolishness now. I'll send Tom to keep an eye on you.'

'Yes, nana,' said the boy. 'C'mon, Joe, I'll get you some stuff to wear.'

Joe followed Simon into the house and Marianne turned back to David. 'You have questions?'

David nodded: 'You said my father 'deserved to have a family'. What did you mean by that?'

'Oh my boy, where do we start?' said Marianne. 'Where on earth do we start?'

'Let me start so that you understand why I'm here,' said David.

He reached into his bag and took out the journal. He explained the finding of it, and what it revealed about this unknown life of his father in Jamaica. 'You are mentioned a number of times, with great affection,' said David. 'But the big question is about his relationship with Maya.'

'Does he tell much about Maya?'

'He tells what he knew about her but she appears something of a puzzle. Seems he could never fathom the depth of her feelings for him. In the end he felt that maybe he'd just been a pawn in a bigger political game she was playing.'

Marianne shook her head: 'I don't think she herself ever knew how to control what she was caught up in. They were difficult and dangerous times.'

'And was it true she was a CIA operative controlled by this American guy, RJ?'

'He was a monster who preyed on her weaknesses, recruited her when we were at college in Miami - used all sorts of bribes to entangle her, helped get her a scholarship and then obliged her to work at the embassy and that's when she found she was in deeper than she realised. And of course she was young and being sent to Cuba on these musical exchanges which then turned into spying missions.'

'In the journal,' said David, 'she seemed to become disillusioned with what she was doing.'

Marianne nodded: 'Will was very perceptive and it was true that Maya was forced to use him by RJ. They had him marked down as soon as he arrived. Will and Maya met on a number of occasions as if by chance but often it had all been carefully choreographed.'

'So she did deliberately use him.'

'Only at first until she became fond of him and started to rethink what she was doing with the Agency.'

David flicked through the pages of the journal. 'And was it his baby she disappeared with?'

Marianne nodded: 'She didn't plan to get pregnant but when she found she was, it affected her profoundly. She talked to me about escaping with Will, to somewhere off the island, starting over but she was frightened for her life, for the baby's life and for Will's life.'

'Did the baby survive?'

'As far as I know but I've had no contact with Maya for years now.'

David groaned, pressed his hand against his forehead. He had assumed they were close to answering the final questions. 'You mean you're not in touch with her?'

Marianne shook her head: 'The last message I got from her was thirty five years ago. She asked me to look after her Uncle Ned when he could no longer cope. That's how I came to live here. He left me his house but I've not heard from Maya since then. In her last message she said she was in danger and had to move on for the sake of her daughter. She said she couldn't contact me as that might allow them to find her and she'd learnt the Agency wanted to 'disappear' her, as she put it.'

'To kill her?'

Marianne nodded.

'But why?' asked David.

'I don't know.'

'So you've no idea where she's living or even if she's still alive?'

'I'm afraid not.'

'I can't believe this,' said David, his head in his hands. 'So near and yet so far. When I realised it was you I thought we were home, that we had finally got there.'

Marianne placed her hand on David's shoulder. 'Give me a moment, will you.'

He helped her to her feet and she went back in the house. David turned round, looked back through the gaps in the trees at the sea beyond. To come all this way and discover this outcome - a blind alley, a dead end. He had hoped beyond hope that he could solve this conundrum. He was sure they were getting closer and he felt so powerfully the presence of his young father in each place they visited. But at least the child had survived - and it was a little girl. That was amazing.

Marianne reappeared and came down the steps to where David was sitting. She held out something to him. 'This is what Maya sent in her final message to me.'

It was a photograph of a child, a small girl, light brown skin, piercing eyes, long wavy dark brown hair. She was holding a teddy bear and smiling at the camera.

'This is the child. All that was written on the back was 'my daughter, aged five'.'

'No name?' asked David.

Marianne shook her head: 'No, I'm afraid not. Maya was so anxious about being traced.'

David took the photograph and held it: 'So this is my half sister.' He couldn't halt the tears from welling in his eyes. 'Oh, little girl, how am I going to find you now?'

Marianne laid her hand gently on his arm. 'Come now, David, let's walk and see the boys. You can help me up the hill. The doctor says I have to exercise so this will be good.' She patted his arm again. 'Come.'

David looked up, wiped his eyes and nodded.

'I have some more photos,' said Marianne. 'We'll see them later.'

They made their way up the track towards the sound of squeals and splashes. This was the swimming place where Will and Maya had bathed, with the plunge pool and the waterfall cascading out of the trees. Joe was standing ready to jump. He waved and then gripped his legs up and bombed into the pool.

'You can borrow a pair of my son's swimming shorts if you want to go in. He's about your size,' said Marianne.

So David stood on the place where Will and Maya had '*chased like a couple of kids*' - he remembered the way Will had described it, and those images of Maya under the water. He jumped from the top of the waterfall, hit the water and swam down into the cool blue depths of the pool. Then Joe's body hit the water and David saw him enveloped in a flurry of bubbles. They surfaced and the sight of Joe's face beaming and streaming with water helped to lift his spirits a little.

Sometime later, after they had all eaten together and the boys were inside watching a movie, David and Marianne sat outside under the light from a kerosene lamp. David found the passage in the journal: 'This was March 28th, 1975, … *Several streams run through the property and Maya led me to her favourite place higher up in the hills. It's where a river drops in a waterfall from a height of about 20 feet into an amazing deep plunge pool. She didn't hesitate to strip off to her bikini and challenge me to do the jump from the top of the waterfall. She jumped first and I watched her dark body swimming under the water to the side of the pool. She emerged, face glistening, her wide smile, the beads of water like so many tiny diamonds caught in the tight curls of her hair. It was one of those moments which imprints itself indelibly…..'*

Marianne nodded: 'She was so full of life, so vivacious and I watched her losing that joy of life, I watched it being sucked out of her and I could do nothing about it.'

'You all went to Mexico,' said David.

'Yes, it was there she became herself again. She was free of the long arm of the Agency and the light and life came back into her eyes. And she and Will became even closer, I could see it clearly and I longed for it to stay like that. But as soon as we were back here she became a lost soul again. It was only in her music that she found some peace of mind. But that never lasted long enough.'

'I visited the cottage at Bermuda Mount where they stayed once,' said David.

'She talked about that place and her wish to escape. Then she found she was pregnant and she kind of went into a downward spiral. She didn't know what to do. She only knew she had to protect the child.'

'But she never told him she was pregnant. Why was that?'

'I don't know. There's so much I don't know.'

'And then there was the shooting. What happened there?' asked David.

'Again, I don't know. I kind of think Maya was going to have it out with RJ, to tell him she couldn't continue any longer. But how the shooting happened I don't know. All I know is that some men brought her to the clinic, we treated her and then the following day some different men came and took her away.'

'And you never saw her again?'

Marianne nodded: 'Yes, that was the last time I saw her. And I have grieved ever since for the loss of her love and her friendship. We were like sisters.'

David stared at the darkness. There were fireflies sparking here and there: 'You know Ned used to call her a 'peenie wallie' - there and then gone.'

'He got it just right, that's exactly how she was - flashing brightly one minute then dark and lost the next.'

'And you think there might have been a contract out to kill her?'

'It's possible, but I've no idea. She may have died already. We have no way of knowing. D'you know that Maya's brother Edward was murdered?'

'Murdered? A friend in England did some searching and found he'd died in a boating accident.'

'It was no accident from what I've heard. Just another piece of a jigsaw of violence and retribution.'

'But the daughter may still be alive?' said David.

'It's possible. I hope you're right.'

'She'd be a little older than me.'

Marianne leaned forward and reached for an envelope on the table. 'Have a look at these; they're the few that I've been able to find.'

They were photographs - Will, Maya and the others in Mexico; Maya with her violin, glamorous in a long crimson evening dress; Maya and Marianne, arms around each other on a beach somewhere; Will sitting on a low wall with a backdrop of the mountains and Maya sitting on the ground, her head against his knee. 'That one's Cinchona,' said Marianne. 'We hiked up there soon after Will arrived.'

'Yes, he writes about it, about waking to the sound of Maya playing the violin early one morning.'

'Those were the good times before it all seemed to change,' said Marianne.

David nodded, looking closely at each photograph again. He sighed and glanced at his watch: 'We'd better go and check in at the Pink Flamingo before we lose our booking. I'll go get Joe. And thanks for the loan of Simon. They seemed to get on well from the start.'

'I'm so sorry, David, that you haven't found the answers you'd hoped for,' said Marianne.

David shook his head, 'No, believe me, you've been very reassuring. I now realise Maya was dealing with so much. When I first read the journal I felt angry that she was using my father, but I now see it was much more complicated. She was also a victim.'

When they left, David hugged Marianne. 'If I find out any more about Maya I'll let you know, believe me, but I can't think that's going to happen. You were my last hope.'

Marianne nodded: 'I treasure my memories of your father and that brief time he and Maya had together. They seemed to find real affection - maybe even love but I'm glad he found love later with your mother. And look at you - a fine young man with a treasure of a son.' She held out her hand: 'Great meeting you, Joe. And maybe you'll write to Simon when you get back to England. He would love to have a pen pal like you. I've written my email address here on this paper. Now don't lose it, will you.'

Joe nodded, took the paper and shook her hand: 'Yes I'll write and send him some football stickers and stuff.' He waved at Simon and gave him a 'thumbs up'. Simon returned the wave.

David put his hand on Joe's shoulder, they turned and started back down the track.

'She was nice,' said Joe, 'and I wish Simon lived closer; and that swimming place was ace, just like Pops described in his book.'

With Joe fast asleep in bed, David got up. It was the early hours. He couldn't sleep. There was a bright moon and the sound of the sea breaking. Quietly, he slid the patio door open and walked out of his bedroom and down to the beach. The Pink Flamingo was not unlike Zion Hill. There were small cottages grouped around a tiny bay which was nudged by rocky promontories. He sat on one of the paddle boards which lay upturned on the sand. He felt heavy, drained. What had given oxygen to this whole venture had been sucked away. The momentum was lost.

To finally meet Marianne was one thing but it hadn't led him to finding Maya and her child. At least he now had an image of them both which he hadn't had before. Maya, young and vivacious, just as his father had described her. When he had first read the journal he had judged her harshly, seeing her using his father as a pawn in a dangerous political game. Now he realised it was not that simple. She had clearly been a troubled soul caught in a mesh of intrigue and manipulation which finally she wanted to escape from. And she had, in a sense, escaped but whether she ever stopped running was another question.

And what of the child - his half sister? Where was she and was her mother still alive? He took the photograph of her from his pocket. Those laughing eyes like her mother's; the long wavy brown hair, the light brown skin, the impish look. Was there anything of Joe in that face or of himself as a child? And David wept again for this child his father had never known, for the love he had lost and the memories he had kept secret and taken to his grave. And David felt again the ache of hearing his father in the care home - 'She's gone, She's gone…' If only he had known, he could have shared his father's loss and maybe eased the pain. Now it was too late.

The following morning they spent some more time with Marianne and Simon before saying farewell and driving down the coast to Boston Bay where Joe had a go at surfing. They tasted the peppered jerk pork from a roadside stall near the beach and drank fresh coconut water from a young man selling from the back of his pick up on the road to Port Antonio. He sliced a sliver from the top of a green coconut with his machete and handed it to Joe who tipped back his head and tasted fresh coconut water for the first time. Joe nodded and grinned as the milk dribbled down the sides of his mouth: 'It's good, dad, really good.'

When it was time to return to Kingston they took the quicker route from Annotto Bay, following the river called Wag Water and past the botanical gardens at Castleton. They stopped by the river and watched some boys fishing for the freshwater crayfish they called 'janga'. They swam in a pool where the river ran fast down from the hills before David started the climb up to Stony Hill and back into the heat of the city.

Violet welcomed them with ice cream for Joe and a cold Red Stripe for David. 'You have a good trip?' she asked. 'You find yuh father friend?'

David nodded: 'We met one of them and saw some of the places he stayed in.'

'So you content then?'

David shrugged: 'A little, and Joe made another new friend, Simon, the grandson of Marianne who lives near San San Bay.'

She turned to Joe: 'So yuh now have someone to visit in Jamaica when you grow up, as well as visit yuh aunt Violet and Lloyd in Kingston, yeh?'

Joe nodded and David warmed at the thought that at least he'd made a connection with Jamaica which Joe might continue into the future.

That evening David emailed Gina. It was good to unburden himself to someone who would understand. He felt played out, lost almost. So much had been pinned on this trip and the more he became immersed in the country, in the wonderful landscape, in these intriguing places his father had written about and which were now real to him - the more he had felt a sensing of arriving - arriving at a resolution; arriving at the place of answers to all the questions the journal had thrown up.

But it was not to be. He was still in the waiting room; still feeling the longing; still trying to imagine a reunion with his sister and Maya; still hoping to put to rest the angst that his father had taken to his grave.

On the morning of their flight home, he received a short reply from Gina:

Sorry you didn't answer all your questions but at least you've sampled something of your father's 'secret life'. And we'll continue the search, you can't let the trail go cold. Give my love to Jamaica and don't forget to bring Appleton and ackees! Looking forward to hearing all. Gx

****

PART THREE: The Weaving

January was always a bleak month; deadness, greyness, winter holding things in an icy grip, the Solway raging at times with violent westerlies that turned the estuary into an angry maelstrom of brown surf and boiling tidal currents. Sometimes the waves broke so high there were ugly flecks of salt foam in the garden. Added to that, the return from Jamaica had been hard to handle. David missed the warmth, the vibrancy of colour, the novelty of it all, but mainly he missed the hope that he'd travelled with, that optimism that finally the trip would lead to answers. True he'd felt the spirit of his young father in the mountains and on the north coast. He'd trodden in Will and Maya's footsteps but had that helped? Maybe it laid some ghosts. They'd found Marianne and now Joe had a new friend - Simon, his internet pal whom he was in weekly contact with. They were playing online games and constructing Minecraft challenges for each other. David had tried to use video calls to Marianne but the signal was poor and so they'd given up. But they were in contact via email and that in itself added a new dimension to their lives. They'd sent photos of home, of the Lake District, of Carlisle and Marianne always replied enthusiastically that she loved the way it was opening her life to the wider world. But beyond that, the hope of finding Maya and her child had all but faded.

Gina had greeted them with a 'welcome-home' meal and David was lifted by her energy and her optimism. 'You mustn't give up trying, David, there must be other ways,' she had said. She was eager to hear all about their travels, the people, the places. 'Sounds like you met some nice Jamaican folks,' she said. 'So there you have a way back, for future visits.'

David nodded: 'I guess so.'

'Think positive, nah man, don' tek it so hard. Keep a likkle light burning!' she quipped as she poured some Jamaican rum into a couple of glasses. 'Come, let's drink to the next chapter in your quest!'

They clinked glasses and Joe smiled at the way Gina cut through the gloom that had hung over his father since they arrived home. He was looking forward to a call from Simon in the morning. To have a new friend and in a place like Jamaica was really cool. His school friends were impressed as he showed off his Rasta wrist band and told them stories of spear-fishing for barracudas and jumping down waterfalls.

On days at his dad's, when he came home from school, he would draw the curtains against the winter darkness, retreat to his room and lose himself in computer games. On his wall he'd created an elaborate collage of the photos they had taken, posters, leaflets and tickets he'd collected. Above the display was a banner of Jamaican scenes and posters of Bob Marley and Usain Bolt.

It was early March when there was knock on his bedroom door. David's head appeared and he edged his way in and sat on the bed. 'I've been thinking. How about we sell my house and move to Pops' house?'

'Really!' exclaimed Joe. 'Could I have the room which looks out onto the river?'

David nodded: 'Whatever you like. There's stacks of room.'

'That's brill, dad. Thanks.'

'So I'll get things moving then,' said David. 'I somehow thought you'd agree.'

He'd made his decision one morning in February when he was cycling round what the locals called 'the Island' - the fist of land which jutted out into the Solway between the villages of Bowness and Anthorn and where the road hugged the edge of the estuary. He had stopped near the old airfield and looked out across the Solway. 'I knew it!' he said to himself. 'I knew I'd seen it before.' And he recalled his first view from the hills above

Kingston, across the wide harbour towards the dome of the Hellshire Hills with the Palisadoes Peninsula thrusting out into the bay to the left. It was this Cumbrian view that had echoed in his mind - the wide spread of the mouth of the Solway, the hump of Criffel and the Scottish hills in the distance and the finger of the Skinburness peninsula pushing out into the bay. It was Kingston harbour in miniature! David nodded to himself: 'So maybe dad had Jamaica in mind every time he saw this view. It could have been the reason he decided on the house in the first place. But it's certainly confirmed my decision.'

One morning Gina texted David with the message: *I have a new idea. See you for coffee Wednesday 4pm?*

Gina was already sitting at the corner table when David arrived. She got up and he hugged her and sat down. 'So, how's things?' he said.

Gina shrugged: 'The usual, work and work and then there's work. But….'

'You've had an idea?'

'I have,' she said and she took a small packet from her bag, placed it on the table and slid it across to David.

'A present?' said David.

'Kind of.'

He opened it and there was a small box. It said *Ancestry - DNA kit*. 'Okay, what's all this about?'

'Simple,' said Gina. 'You do a DNA test, send it off and see what happens?'

'I've heard of this but never really understood how it worked. I thought it was a medical thing.'

'It can be but this test will give you a profile of your ethnicity. It goes into a huge database and you get matches with people whose DNA is similar to yours. The closer the match the more likely it is that you're closely related.'

'So I could get a match with my sister?'

'Depends on whether she's done a DNA test. If she hasn't then there's no chance. But it's gaining in popularity all the time. It's very big in America, so you never know.'

David opened the package. There was a leaflet and a small plastic container with a screw top. He held it up quizzically.

'No, it's not to pee in,' she laughed. 'You spit into it.'

'And that's it?' David was frowning.

Gina nodded: 'That's it. It goes off to the lab and in about six weeks or so you'll get the results.'

'Well, nothing ventured, as they say. But I can't believe it'll take us anywhere.'

'Don't be so bloody pessimistic. We have to live in hope.'

'I know, I'm sorry. I just feel so let down after that amazing trip which didn't give us the answers.'

'But you met Marianne, and you got to know about your sister and you have the photograph. And you went to all those places your dad talked about in the journal. Surely that was a help.'

David nodded: 'Of course it was.'

'And Joe had a great time and he's met Simon. Just think where that connection could take him in his lifetime.'

'You're right, as usual,' said David. 'I need to feel half full instead of half empty.' He stretched across the table and patted the back of Gina's hand. 'Thank you for sticking by me. I'm an ungrateful sod, aren't I.'

'Yeah, sometimes you are. But despite that I'll still buy you some more cake and another coffee.'

By mid April David and Joe had virtually moved into Pops' old house. The other house was up for sale and when Joe stayed over he now had the view across the Solway to wake up to. The geese were already leaving, great skeins of grey birds high up in the sky heading north to Scandinavia. Joe watched them through Pops' binoculars, watched the way they kept their V formation, although there was always the loner out of line, honking to catch up and keep in the slipstreams of the others, like the kid at school who's clumsy and hopeless and is always the last to get picked when they're choosing footie sides. It always made Joe smile.

He loved his new room. There was more space and he and David had done a quick emulsion job on the walls before he was able to put up his collage of photos, his posters and banners. He was in contact with Simon regularly during the week as they swapped ideas for developing their Minecraft constructions and challenged each other with new computer games.

David had been distracted by the move but at the back of his mind was the thought of his DNA sample being processed and the possible clues it might generate. He wanted to go back through the journal and note any other clues as to where Maya and the child might have gone. Initially he'd assumed they'd be in America, she being a CIA agent but then, when he looked again he got the impression that maybe that's the last place she would go if, as the journal hinted, she had become disillusioned and changed allegiances. She had talked of her affection for Mexico and it was a place she had gone to with Will and been happy. *'This is my kind of place, Will,'* she had said when they had visited the Yucatan on that second Christmas in 1975. They had made love on the beach and maybe that was when the child was conceived? Maya spoke Spanish and if she wanted to disappear it was a big country. But where would you start looking?

David quickly dismissed the idea. Another long haul trip with only a wing and a prayer and more probable disappointment was not what he needed. No, he would see what came of the DNA venture first.

He bought frames for the photos that he'd brought back from the trip - the one of the child which Marianne had given him and also the one of his young father and Maya that Frank, the old Jamaican, had shown him at Bermuda Mount. He placed them on the table by his bed, a reminder that the search was far from over. He bought an album for all the photos he'd taken on the trip which he must get printed, but projects at work were pressing and there was much to do to upgrade his father's house. The quest to find his sister and Maya would have to wait.

***

Luciana Torriega watched a tanker making its stately progress down the St. Lawrence - incongruous in its monstrous size, pushing a huge bow wave ahead of it and dwarfing the islands and small boats which dotted the Seaway. She and Sonia were staying at a small resort just out of Selton, the Canadian side of the Thousand Islands. The far side of the Seaway was the United States and the border ran down the centre of the river. They had flown for a two week vacation from Merida to Montreal a few days earlier and driven along the river as far as Hill Island. This was an area Sonia knew well having spent a year at the university in Montreal some years ago. It was tantalising to see the border crossing on Wellesley Island just a few miles away but they weren't going to chance it. Since Trump had arrived in the White House, Mexican passports were like a red flag at the border. So they were renting a cabin on a small bay on the Canadian side, just off the main Seaway.

'I'm worried about momma,' said Luciana.

'Why, what's happened?' Sonia looked up from her book.

'When I said we were coming here and I told her it was on the border, she said, 'You won't go over will you? Promise me, you won't cross over.' She held my wrist very tightly and her eyes were staring in a weird way.   She has this thing, always has done, about not setting foot in the U.S.A.'

'But I thought she went to college in Miami.'

'She did,' replied Luciana. 'Then she went back to Jamaica but left in the Seventies and has never been back there either. And there are other things too. She's sleep walking and murmuring in her sleep - all sorts of weirdness that it's difficult to understand. In the morning she looks hollow eyed and vacant as if she's been travelling all night.'

'Sounds like she has, in her dreams.'

'It's since she retired from running the school. She seems to have no focus anymore.'

'Does she still play?'

Luciana nodded: 'Yes but it seems to be the same pieces over and over - often it's Satie and that Andante by Shostakovich. You know she composed an arrangement of the Andante once for violin and guitar so that we could play together. It was a concert in Mexico City - the audience loved it but at the end momma was in tears and I mean real tears. She was almost inconsolable.'

Sonia sat up, and pulled her knees under her chin: 'So what are you going to do?'

Luciana shook her head slowly and then shrugged: 'Go for a swim, I think, try to clear my head.'

She stepped lightly across the rocks to the smooth granite platform which fronted onto the water. The water was clear and deep and she dived and swam for a while underwater before surfacing a short distance away. 'Oh my god!' she shouted to the sky and threw her hands up in the air.

Sonia shook her head as she watched her friend moving away through the water with her long, gliding strokes.

Luciana swam to the small rocky island in the middle of the bay, climbed out onto one of the smooth boulders and did some yoga stretches and deep breathing. Her mind felt a little calmer. She dived again and swam across the bay to the beach where the sailing dinghies were moored. She rigged one of the Sunfish sailboards, slotted in the tiller and pushed it out onto the water. Yoga was one kind of therapy but for her, sailing was the ultimate. Where it came from she didn't know, this wonderful exhilaration that she felt when she was alone with just a simple sailboat, the wind filling the sails and the bubble of the surf streaming out from the wake - she just felt the thrill of being alive. It was almost as if it was in her blood. She had first sailed on the lagoon at Punta Blanca, south of Valladolid where years ago her mother had bought a small cabana close to the beach. One of the local boys had taken her out in a dinghy when she was about eight years old and something inside her clicked like a sluice gate being opened to let the water flow. She felt a thrill deep inside her, the thrill of a type of freedom and connection with the gods. And now, as she tacked out of the bay into the Seaway itself, the feeling was the same. Out from the shelter of the bay the wind was instantly stronger and she had to keep checking the pull on the mainsail sheet, being ready to ease it to spill the wind from the sail if a sudden gust came. She watched the surface of the river ahead for the tell-tale dark patches which signalled wind on the water, checked the curve of the sail, eased her weight to keep the boat tilted into the wind. It was wonderfully all-consuming this total focus on the wind, the water and the movement of the boat, all other thoughts eclipsed.

When she got back to the cabin, Sonia had already started the barbecue. 'You were loving it out there, I could tell,' she said.

Luciana shook her head as she towelled herself: 'Don't know what it is but I just love being alone with the wind in the sails.'

'You're just an incurable romantic.'

'Something like that. Maybe I take after my mother. I think she was a romantic once, before the shooting.'

Sonia spread the charcoal on the barbecue and laid kebabs on the grill. 'What happened? You've never told me much about it.'

'I don't know any details, really. She's never opened up. Just know that when she was pregnant with me she got caught up in a shooting incident. It was at that time when the rival political gangs in Jamaica were shooting the hell out of each other. She was just in the wrong place at the wrong time. Lucky she didn't get killed or I wouldn't be here to tell the tale.'

'That's when she left Jamaica?'

'I think she was traumatised by it all. Says she doesn't remember much about it.'

'And that's when she came to Merida?'

Luciana nodded: 'Yes, she says she'd been a couple of times before on a concert tour with some musicians and a boyfriend. That's when she first discovered Punta Blanca and kind of fell in love with Mexico.'

'What happened to the boyfriend? He wasn't your father, was he?'

'That's the big unknown. She's only ever said that when she fled after the shooting she lost touch with him. It's nagged at me for years.'

'D'you know anything about him. I imagine he was white, looking at you and your wonderful skin tone, you lucky thing.'

'He was English and his name was William. And that's all I know.'

'William what?'

Luciana shook her head: 'She won't tell me. Says to leave him alone, that he's suffered enough without having some stranger from Mexico trying to upset his life.'

'And how d'you feel about that?' asked Sonia.

'I feel cheated. I would like to know about him, whether he's still alive and what happened to him when momma left Jamaica.'

Sonia nodded, forked the food on the grill and put a couple of plates on the table. 'Pour the wine, will you?'

They sat eating and watching the sky redden across the water, watched the lights from the navigation buoys winking green and red, heard the wing beats of the geese flying out to roost on the islands.

'It would kill me not to know,' said Sonia.

'I think it's kind of killed a part of me already,' added Luciana.

She got up and went into the cabin. She came out with her guitar. 'Didn't know I'd bought a little Martin, did you,' she said.

'A Martin?'

'It's a beautiful little thing, nice and small for travelling with and you know that Ed Sheeran plays one.'

'Oh well, if Ed Sheeran plays one then it's a no brainer,' smiled Sonia.

'Made in Pennsylvania,' said Luciana.

'Well then, that's definitely one reason for visiting the U.S.A.'

Luciana checked the tuning. Then she adjusted her seat and the position of her hands and started playing. The sound was light on the evening air; first a little study by Fernando Sor and then a haunting melody by Giuliani. The sound was mesmeric and when she stopped Sonia waited for a moment to let the last notes of the music drift away on the wind. Then she said: 'Can you play that piece you mentioned, the one your mother's often playing.'

'The Shostakovich?'

'Yes, that one, I'd love to hear it.'

Sonia leaned back in her recliner and let the music start to float her away. The melody was seductive in its simplicity, the harmonies sublime, the sort of sound that when you stared up at the night sky made you feel you were drifting out to some supernova in a far off galaxy.

'You play that beautifully,' murmured Sonia. 'What an exquisite piece.'

'When she's down at Punta she often plays in the evenings - sits down on the rocks and plays. I watch her and wonder where she travels to when she's playing. She looks so distant and sad sometimes, and I see her wiping away tears. I just wish there was something I could do.'

'She loves that little cabana, doesn't she,' said Sonia.

Luciana nodded: 'She tells me that she bought it when I was just a toddler. There wasn't much settlement at Punta back then. Just a few other cabins on the edge of the bay. It's where I learnt to sail. There was a local boy, Enrico, who was older and he had a sailboat. He showed me how to set the sail to catch the wind and the best places for spearing lobster. It's changing though; new roads, lots of new building but it's still a great place to go. I love it down there.'

'How's it going to be now that she's retired from the school?'

Luciana shook her head: 'You know she started that school with just four students, teaching them music. When she retired there were two hundred and fifty with ten staff. There were a lot of tears at her leaving celebration I can tell you, me included.'

'What will she do?'

Luciana shrugged: 'During her last year I noticed a change and Patricia, one of her closest colleagues, said she had become forgetful, couldn't seem to concentrate like she used to; would talk to herself as if nobody else was there. And it's getting worse. She seems plagued by nightmares and sleeps badly. I'm really worried about her. I may have to postpone my PhD for a while.'

'But you're so close to finishing.'

'I know but she needs my attention especially in the evenings when she's tired, and that's when I work on my thesis.'

'Doesn't she still play in that little quartet?'

Luciana nodded: 'Yes, that's what's saving her at the moment. They come to the house on a Thursday and they're preparing for a concert in the fall and for the festival at Christmas. She plays mainly from memory and so doesn't have the problem of having to learn new stuff.'

Sonia poured them each another glass of wine. 'Didn't you once say she's never been back to Jamaica?'

'Like she wouldn't ever go to America - going to Jamaica would be completely forbidden for me. I don't know what happened there but it's marked her for life. She won't even talk about the place.'

'And yet I guess it's probably where you were conceived!' exclaimed Sonia.

Luciana nodded: 'I know, I know. I just wish I knew about her life over there. I've looked at photos and video clips online and it looks a beautiful island but it's totally off limits. She won't even hold a conversation about Jamaica. It's really weird. There's so much I'd like to know but I just hit a blank wall every time.'

She threw some sticks onto the barbecue and flared it into a small campfire then placed some bigger logs on the flames. She sat back in her chair and stroked the strings of the guitar.

'What have they got you doing at work at the moment?' asked Sonia. 'Still classifying artefacts?'

'No, the museum's panicking because they're getting some bad reviews on Trip Advisor and might lose government funding. Visitors are criticising the lack of information in English, so I've to revamp the displays and do a massive translation exercise on all those individual cards which go with the artefacts.'

'Will you stay at the museum when you've got your PhD?'

Luciana shrugged: 'I had my hopes set on a lectureship at a university, but I'll have to see how things develop with momma. I worry that she won't cope if I go away.'

There was the sound of an owl far off in the woods and the distant moan of a fog horn on the Seaway. A mist was drifting over the water, dimming the lights from the islands.

Sonia got up and brought blankets from the cabin. 'D'you ever see Ricardo?'

Luciana shook her head. 'Not since the last visit to the fertility clinic. You know we've failed twice now. It's been hard on both of us. When you're desperate for children and it doesn't happen, then what?'

Sonia shook her head: 'I didn't know you'd tried twice.'

'When he said he was moving out, I said to him, 'So you're taking your sperm elsewhere then?' I don't think he was amused. He just shrugged and said, 'Something like that.' Ten years we were together and now he's gone with no word since.'

Sonia leaned over and put her arm round Luciana's shoulder. 'I'm so sorry,' she said.

'So I've decided, if I can't have my own children, I'd better search for my father. He may be a way of me finding a family.'

'I so wish I could help,' said Sonia.

'You can. You can join the search. The first thing is to get a name from my mother. I only know it's William. But a first name doesn't give you a lead. She must tell me more about him. I don't care if it upsets her. I just have to know.' She stretched and drained her glass, then checked her watch. 'We need to set off early in the morning. Flight's at 11.'

Sonia nodded: 'I've so enjoyed this break. Haven't been back here for so long.'

'And don't tell momma we contemplated crossing the border. She'd never forgive me.'

'Don't worry,' replied Sonia. 'Our secret.'

*

Maria Torriega scribbled a quick note. *Gone to Punta. Need to breathe sea air. Hope your trip went well. M xx* Looking in the mirror she patted her greying hair. Once it had been waves of jet black. Sadly no longer. She closed the kitchen door and put the key in the plant pot near the step. The seats of the car were hot and she spread a towel across the driver's seat before getting in. She should be there by lunch time. It normally took about four hours if she stopped in Valladolid for a break. She had loaded the cooler with ice, food and drink but there was always Francisco's little store in Punta where she knew she could stock up on basics which she might have forgotten.

She didn't need to think about directions - the car had done this trip so often it almost steered itself. But it could be confusing if they had opened a new road which seemed to be happening almost monthly. So much development. So much change. So many new people. But she still gave thanks that Punta didn't change much. A huddle of cabanas, some cantinas, a couple of hotels, some new dive schools and fishing outlets but essentially it was the same place she had fallen in love with all those years ago.

Her own little cabana had not escaped the ravages of time. When she first bought it from old Antonio it was a simple two roomed wooden building with a palapa roof, a sand floor and a porch. She and the baby slept in hammocks and they washed in a lean-to shelter behind the house. In the early years she had improved it a little but it was hurricane Gilbert in 1988 which had prompted a rebuild. Many of the buildings in Punta had been damaged or flooded when the hurricane hit the island of Cozumel and it was then that she decided to get some professional help in the reconstruction. So Cabana Luciana was now a single storey building raised off the ground on five foot stilts and having a wrap around balcony which led off the two bedrooms and the living room. The rooms had hard wood floors, paddle fans slung from the roof beams, hammocks and porch chairs on the balcony which had a wide view of the bay. She was told she now owned some prime real estate but the idea of selling never entered her head. No, this was her bolt-hole, the place where she felt most safe.

She went inside and opened the shutters to let out the stale heat. She hadn't been here for a couple of weeks and she checked the interior to see that everything was in its right place - the patterned cushions, the woven throws on the sofa, the carved figurines, the pottery which brightened the shelves in the kitchen, her precious books on the bookshelves in the sitting room and her musical instruments - her guitar, mandolin, her Peruvian harp and several violins. All appeared to be in order and she breathed out slowly, calming the anxiety she always felt when she arrived. If anything happened to this cherished place she didn't know how she would cope. Punta had saved her sanity all those years ago when she first arrived from Jamaica. Now she seemed to need it even more.

She went down the steps which led from the kitchen at the rear of the house to her little garden. She must check on her precious herbs, the most important part of her family of plants. She knew each plant intimately, they were like her offspring, needing nurturing, disciplining when they got unruly, cherishing when they were ready for harvesting. She stroked the rosemary and smelt the dry scent on her palms; brushed her hands over the oregano and cilantro and crushed mint between her fingers. She loved the rush of its sweet scent and anticipated the mint tea she would make later. There was a bamboo fence which Eduardo's grandson, Diego, had made for her with fishing net pinned along it to keep out animals which might try to steal her tomatoes, peppers and chillies. She paid him to tend the garden when she was away and keep it watered.

She opened the little gate and went through to where she kept her baskets. Taking the one she had bought in the market in Puebla years ago, the one with the zig-zag pattern, she picked a selection of things for later - a couple of avocados, tomatoes, green peppers and sprigs of rosemary and cilantro. She dug up onions and collected chayote and zucchini to add to the fresh corn, oranges, limes and bananas she'd bought from a roadside stall just outside Valladolid. As she closed the gate behind her and carried her basket back to the kitchen she pictured the meal she could make later; plenty of fresh comfort food was what she needed.

But then, thinking of Diego, the name - it triggered a flush of heat to her face and she staggered a little and gripped the banister of the staircase. She sat down on the top step and dropped her head into her hands. 'Diego' she said to herself. Hadn't he been with her in Cuba all those years ago and hadn't he been with her that night in the hospital when they carried her out to an open truck and they drove through the night? 'Diego' - what had happened to him? He had been with them when they hiked in the Blue Mountains. She could only vaguely hold his face in her mind for a moment and then it was gone. Her heart was racing and the sweat was cold on her face. She had to get up, get inside where it was cooler. Grasping the banister she heaved herself up and stumbled through the door into the cool of the kitchen. She put down the basket, hung her head while she filled a glass with water. Then she went through to the living room and slumped down onto the sofa. Her heart was still racing but the light headedness was fading and she wiped the sweat from her brow with a towel and sipped the water slowly. 'Diego,' she murmured.

These flashbacks which came from nowhere and then vanished. They were becoming more frequent and more disturbing. Flashbacks from a part of her life she had blocked out for so long. Why was it happening now?

She slept a little and when she woke the sun was starting to go down. She looked out from the balcony which faced the bay. The fishermen with their kerosene lights were setting out from the beach, heading for the channel which cut through the reef and led to the open sea. A cooler wind was blowing now and she closed the shutters and went through to the kitchen to prepare her meal. She thumbed through the selection of CDs she kept in the kitchen and chose the one Luciana had bought her recently - a young guitarist friend, Francesca Di Silvio, playing Tarrega's Capricho Arabe. It was gentle, soothing and it helped to smudge away the shadows in her head.

Once the pisto was bubbling away in the saucepan she poured herself a glass of wine and found her handbag. She wanted to look over the photographs of her retirement again, to remind herself. As always it was the faces of the children which warmed her the most. Yes, she valued her colleagues but it was the children she had always done it for.

And she remembered the first children and how it had all started. She had not long been in the country and she feared she would never play the violin again. The bullets had grazed her right arm, her bowing arm and for a while she could not lift it. Luciana had not yet arrived and she was in a strange waiting place - waiting for the baby, hiding in a foreign town where she knew no-one and constantly haunted by fears of a knock on her door and a gun being put to her head. And then came the morning a few weeks later when she tried again to lift her bowing arm. She felt some new strength there and she could grip the bow. She had lifted her violin, put it under her chin and drawn the bow across the strings. Something in her soul breathed again. Within a few days she was able to play, tentatively at first, but then with more confidence. And one morning when she had been playing near the open window, she looked down into the street and there were two children looking up at the balcony of her apartment. She had waved and smiled but they were shy and ran away.

But then a few days later the children were back, and now there were four of them, standing listening to her playing and one of them was holding a violin. That's how it had started - a school of four children who came to her once a week and learned to play their violins. She met their parents who told their friends and more children started coming until she rented a room and while Luciana slept in her cot Maria Torriega tutored her little ensemble.

She looked through the recent photographs at all the children assembled in front of the school building and her staff who had helped her establish the Bermuda Mount Institute of Music. 'Why 'Bermuda Mount'?' one of her staff had once asked. She had smiled: 'It was a very special place in a previous life.'

And now she remembered it again - the mountains, the humming birds, the little cabin on the hillside and the young man from England whom she had loved and lost.

But not entirely. He still lived on in Luciana; in her eyes, in her wavy brown hair and her light skin. And she remembered that first encounter - diving for lobster at those islands off Jamaica - his face, his eyes, his smile, the water streaming down his fair skin. And then she remembered her betrayal of him and the monstrous American who had pressured her to do it.

She shook her head, poured herself more wine and looked for her bottle of pills. Somehow she had to push away these dark thoughts. The music soothed her and she got up and went across to the balcony. The tree frogs and cicadas were loud in the darkness. Sometimes there was the bellow of a howler monkey or the screech of the parrots away in the forest. Tomorrow she would walk to the cenote and swim before any of the tourists arrived. It was only a small sink hole compared to the Grand Cenote at Tulum and smaller even than the quieter Cenote Zaci at Valladolid but it was her favourite which she'd discovered years ago. Then it had been their own private swimming place where Luciana had learnt to swim and dive. Now it had been discovered by others and steps and ropeways had been constructed for the safety of visitors.

She had once organised an outdoor concert in a cavern at the Grand Cenote with an orchestra of twenty musicians. No-one had ever tried it before and the tourists and local people were spellbound by candlelit caverns and the sounds of the strings echoing along the tunnels and round the cavern walls. It was as if the stalactites themselves were ringing like tubular bells, vibrating the sound waves in a curious symphony of sound and flickering light. And Luciana, aged fourteen, had played a guitar solo which the local newspaper had described as being 'like the whisperings of Xtabay', the goddess of the jungle. It was on walks to the cenote along the forest paths that they came across ancient mounds and Mayan stellae encrusted with lichen and creepers, standing like sleeping guards. It was this that first stirred Luciana's curiosity and then when she was older and they visited the ruins in Guatemala at Tikal where the jungle clutched at the soaring pyramids of the Central Plaza and the Acropolis and where the mystery of the city lost beneath the jungle undergrowth teased her imagination - then she was hooked. She had studied hard and graduated in anthropology from the universities of Mexico and Lima and was soon to gain her doctorate.

How proud her father would be if only he knew. The guilt hung like a dead weight. Was she to blame for what happened? She only remembered fragments of those events - of the embassy intrigues, of the duplicity, not knowing who to trust, the tangled web of relationships with Cuban agents, Americans who chewed gum and carried guns under their smart suits. What she did remember was the clumsy touch of the American, his stubby fingers, his gross belly. He had groped her when she was a student in Miami, had held a gun to her head in Jamaica when she tried to plead with him. And finally she had led them to him.

And what a price she had paid. She had lived a fugitive life, changing her name, always glancing over her shoulder, never sure if it might end with her blood on the blade of a knife or the life of Luciana being stolen from her. And more than that, she had betrayed her only love - that young, naive, fresh-faced Englishman. His touch she remembered too. Their nights under the stars - at Ned's cottage, at the place in the mountains where the breezes nudged the leaves of the eucalyptus trees and they brewed coffee over the open fire. She had searched for a gift for him and bought him a book. And they had planned to meet there again when she would explain and confess. But it had never happened and for forty years she had lived with the ache of it.

She tensed at the flicker of car headlights and the sound of tyres on the gravel outside. The slam of a car door and footsteps up to the balcony. For a moment her heart was gripped with the old fears but then with relief she heard Luciana's voice: 'Momma, it's only me.'

After they had eaten they sat watching the lights swinging on the fishermen's canoes and the moonlight dished in the waters of the bay, as they sipped coffee and chased it with rum.

Luciana decided it was now time to confront her mother. She turned to her: 'Momma, since Ricardo left me after my attempts to be a mother failed again, I decided I must try and find my father. I need to know, momma. It's eating away at me.'

Her mother shot a glance at her, then looked away. After a few moments she sighed and nodded slowly: 'I've been thinking too. When the doctors said I'd got this heart murmur I gave it a lot of thought. You're right. You should know more. It's just that I wish I could remember clearly. There are fragments. My memory is like a hallway of opening and closing doors. I start to remember and then the door closes and I'm wandering in an empty place again. I'll open another door and there's an empty room and then in the distance I see a figure disappearing. I catch a face for a moment and then it's gone, but I'll tell you what I can.'

She explained about going to study music in Miami with her friend Marianne. Of the meeting with the man from Texas who got her the job in the embassy in Kingston.

'What was he like?' asked Luciana.

'You don't want to know. He was a monster.'

'What happened to him?'

She hesitated: 'He was killed at the time I got shot.'

'And that's when you left Jamaica?'

She nodded; explained what she remembered of the gang warfare between the rival political parties.

'But what about my father? That's what I really want to know. Please tell me about him.'

She told what she remembered; about meeting Will, their trips to Mexico and time spent in the Blue Mountains. 'That's where the name 'Bermuda Mount' came from when I named the school. It was a very special place for Will and me.' She got up and went across to the dresser, opened the middle drawer and pulled out a small parcel wrapped in tissue paper. 'When we first came down here on that second visit to Yucatan, a young Mexican girl sewed this for me.' She unfolded the little scarf with the name 'Maya' embroidered next to a flower and a humming bird.

'Who's 'Maya'?' Luciana smoothed her fingers along the edge of the scarf.

'I'm Maya. That's my birth name - well it was Mahalia, but I was always called Maya.'

'So why do I know you as Maria?'

'When I left Jamaica I was forced to change my name. They gave me a new identity - Maria Torriega. It had been Maya Tennyson, but it was too dangerous to keep that name.'

'What!' Luciana threw up her hands: 'I don't believe this! So who gave you this new name?'

'The people who helped me escape. I don't know who they were but they arranged it.'

'So my real name is not Torriega?' said Luciana.

'Yes it is. Well that's what's on your birth certificate.'

Luciana leaned forward and stared hard at her mother: 'So what should be my real name?'

Maya shook her head, and sighed: 'My darling, that has to be your real name - Luciana Torriega.'

The young woman got up, paced the floor, banged her fist against the door frame. 'I just don't know what to think. I don't know what's real and what's not. I don't know you, I don't know my father. And now I don't know my own name!'

'Please, my love, sit down, let me finish explaining.'

She paced a little and then forced herself back on to the sofa. 'Go on, you were saying about coming down here with my father.'

Maya took Luciana's hand and continued: 'We stayed in a little hotel for a couple of days and that's when I realised I didn't want to go back to Jamaica.'

'You wanted to stay here with Will?'

Maya nodded: 'Jamaica was getting so dangerous and my job was all about destroying the government. I hated what I was doing and what it was doing to my friendships and my honesty with people. And I feared for our safety, for your safety.'

'So what happened to him, what happened to my father?'

Maya hung her head: 'I don't know. I was rushed out of the country after the shooting and had no way of contacting him. It was all too dangerous.'

'What about your uncle Ned and your friend Marianne?'

Maya shook her head: 'I don't know. I was afraid to go back or make contact with anyone there. I feared for our lives, yours and mine.'

'Because of the shooting?'

Maya nodded. 'I told Marianne she must not try to contact me in case people were after me.'

'But the shooting wasn't your fault. You didn't cause his death, surely?'

'I did. I was followed and led them to him.'

'And you've lived with that fear ever since?'

'When you betray the CIA they don't forgive or forget you.'

Luciana gasped, her hands covering her mouth: 'My god momma, I thought you just worked at the embassy. I didn't realise you were working for the CIA!'

My nodded: 'So now you know. That's the shadow I've lived under all these years. Even now, when I saw your lights and heard the car, I still panic.'

'And that's why you've never gone back and why you forbid me to go to America?'

'I just don't know whether it will ever be safe.'

Luciana paced the room shaking her head. 'My mother, a secret agent. Wow!'

'And you say nothing about this! Promise me.'

'Did Marianne ever know?'

'Promise me, Luciana!'

Luciana dropped to her knees beside her mother and held her hands: 'I promise, momma. What about Marianne?'

Maya shook her head. 'My dear friend Marianne. Yes, she knew. But I've had no contact for many years. I feared contact with her might lead them to find me. I don't know whether she's still alive.'

'Did my father know about your work?'

Maya shrugged: 'I'm not sure. He never said anything, but maybe he suspected.'

'And you won't tell me Will's other name?'

'What good would it do if you found him? I probably ruined his early life. I don't want to ruin the rest. I've wrecked so many lives in my foolishness. Leave him in peace, please,' she cried. She put her hands to her face and sobbed, her chest heaving with each breath.

Luciana knelt in front of her mother and wrapped her arms around her. She felt the sobbing against her own chest; felt her mother's tears on her arms. Was there nothing that could be done to soothe this pain and this fear?

And what of her own pain? To know her father, to see him, put her arms around him. That pain went even deeper.

She left her mother sleeping for a while, went out of the house and sat on the rocks where the waves were breaking onto the sand. There was a near full moon, its light scattered on the surface of the sea in silvery fragments. A cruise ship with its lines of flickering lights was moving south, probably setting out from Cancun, taking its shipload of tourists to some other destination. And what of her destination? Ricardo was gone, the possibility of having her own baby was gone and she was forty one. Her own life was passing. Time was moving on. And maybe soon, her mother would be gone - ten years perhaps and then she would be alone with no family.

Somehow she must try to find her father.

*

The autumn of 2016 had brought tropical storms to the Yucatan. No hurricanes but the area round Punta had suffered flooding and some wind damage. Luciana had driven down to check on the cabana. They had locked it up and prepared it for the rainy season back in September and when she drove down in late November she was relieved that all was looking safe and secure. Since the summer she had focused on getting her thesis finished and by December it was almost ready to be submitted. They were rehearsing for the Christmas festival in Merida and she was pleased that her mother was able to focus on something specific. For the past few months Maya's behaviour had become increasingly unpredictable. Fits of depression, panic attacks and sometimes just a staring vacancy. But when she picked up her violin it was different. Her mother could still conjure that sublime magic from those strings, mesmerise her listeners and lose herself in the music.

At work Luciana was concentrating on the project to revamp the displays and increase the footfall of visitors at the museum in Merida but she still went out to visit the sites, to take new photographs and double check some of the data she was using in her thesis. Her focus was what was called the Early Postclassic Period - A.D. 925-1200. It was the time when the more militaristic Toltecs took hold over the Mayan culture and their centre of power focused on the site at Chichen Itza. Luciana was looking at the way Toltec symbolism was superimposed on the earlier Mayan structures and the image of Quetzalcoatl, the plumed serpent god, became a recurring motif. It was prominent at the foot of the stairway of the Temple of Kukulcan but recurred within the smaller glyphs, those square stone picture tiles which held the key to the Mayan language. It was like probing the Mayan DNA, trying to unravel the hidden mysteries of this intriguing civilisation.

One morning in early December, she was sitting on the steps of the temple checking some of the photographs she had taken when the thought came to her. Here am I searching for the Mayan DNA - why not check my own as Sonia has done. Sonia had mixed Mexican Indian and European parentage and her DNA results had revealed a fascinating amalgam of ethnic roots. Why shouldn't I do the same, thought Luciana, cast my DNA out into the world and maybe I might find a match; a Jamaican mother who might have African roots and an English father with European ties might make for an interesting profile. Luciana wasn't sure how it worked but from what Sonia had told her it was like throwing a pebble into a pool and setting up the genetic ripples. She phoned Sonia and arranged to meet her.

'So how does it work?' asked Luciana. They were sitting at a little cafe on the edge of the square in Merida. It was late afternoon, people were strolling after work and a marimba band was playing near the fountains where the ice cream sellers had set up a stall.

'You pay a fee, around eighty dollars and they send you a kit. You can send a cheek swab or just some saliva in a container. It goes off to some lab in California where they keep this global database and then you get a profile and you're notified of any close matches.'

'And does it work? Sounds like a possible con to me.'

Sonia nodded: 'I found a cousin in Washington State and we've been in contact. Seems her grandmother was related to my great aunt.'

'And that all comes from spitting in a bottle?'

'The wonders of science and technology,' said Sonia, nodding. 'You might even find your father.'

'You mean it can be that precise?'

'Apparently, it can.'

Luciana sat back and looked out across the square. Someone was flying a kite with a long tail of coloured streamers. The wind was tugging at the wings of the kite and a small boy was holding on to the string and closely watching the movement of the kite. She was a bit like that kite, straining to get free but she had deferred to her mother's wishes not to search for her father. Maybe it was time to break free.

'Mother won't be happy if I do this.'

'She doesn't need to know and it may come to nothing,' replied Sonia. 'And anyway, she's had her life; you have a right to chase this thing down. You haven't had peace of mind for forty years.'

'I don't think I was agitating about it in my cradle,' smiled Luciana.

'You know what I mean. You have a right to find out what you can.'

Luciana nodded: 'True. It'll still feel like I'm going behind her back, though.'

Sonia shrugged: 'You need to make the decision. No-one else can make it for you.'

And just after Christmas, as she was sitting in the cathedral waiting for the third chime of the Angelus bell, she made her decision. New year, new resolution. And on January 10th, she sent off her DNA sample.

***

Buried beneath the Yucatan Peninsula is an impact crater. It was formed when a huge asteroid struck the earth about sixty six million years ago. It's called the Chicxulum crater, named after the town of Chicxulum where its epicentre is located. The impact changed the Yucatan landscape for ever.

Today a different kind of cataclysm was occurring.

Luciana stared at the screen of her laptop. 'What does this mean?' she said.

'You have what's called a 'Close match',' replied Sonia, 'with someone called David Pearson. You share 1750 cMs with him.'

'Is that good?' said Luciana.

'Not sure. We need to find out what that means,' said Sonia.

Luciana's hand was shaking and Sonia took hold of it to calm her down. 'Let's take this slowly,' she said. 'Not jump to conclusions.'

**

Three thousand miles away another meteor had struck.

'Hello, Gina, hey, I got a reply!' called David. 'But I don't quite understand the data.'

'David? What are you talking about? I'm at work and have a meeting. Can't really talk.'

'Sorry, let's meet.'

'4.30. Usual place.'

'This is so exciting…!'

'Gotta go, sorry.'

The email from Ancestry gave a login code which took David to a screen which said *Hello David*. There was a link to a map. It showed he was 80% North Western European, 10% Scandinavian, 5% Spanish and 5% Portuguese. Then there was another link to *DNA Matches*.

He clicked on this and there was a name: *Luciana Torriega* alongside which it said : *Close match - Shared DNA: 1750cM.*

'Luciana Torriega'? An intriguing name. But it meant nothing to him. But then it was a 'Close Match,' whatever that meant.   He Googled 'cM' to try to find out what the number 1750 referred to. The answer appeared - *centimorgans - a measure of shared DNA. Half siblings are likely to have around 1700cM.*

A half sister? Could he contact this Luciana Torriega to find out more? He searched the screen and found 'Message'. There was an option to send a message to this Luciana person. But what would he say? And should he rush into this? Maybe this person knew nothing about a connection with a half brother. Why would she? If Will left Jamaica when Maya was pregnant then the baby would have no knowledge that a half brother had been born. And anyway, Luciana may not be the person he was searching for. But there was this apparent close match with 1750cMs. Oh, this was so confusing.

Below the name of Luciana Torriega there were other matches; more distant, fewer cMs. No names that rang any bells. Presumably they were related to his distant aunts, cousins, great uncles. It was all strangely unsettling to know he was somehow connected genetically to this wider network. He wondered where the Scandinavian connection came from, and the Portuguese. It all added up to a more exotic self image than to think he was simply 'English'. We're all mongrels when it comes down to it, he thought, a pot pourri of wild genetic ingredients.

He stared again at the name *Luciana Torriega* and his fingers itched to send her a message. But he held back, closed his laptop, locked the house and drove to the cafe to meet Gina.

She was already there when he arrived. She nodded as he came in smiling broadly: 'You're like the cat that got the cream. Go on, what's happened then?'

'Just look at this,' said David. 'I think we may have found her.'

'Who, Maya?'

'No, my sister.'

He logged on to the Ancestry site and showed her the window with Luciana Torriega's name. 'And I can send a message, look, it doesn't go directly but through Ancestry. I was itching to send one but then thought I'd wait and see what you thought.'

Gina scanned the screen and nodded: 'It says 'Close match' which sounds promising. But this means that this Luciana is doing a search to find ancestors or relations. She doesn't know anything about you, doesn't even know that you exist. You can't just storm in and announce yourself to her. You've got to be sensitive about how you do this.'

David rubbed his hand across his face and nodded: 'You're right. Of course you're right.'

'You've got to tread carefully and slowly; step by step,' said Gina. 'You might be messing with someone's life here. For her to suddenly learn about a half brother and a father who's died could be really upsetting for her. I know it's exciting for you that you might have found your long lost sister but think of it from her point of view as well.'

She looked across at David and put her hand on his arm. 'C'mon, though, let's try and send her a message.'

They worked on it for several minutes to get the tone right and then it was done and ready to send.

Hello Luciana. I just received information from Ancestry that we might be related. I've been researching to find someone called Mahalia Tennyson, who went by the name of Maya and lived in Jamaica. She had a daughter, born in 1976, and I wondered if you could tell me if you know anything about them. Kind regards, David Pearson.

David scanned the message again. 'Sounds a bit impersonal, don't you think?'

Gina shook her head: 'No, I think the first contact needs to be a little formal. Ease her in gently. No sudden shocks.'

'Shall I send it then?'

Gina nodded: 'Yes, do it,' and she squeezed his arm reassuringly.

*

Sonia had taken over the computer and was searching to find out what '1750cMs' meant. Luciana was finding it difficult to calm her excitement. 'Here it is,' said Sonia, 'cMs is the measure of DNA connection between people. The higher the number the closer the match.'

'So what does 1750 mean?'

'It's the number that would connect a brother and sister.'

Luciana gasped and put her hand across her mouth. 'So this David Pearson could be my half brother?'

'Possibly.'

Just then, the computer pinged and a notification came through that a message had arrived.

Sonia opened the message and they read David's words: *Hello Luciana.....*

Luciana shook her head. 'I have to reply to this. What am I going to say?'

'Now wait a minute,' said Sonia. 'Let's remember your mother's lived a lifetime in fear of being found. As much as this looks genuine, it could be a scam to locate her. We need to be careful about giving away too much information.'

'To hell with that,' said Luciana. 'I'm going to take that chance. I've been aching to know about my father for a lifetime and this is the closest I've ever got.'

'Okay,' said Sonia, 'let's think about this. This David is asking questions about your mother and actually knows her real name. But you want to find out about his father, whether or not his name is Will.'

Luciana nodded: 'Yes, yes, that's right. This could be it, what I've been hoping for all these years.'

'Okay then,' said Sonia. 'Let's take this slowly. How are we going to answer this?'

They worked on a reply for a while and then were ready to send it.

Hello David. I think we might be related. My mother lived in Jamaica in the 1970s but left when she was pregnant with me. I've been researching to try to find my father whose name was William. I never knew him and he never knew me. Please can you help me with this? Agape, Luciana.

*

'What does agape mean?' asked David.

'It's Greek - a term of endearment. Refers to a kind of spiritual love, I think,' said Gina.

'I love that,' said David. 'Makes me feel quite tearful.'

'So what are we going to say?' said Gina. 'How about if we send her your email address in the next message and then we can bypass this Ancestry site. It'll be more direct and quicker.'

'Let's do it,' said David. 'I feel we're so close now, to finding out.'

Hello Luciana, I'm finding this very emotional. But let me explain what I know. My father, William Pearson, was an architect who worked in Jamaica from 1974-76. He left during the political troubles in the summer of '76 but he had a close relationship with a young Jamaican called Maya. She left Jamaica very suddenly without warning and he lost contact with her but he learned that she was pregnant with his child. However, he never knew whether or not the baby survived. Sadly, he died last year but he had very fond memories of Maya for the whole of his life. I'm his son and I only learned about my father's time in Jamaica after he died. Since then I've been desperate to find Maya and her child. Yours, David.

*

Luciana had to read it twice and then she felt the numbness. 'No, no, oh please no, not this, after all this time!' she cried, her voice rising. She thumped the table with her fists and the tears began to blur her vision.

Sonia put her arm round her friend's shoulder and tried to soothe the sobbing. 'C'mon, querida, it was likely to be like this. He would have been around seventy and who knows whether or not he was in good health.'

'But I feel so cheated. I have never felt a father's love, never felt the strength of a father, never felt a father's pride or his arms around me. He never knew about me, never heard my music, never watched me growing up, seeing me graduate.'

'And he must have suffered too,' said Sonia. 'He was cheated of all that, as well. What sort of a life did he have knowing he had a child that he would never see? Why did your mother deprive him of that? Why did your mother deprive you of ever knowing him?'

'She says she's lived in fear. She felt she was a fugitive, on the run, never safe. I could never argue against that. I'm not inside her skin, I haven't gone through what she's gone through. Oh Christ, what a mess this is.' She stood up and clutched at the sides of her head. 'If there's a God up there he certainly likes to play his games.'

She went and stood on the balcony which overlooked the street. There were children playing ball in the twilight, high-pitched voices full of laughter and innocence. Smoke was rising from the tortilla sellers whose stalls lined the roadside near the square. They squatted in the glow of their charcoal fires, wafting the heat, coaxing the flames. Luciana sighed and turned to Sonia who was watching her: 'But it seems I have a brother,' she said, wiping her eyes. 'I wonder where he lives and what he looks like and what he can tell me about my father.'

Sonia nodded: 'Shall we ask him?'

Luciana came across to the table and sat down again. She nodded: 'Yes, I need to do this.'

*

David's pulse quickened as he read the email from Luciana:

My dear David, or can I say my dear brother? I am devastated to learn that our father has died. I had hoped I might find him and get to know him. But that will never happen. All I can hope for is that you can tell me about him, about his life, the type of person he was, the sort of life he led. Apart from my utter sadness about the loss of him, I am thrilled to learn that I have you as a brother! I want to know all about you and your life, all about our father's life. As for me, I am 41 years old, I'm an only 'child' and I live with Maya, my mother in Merida, Mexico. She's just retired from running a music school in Merida, she's a brilliant musician and I've tried to emulate her virtuosity on the violin by my own playing of the classical guitar……

There were more exchanges of emails and Luciana was intrigued to hear about David's trip to Jamaica and meeting with Marianne; that he'd visited the original 'Bermuda Mount' and met old Frank who had known Maya and Will all those years ago. And when David then phoned Marianne and gave her all his news she was overjoyed to know that Maya was still alive and that Luciana was also a talented musician.

'We have to meet,' said Marianne, excitedly, 'we have to have a grand re-union. But let it be a surprise for Maya. It sounds as if she's very anxious and she'll worry about it. So let's keep the arrangements quiet. Oh I can't wait to see her, to hug her, to know her again.'

When David mentioned to Luciana Marianne's idea for a reunion she agreed it needed to be kept quiet. Maya had recently been diagnosed with a heart murmur and so any anxiety should be kept to a minimum.

But Luciana was overjoyed at the prospect of meeting her brother and her new nephew, Joe. 'I think he's going to like it over here,' she said in a phone call to David. 'There are some great swimming and snorkelling places I want to show him. I think he'll love it.'

*

Joe watched the armadillo trundling along the sand. It had waddled out of the bushes behind Cabana Luciana sniffing for food. Joe had never seen one before, this little creature which looked like some robot extra from a Star Wars film. He called Simon to come and look and the two boys crouched down and Simon prodded it with a small stick. 'Armadillos are fine,' Luciana had said, 'they won't trouble you but don't upset our little porcupines unless you want to be pierced with spines and stink for a week.'

He loved this place and he loved all these new people. Luciana, his new aunt was great fun, her mother Maya was nice too. He had watched her and tried to think of her as that young woman, the person that Pops had known when he was young. He had seen the photo of the two of them which old Frank had given to his father when they went to Bermuda Mount. How strange to think of Pops as so young before even his own father was born. It was a tangle to get your head round. And now they were all here and the only person missing was Pops himself. Joe found a piece of drift wood and carved the name in the sand. He found a longer branch and stuck it through the 'o' in 'Pops'. It was then that the idea came to him.

Luciana stood watching the boys playing together - her new extended family. She had met David and Joe at the airport. Both she and David, in their separate ways had been excited and nervous about this first meeting. Communication by text and telephone had helped prepare them but face to face was different.

When David and Joe emerged from the Arrivals lounge into the throng of taxi drivers and welcoming parties, David scanned the faces for his first glimpse of Luciana. And his neck prickled when he saw this vivacious young woman with her long wavy brown hair, her face alive with excitement and her eyes meeting his for the first time. Here was his father's daughter, his half sister, Luciana. They approached each other with outstretched arms and clung together in an embrace which erased the years, the longing, the ache of the searching. They separated and through tears of joy scanned each other's faces. 'At last,' said Luciana, 'my heart's found a home.'

David nodded: 'I know,' he murmured, 'I know.'

Joe watched them and then Luciana turned to him: 'And this is Joe! Joe, my love, welcome to Mexico. I'm your auntie Luciana and I'm so pleased I can give you my first hug.' Joe didn't know quite how to respond. He had gone to shake her hand but found himself engulfed in this tight, warm embrace. He nodded shyly and said, 'Hi.'

'Sorry, Joe,' said Luciana. 'This is all a bit mad isn't it. But you see I've never had a brother and now I have one and a new nephew too. It's like a bundle of Christmases has arrived all in a rush.' She took his hand. 'But come, I've so much to tell you and show you both. You're going to have a great time, I promise.'

A few hours later Marianne's flight arrived and Luciana was able to experience the warmth of this person who had been so close to her mother. And then there were her mother's tears when she saw Marianne. It had been forty years. She was overcome when Marianne came in through the door of the cabana. She cried, she laughed, she clapped her hands, she wanted to know how this had happened, who knew about it, how she hadn't had time to prepare herself and how she must look a sight to her old friend. Marianne hushed her and just calmed her with gentle hugs and a stroking of her hands. 'It's a long, long story,' Marianne had said. 'Just accept that God works in mysterious ways. Go with it, my darling. Everything's fine and you're safe and I'm back in your life.'

Luciana had said nothing about the reunion to her mother. David, Joe, Marianne and Simon had flown in a few days earlier and checked into a small hotel in Punta. Marianne would go in first and a short while later it would be David's turn. They knew that meeting David and hearing about Will would be the greatest shock for Maya so they allowed half an hour to pass before he made his way up from the beach to the house.

'There's someone else for you to meet, momma,' said Luciana. She sat close to her mother with Marianne on the sofa opposite. 'I've kept you in the dark these past months but you know I've been desperate to find out about my father.'

Maya nodded: 'And I haven't made it easy for you.'

Luciana continued: 'Well I made enquiries, I did a DNA test and I found a new brother I didn't know I had.' She turned as the door opened and David entered. 'This is David, Will's son. He's come from England to meet you.'

Maya turned, looked, strained her eyes to see; her hand went to her mouth and she gasped: 'Will, is it you?'

'No momma, this is David. This is Will's son.'

David came across and knelt in front of Maya. He took her hands in his. 'At last,' he said. 'I can't believe this is happening. I've been wondering about you for so long. You've no idea. I so wish my father could be here, but he hadn't been well these past years and, sadly, he died last year. I'm so sorry to have to tell you that. But I can tell you, he never forgot you in all those years. You were his first love and he cherished the memory of you.'

Maya stared through her tears into David's face. She shook her head slowly: 'I was cruel to him and I so wanted to make things right. But it was not possible.'

'I know,' said David. 'You don't have to explain.'

'But then he married and had a son?'

David nodded.

'Thank goodness he found happiness. I feared I'd ruined his life for ever.'

'You didn't, and I don't think you were ever far from his thoughts.'

Maya stroked her hand down the side of David's face. 'He was a wonderful young man, not unlike you to look at. We knew each other for such a brief time but he was a joy to be with and a comfort when my life was falling apart.'

'I know something about it,' said David. 'He wrote a journal while he was in Jamaica. I only recently found it. It's very personal and tells the story of that time in his life when he met you.' David opened his bag and pulled out the journal. He handed it to Maya. 'I brought it with me for you to read.'

Maya took the book, smoothed her fingers across its cover and then opened it. She saw the title:

THE JAMAICA JOURNAL OF WILL PEARSON
My first venture into serious writing.
Here's to posterity!

She looked up at David: 'This is such a treasure. I know I shall relive those times with both pleasure and pain. Thank you, David, so much.'

Luciana felt it was time to interrupt: 'Come now momma, there's plenty of time for catching up. David and Marianne are here for ten days. We have to celebrate and there's a feast arriving soon so you need to go put a party dress on and glam yourself up. Then there are two hungry boys who you haven't met yet. I'll tell you about them while I help you dress. And you need to dust off your violin. We're going to play some music.'

Maya allowed herself to be helped up. She took Luciana's arm then turned to David: 'I'm so glad my Will found happiness. I've lived with my guilt for so long. You've lifted a great burden from me. Thank you, David.'

There was the crunch of tyres on the gravel outside. It was the van from the local cantina. Two young men quickly set up a table on the terrace in front of the house and then carried food from the van to the table. There was a spread worthy of a Mexican fiesta - plates of charred corn and flour tortillas, pork canitas, dishes of guacamole, grilled corn, salsa dips and dishes of various taco fillings - shredded beef, lime grilled chicken, shredded fish alongside beef and chicken fajitas. But it was the churros which won the day with Joe and Simon. Dipped in warm chocolate they were little sticks of sugary heaven and the boys were in their element dancing around the table with chocolate oozing from the corners of their mouths.

After they had all eaten and several beers and margaritas had been downed, Luciana took up her guitar and played some stirring flamenco flourishes. Marianne and Maya clapped and hugged and laughed and David watched and marvelled at the way the threads of their lives had come together to make this moment. His father would have loved it.

When the excitement had quietened a little, David held up his hand and said: 'You know, in a way, this all started with a particular piece of music which I heard one day when I was visiting my father. He mentions it in the journal when he first set eyes on you, Maya. You were playing the violin at The Little Theatre and he was hooked by the music and by the sight of you. I wonder if the three of you could play that Shostakovich piece for me and for my father's memory.'

The sun was going down and the breeze which had been swaying the tall palms was melting away. The fishermen were loading their gear and fixing their lamps to the sides of their boats before pushing off from the beach. Maya and Marianne tuned the violins to Luciana's guitar and sat in a triangle facing each other. Maya nodded, raised her bow in an upstroke and the first notes were sounded.

David closed his eyes. This musical thread, sublime as always, drifted on the night air, met the whirr of the cicadas and the bubbling thrust of small waves which were breaking onto the sand below the house. It had drifted through time and woven a pattern round their lives and when the last note sounded and the three musicians held the moment before breathing out, so it felt that finally, a circle had been completed.

'Thank you,' said David. 'I'm sure my father was listening to that.'

It was as they were getting ready for bed that Joe told David his idea: 'Dad, I've been thinking. I was wishing Pops was here, and sad that he was missing all this. What about we plant a tree for him, like in his memory, so that when people look at the tree they think of him? And as it grows it's almost like he's here.'

David nodded: 'What a lovely idea. Yes, that would be something wouldn't it. To get a tree which would grow big and spread its branches, give shade and shelter and comfort. That would be Pops, all right. He would like that.'

'Can we do it then?' said Joe.

'I'll talk to Luciana and Maya in the morning.'

And at breakfast the following morning the decision was made.

'I love you for this, Joe,' said Luciana, hugging him tightly. 'I love you anyway but I love you even more for this brilliant idea. We could call it 'Will's Tree' and get Eduardo to carve a little sign. He's brilliant at wood carving.'

There was a movement from the end of the table as Maya raised her hand: 'Could I choose the kind of tree?' she said.

They all turned to look at her.

'What would you choose, momma?' asked Luciana.

'Well, there's a tree which grows in Jamaica, a tree that I always loved when I was growing up. It has bright yellow blossoms which come before the leaves appear. In fact I think it's the national blossom of

215

Venezuela where it's called El Araguaney. In Jamaica it's called a Poui tree.'

Joe almost giggled at the name. Luciana noticed and added: 'Yes, Joe, it sounds a bit weird, I have to say. But if momma wants a Poui tree let's see if we can get one. It'll bring a little of Jamaica to Mexico and that's what we want, don't we, momma?'

Maya smiled and nodded: 'Yes, that's exactly what we want.'

They checked online for the nearest tree nursery and Luciana made some phone calls.

Later that day, the phone rang and Luciana's face broke into a broad smile. She called from the balcony: 'Good news everybody. A mature Poui tree is to be delivered tomorrow! So let's get organised. We need to prepare for the great planting of Will's Tree. We've got to think carefully about where to plant it. From what I've read this tree grows big and has spreading branches which can offer shade, so we need a spot not too far from the house.'

The following morning a truck arrived from the nursery and the tree with its root bole wrapped in sacking was hoisted from the truck and lowered to the ground. While a small digger was being used to excavate a hole, preparations were made for the planting ceremony.

Luciana's friend Sonia had driven down to join the party and she and Luciana were laying out the cakes and pastries she had brought. David was setting up a tray of glasses for the drinks. Maya was sitting watching from the sofa.

'I seem to remember in the journal that there was some ceremonial pouring of white rum when they did the foundations for the project dad was working on. Would that be right, Maya?' asked David.

She nodded: 'Yes, there was lots of superstition in Jamaica; pouring the blood of a newly slaughtered chicken along with white rum - yes that was quite common.'

'Well we're not slaughtering any chicken,' said Luciana, 'but we could pour some rum and tequila into the hole before they drop in the tree; bring Jamaica and Mexico together. How about that?'

And as Maya poured white rum and Luciana and David poured tequila into the hole and the tree was lowered into position so Joe took photographs with David's phone which they could send to Gina.

Later David phoned her and described the events.

'Thanks for the photos,' she said. 'Looks like you found a new home and a new family,' said Gina.

'It would be good if you could see it for yourself,' said David. 'This is some place, I can tell you.'

'I'd like that,' replied Gina. 'I'd like to meet everyone. Maybe a double trip to Mexico and Jamaica then I could really take it all in.'

*

Early the following morning David was dressed for a quick jog round the bay. Joe was still sleeping and David quietly slid open the balcony door and went outside. Below, he spotted Luciana. She was standing next to the tree running her hand down its trunk, spraying its base with water from a hose. She spotted him, waved and then beckoned.

Her voice was hushed so as not to wake those still sleeping. 'What a wonderful idea of Joe's to get a tree - Will's tree.' David stood by her side and she linked her arm in his. 'It's as if he's back and he's with us.'

David closed his hand over hers, stroked it gently. 'I could never have imagined how this would be. The strangeness of finding you, and after visiting those places where they spent time together.'

Luciana nodded: 'Yes, I want to see all those places he writes about in the journal and where he lived in England. I want to get to know him better. And I want to get to know my mother when she was young. She's still something of a mystery, you know.'

David looked into his sister's face. 'What a miracle you are, that you survived all that happened - the shooting and everything. And here you are, my big sister.' He kissed her on the side of her head.

'Yes, you may be taller than me but you are the little brother, that's true.' She looked up at him and touched the side of his face. 'We've got so much to catch up on. But first I'm taking the boys sailing. You must join us.'

'Of course,' said David. 'I'm just off for a quick run.'

'Okay. See you later then… brother.' She clapped her hands: 'Oh, I so love saying that word.'

David waved and set off along the track which followed the curve of the bay. Jogging helped him to collect his thoughts. So much had happened. So much to think through. The sun was just rising, the air still cool, the scent of sea salt fresh and invigorating. There were sailboats out at sea, a cruise liner away near the horizon, some local fishing boats heading in to shore. A new day had dawned.

When he got back to the house he stood for a while and watched Luciana with the boys down near the water's edge. How his father would have loved to see this - his grandson and his daughter together rigging a sailboat. So sad that his father died knowing nothing of this legacy, only the pain of loss and seeming betrayal.

But David needed to try to forget that and see only the joy of it; be thankful that his father's adventures had led to this moment; that he could be standing here on the shores of the Caribbean looking down on Joe and Simon rigging a boat with Luciana. Yes, this was his father's true legacy - that the fragile threads which shape our lives could lead to an exciting new future for them all. Luciana was planning a visit to England with Marianne and Simon and hoping Maya would join them. Joe and Simon were already planning escapades back in Jamaica.

David shook his head at the wonder of it all. He stretched, closed his eyes to the sun and sighed. He took off his running shoes, felt the sand warm between his toes and jogged down the beach towards where they were rigging the sailboat.

Maya and Marianne walked slowly, arm in arm, along the path on the edge of the bay.

'So will you come? Will you come and visit,' asked Marianne.

Maya looked down, measuring each step: 'I finished reading Will's journal last night. I wept for hours, sobbed myself to sleep. It brought back so much that I lost back then, so much pain, so much confusion but also so much pleasure. Those hikes in the mountains, the sailing, the beauty of the rivers, the waterfalls where we swam, the music that we played and my time with Will which was so new and so precious. But it all got tangled in fear and dread and in some ways Will's writing untangled it for me.'

'So you'll come back, say you will.'

'I'm still not sure. These days my mind plays tricks, my dreams can haunt me the whole day so that I just want to be safe. And it's here that I feel safe. I know this place in a way that I didn't know Jamaica; could never find its truth.'

She turned and placed her hands on Marianne's shoulders, looked into her eyes: 'I'm sorry my dearest friend but I'm not ready to go back just yet.'

Marianne leaned her head on Maya's shoulder. 'I understand,' she said.

'But I'm sure Luciana will go visit. She needs to see her mother's country.'

'What about England? Will you and Luciana go and see David?'

They started walking again: 'Now that's different,' said Maya. 'Luciana can't wait to see more of her new brother and her little nephew and see where her father lived.'

Marianne smiled: 'Isn't it lovely to see the two boys getting on so well. See them down there.' She pointed to where Joe and Simon were carrying things to a sailboat which was pulled up on the sand.

Maya nodded: 'I never could have dreamed of this.'

Luciana was sorting out the rigging and David started clipping on the sails. 'Okay, listen now boys,' she said. 'I'm going to show you the bay and we'll head out close to the reef where you can jump in to do some snorkelling.'

Simon and Joe were hopping with excitement. As he was uncoiling one of the ropes, Joe said: 'Pops taught me to sail, when I was only six. He had a sailboat called 'Jamaya'. My dad thinks it was named for your mother.'

'And Jamaica?' replied Luciana.

Joe nodded: 'Yes, the two put together. Clever name wasn't it.'

The boys climbed aboard, Luciana checked the tiller was locked in its slot and hoisted the main sail while David unfurled the jib.

'So Will taught you to sail did he, Joe?' said Luciana as she pushed the boat into the water. 'Well, I reckon he must have taught me as well cos somehow, sailing's in my blood, it's in my DNA and I reckon that could only have come from one person.'

She caught the tug of the wind, the mainsail filled, David tightened the jib and the boat took off from the shore like a kite set free. Luciana felt the wind in her hair, heard the hiss of the wake, looked at David and the boys and shouted to the sky: 'Thanks Pops, we love you!'

****

THE THREAD OF MUSIC

Music is an important thread within the storyline. To appreciate its hold over the characters why not listen to the *Andante from the Piano Concerto No.2 in F Major* by Shostakovich. You can listen via 'You Tube' by a simple search for '*You Tube: Shostakovich, Andante*'

JAMAICA - follow up
All the locations mentioned in the novel are actual places. You can Google them or search You Tube for video clips.

For an interesting detailed exploration of modern Jamaica try Ian Thomson's *The Dead Yard*. 2009 Faber

And of course there's *A Brief History of Seven Killings* by Marlon James (2014) - winner of the 2015 Man Booker prize.

ACKNOWLEDGEMENTS

Thanks, as always, to my wife, Sue, for her insights, sensitivity to the needs of the narrative and patient proof reading.
Thanks also to reviewers Ray Wirth, Serena Field and Rachel Laverack for their critical comments which have helped to shape certain aspects of the narrative.
Thanks to Joby Davey for his cover design.

Cover photo 'Sunset over Criffel and the Solway Firth' is by BD

ABOUT THE AUTHOR

Barrie Day is an eclectic writer. He has published articles for newspapers and magazines, and in 2001, Oxford University Press published his *Mixed Media*, a school text book on media education which attracted a worldwide audience.

In recent years he wrote a lively autobiography, *Not Behind The Bike Sheds,* which describes personal and family adventures and captures the ups and downs of 40 years in education including his time living and working in Jamaica and Florida.

His first novel, *The Breath I Would Give You,* earned glowing reviews and his latest novel, *A Thread in Time* weaves a number of fascinating themes and draws on his early life living in Jamaica in the 1970s.

The musical motif which runs through the novel reflects his love of music and its power to inspire and transform lives.

Although born in the English Midlands, for the past forty years he has lived with his wife, Sue, in Cumbria, his favourite place on the planet. He has two children, Katie and James and five grandchildren who are a constant source of joy and inspiration.

For more info. go to: www.barrieday.co.uk.

The books mentioned above are all available from Amazon.com and Amazon.co.uk

AFTERWORD

Months before starting work on *A Thread In Time* I'd come across John Steinbeck's *Journal of a Novel.* This intriguing series of letters, Steinbeck wrote each morning to his editor, Pascal Covici, while working on his classic, *East of Eden.* They take us into Steinbeck's mind and the creative journey involved in writing a complex novel.

The production of a work of fiction is a mysterious process for the writer. How it germinates in the first place, how it develops and progresses and how it's completed is a curious alchemy which I certainly can't fathom. You start with the the germ of a story, you set up scenarios, introduce characters and then the momentum starts to build as the characters begin to assert themselves. You weave the plot and the characters kind of take over. They'll only do what that type of character would do. Where the characters come from in the first place is a mystery - they're amalgams of traits, characteristics you've seen in certain people which as the writer you reform into someone who's going to meet the needs of the plot. Then the plot has to resolve itself in some way and you have the characters' voices in your head; you have the voices of readers with their questions in your head and all the time you're trying to bring these competing demands to a satisfying conclusion. And when it's done the whole text sits there in front of you and you think - How did that happen? Where did this thing (for it's now a definable, finite 'thing') come from?

In order to try to capture that 'mysterious process' I attempted to keep an intermittent log when writing *A Thread in Time.* It wasn't a letter each morning like Steinbeck wrote but it was an attempt to capture the vagaries of the creative process - to remind myself about the queries and questions which had spun in my head for almost a year during the writing of the book.
So here it is. Make of it what you will.

October 2018.

Early thoughts/themes:

Do we ever know our parents? What if, after death, things are discovered which reveal aspects of a parent which are a surprise/shock?

Dementia - the memory of my father in the care home, his wonderful musicianship lost - but it was the last thing to go. So maybe work in a musical theme. Heard on the radio the exquisite Andante from Shostakovich's Piano Concerto No. 2 in F major and wondered if that might be a motif through the book.

Want to use Jamaica as a prime location - such a rich fund of landscape and cultural features as well as the drama of the political upheavals of the 1970s. Will set the English scenes around Lancaster, I think.

Want to work in a grandparent/grandchild relationship. So need to have a younger character as a vehicle for this.

November 2018.

Decided to set the story in 2016 which means the contemporary characters can use internet/Google online research.

Have relocated from Lancaster to the Solway Estuary. Some personal resistance at using a location close to home but then I wondered why when I know the Solway area so well in all its moods/seasons.

Part 1 is going well. Using 11 year old Joe as a useful vehicle for moving the plot and developing the character of the older Will through his relationship over the years with Joe.

Google is amazing at helping my research into events in 1970s Jamaica as well as modern Jamaica. There are online news reports, You Tube clips of travelling round Jamaica, instant Wikipedia verification of events/people etc..

December 2018.

Progressing well. I'm enjoying revisiting my memories of Jamaica but fleshing them out with background checks on the political/dramatic events of the time.

I'm resisting indulging the descriptions of places and events. Have to remember, Will's journal is just that - his observations/reactions etc.. He's not a seasoned writer writing a literary text, therefore the journal entries can be brief, chatty etc..

Feb. 2019.

Where did the character of Maya come from? She's a blend of smart young women whom I've encountered but the idea of her being a violinist was inspired during a holiday in Montenegro in October 2018. We were in the old Venetian town of Kotor and came into a small square where a tall young female violinist was playing solo to no-one in particular - just caught up in the music. And then I had it! Maya began to come alive for me and I started to think how I could use the music element in the narrative. As for Gina - the young black English lawyer - she's again an amalgam of people I've known as well as the many feisty women of colour I've seen in the media.

March 2019.

Gina's proving to be a useful character - provides a more pragmatic/practical counterweight to David's reflective, indecisive approach to the issues which are arising. She's not emotionally involved in the way that he is which sets up a useful dynamic between them.

April 2019

This creative process is a mystery. When I start in the morning (mornings are my chosen time to write) I obviously have the threads of the previous writing session to pick up on but beyond that, who knows what is going to spill onto the page! I listen to the voices of the characters, picture their physical presence, think of what they would do as dictated by the personal traits I've given them. Initially it's all rather tentative, as if they're coming on stage for the first time but once they're there, then they push the plot and influence the mood/dynamics of what happens.

May 2019.

Got to get the timings right so that when Maya disappears pregnant it can be credible that Will wouldn't have guessed. So the baby has to be conceived around Feb/March.

28.6.19

Yesterday I left David re-reading his father's journal from the balcony of a guest house in the Blue Mountains. The following morning he's going to try to find the cottage where his father brought Maya and where the baby was probably conceived. So, since finishing writing yesterday, a little room in my mind has had David on the balcony waiting for his next move.

And I was thinking about how a novel progresses. Early on the scenarios are being set up. New characters are introduced - like Gina for instance - she came out of left field when David was in a cafe. Why she emerged is probably because I knew I needed a character who would be a companion for David, someone to help in his quest. And so from nowhere Gina emerges and then becomes an accepted integral part of the storyline. And each character imposes a kind of logic into the way the story develops - they insist on behaving in a certain way. And each day I come into the study, sit, open the computer and wait for the threads to start finding their pathways.

David's about to get up, early morning and go with Joe to find Bermuda Mount cottage. Thereafter they'll continue the journey to the north coast and Port Antonio to try to find Marianne. Haven't worked out where and how that encounter will go, but I have faith that my imagination will weave something coherent and believable and which the reader will feel is authentic and plausible.

So David gets up and I'm keen for him to be on the path to Bermuda Mount. But of course, I have to think what

David would do first thing in the morning - he would shower, have breakfast - of course I could leave all that out and move the story along more quickly but then for the reader these small details of realism are probably important. So he has a dialogue with Miss Olivia and they talk about her singing and the coffee she's serving and I hope this brings realism to the scene. 'Show it don't tell it' - I try to keep that mantra in mind...

7.7.19

I come into the study and prepare to reenter that world I left yesterday, where two of my characters David and Marianne were talking, where David had just made a new discovery and realised a painful truth. Their conversation has, for the past 12 hours, been tucked away in that backroom of my mind marked 'writing project', they've still been quietly conversing in my subconscious but nothing loudly coherent until just before bed a new idea popped from nowhere into my head. I went downstairs switched the living room light back on, opened my lap top and typed a couple of sentences to capture this thought that I didn't want to lose. Now here I am with a couple of hours to shape that thought into the narrative and continue where I left off..

9.7.19

Virtually finished Part 2 where David leaves Jamaica having failed to find Maya. So now I'm thinking about Part 3 and fear that this could fall flat. The tension of finding Maya is still there through the DNA search but is it enough to hold the reader?

Then talking with Sue, I started thinking about Maya's daughter, Luciana. She'd be 41. How about changing the perspective of the narrative and telling things from her point of view? Where is she living? What is her work? What is her relationship with her mother, Maya, who is now 65? So now I've been trying to visualise Luciana, what does she look like - she's mixed race, speaks both English and Spanish as she's been brought up in Mexico. I have toyed with different locations for Maya to have settled but decided Mexico gives the narrative an exotic feel as long I can write convincingly about Mexico!

Decided Luciana works in the anthropological museum in Merida, having studied anthrop. in Mexico City and in Lima? She plays classical guitar, has a Martin (Ed Sheeran) guitar, has had a failed marriage/relationship and is on vacation at the Thousand Islands when Part 3 starts.

Having decided on this tack I'm now trying to answer a string of question which the reader might ask.

Why hasn't Maya been back to Jamaica? What has she told Luciana about her father? His name? Has she seen photographs of Will?

Is Maya suffering from PTSD? thinks Luciana.

Should I tell Maya's story as well or keep Luciana as the central focus and just refer to Maya via Luciana, the worried daughter's point of view?

Maya - started teaching music and gradually built up a music school which she's run for many years in Merida?

Does Luciana ask Maya directly about trying to find Will?

Does Maya say categorically - No! Because she feels she betrayed him and she shouldn't intrude on his life?

Does Maya, through the PTSD believe she caused the death of RJ? - by things she said, without deliberately informing for the PNP. Who got her out of Jamaica? Do I need to answer this question?

9pm same day.

And we're off! Luciana has come to life! And I'm beginning to get to know her - picturing her, giving her various facets which are then starting to drive what she says and what she does. And she's dynamic where David was never dynamic. She's going to be a force to be reckoned with. She's concerned about her mother (Maya) who's now an old woman and suffering from delusions and symptoms of PTSD. Gone is the vivacious Maya. This older version has taken over.

But then how much should I get inside the mind of the older Maya? Capture her delusions, her dreams, her memories and nightmares?

The English thread - Joe's connection with Marianne's grandson, Simon. They trade games, play over the internet, send photos etc..
David and Gina….She instigates the DNA idea.

Does Luciana find photographs of Will?

Curious how characters reveal themselves. You start with an idea of a person - give them a name and then start to flesh them out - you picture them probably from the myriad of people you have known personally or seen in the media and start to endow them with personality traits which will fit the needs of the plot. Then probably the name comes because certain personalities suggest a name - or is it vice versa? Then you introduce the character into the ongoing plot and they then start to assert themselves - they say and do things which would be appropriate to that personality and if you try to get them to say or do things which are 'out of character', they'll soon tell you!
29.8.19
Now switched the narrative to focus on Maya and I've been struggling a little to visualise 65 yr old Maya living in Mexico. It's a question of feeling empathy for the person and the place where they're functioning - in this case Merida and Yucatan coast and picturing the physical appearance of the character too. And I have to fill out her past 40 years since she arrived in Mexico after the shooting. Who took her? Who cared for her? What sort of life did she establish - a young black woman with a new baby?

30.8.19

It's done. Not so difficult once I got started. Still find it difficult to picture Maya's face but I've fleshed out her past and Luciana's relationship with her. Think I may have finished Part 3. Now back to the Solway.

2.9.19

I have to start to finally bring David and Luciana together. Does she come to England for a museum conference? Does he go to Mexico after Gina finds 'Bermuda Mount' Music Institute newspaper ref. ? Does Luciana go to Jamaica? Or do they just come together through the DNA match. Or do they then agree to meet in Jamaica at Bermuda Mount?

4.9.19 (morning)

Have written the DNA sequence and it seemed to generate more tension than I'd realised. I lie in bed just after I've woken and pick up the scene I arrived at the previous day. I visualise the next scene, the characters, project into their minds and their feelings, weigh it up from the reader's point of view. And now I feel I'm ready for the final chapter which will be a reunion in Mexico. Maya hasn't been told about the connection between Luciana and David as Luciana fears the shock of it might affect her weakened heart. So I've got to write the reunion scene, with some sentiment but not too much.

4.9.19 (evening)

Think it's finished!! Not sure whether the final section is too brief, too rapid, whether things are tied up too quickly. But I wanted to end on an upbeat note, not over sentimental, hence the final scene with Luciana taking the boys sailing.

5.9.19

Thought I was finished but two of my characters, Marianne and Maya are having a conversation in that backroom of my mind which I must attend to. The ending was too swift and there needs to be more time for reflection for the reader prompted by what the characters talk about.

Music epigrams needed?

7.9.19

Re-read the whole thing and I don't feel the end section works. To suddenly introduce Luciana at the start of Part 3, and immediately after David's downer in Jamaica didn't feel right. We need to see him back in England first so I'm switching the Luciana section to later. Hope this works. What it reminds me of is that, as I write, I'm not only in the mind of the character and considering their motivations driven by their personality but I'm simultaneously in the mind of the reader, trying to assess how the reader's going to react. It's an interesting process of mental gymnastics!

Right - done the switch and it 'feels' right - there's time for the reader to absorb David's disappointment before I reveal the life of Luciana.

In the light of comments by friend Ray about the opening section when the journal is found, I've changed the place and circumstances of the discovery. In the first draft the journal was locked away as if it was all a secret, but as Ray said, why would it be such a secret that Will worked in Jamaica as a young man? So now Joe finds the journal in the drawer of Will's desk in his workshop quite by chance.

January 3rd 2020

Reviews by Rachel and Serena have drawn attention to racial tension that Will feels when he's with Maya and whether I'm labouring this too much. This is a tricky area to deal with but I feel strongly it has to be explored. Been reading Reni Eddo-Lodge's *Why I'm No Longer Talking to White People About Race* and Gina Miller's *Rise* which confirms to me that I must try to get this right. I'll use Will's sensitivity to Maya's colour and David's reaction to what he's reading as a means of provoking the reader to reflect on this. Maybe I'll use dialogue between Gina and David to try to explore this further.

Jan. 4th

Have inserted dialogue between Gina and David re. the 'skin factor' that Will often refers to. Hoping this piece of 'lecturing' by Gina isn't too 'clunky' and clarifies some of the issues.

Jan. 6th

Finally, (if there ever is a feeling of finality) here it is - my new baby waiting to be launched into the world. How will it be received? I can only think of the flaws in the novel (inevitably there will be some) .

So now it's over to the readers and out of my control. And for the first time for 18 months my head is empty of narrative threads and the gristle of unresolved plot lines. It's a kind of limbo where I'm no longer sharing scenes with my characters or conjuring the next thread of the narrative. It's a relief but also a feeling of loss.

Now, I look forward to holding a copy of the finished novel, turning the pages to check for technical errors and then setting it free to make its way in the world.

BD Jan. 2020

***

Printed in Great Britain
by Amazon